THIRTEEN HOURS

by

Meghan O'Brien

2008

THIRTEEN HOURS

ISBN 10: 1-60282-014-7
ISBN 13: 978-1-60282-014-2

THIS TRADE PAPERBACK ORIGINAL IS PUBLISHED BY
BOLD STROKES BOOKS, INC.
NEW YORK, USA

FIRST EDITION: MAY 2008

CREDITS
EDITORS: JENNIFER KNIGHT AND STACIA SEAMAN
PRODUCTION DESIGN: STACIA SEAMAN
COVER DESIGN BY SHERI (GRAPHICARTIST2020@HOTMAIL.COM)

Acknowledgments

First and foremost, I would like to thank Radclyffe for the opportunity to join the Bold Strokes team. I've received such a warm welcome, and the future looks bright. I would also like to thank Jennifer Knight for lending her mad editing skills to another of my novels. Each time we work together I learn so much, and I'm forever grateful for this continued education. I'd also like to thank Stacia Seaman for finding all my boo-boos and helping to make this book the best it can be. And as always, I need to recognize K.E. Lane for her constant willingness to read my work and offer thoughtful suggestions.

On a personal note, I want to thank my partner Angie for her unwavering support. I know it's not easy to be a single mother when I'm busy writing and/or editing, and I appreciate you giving me time away from being mommy so I can work. Thanks also to Ty, who has encouraged me from the beginning and always has good advice when I need it. And a hearty thank you to my sister Kathleen, for always being there.

And last but certainly not least, I want to thank my parents. I've felt strange about acknowledging them in the past, but only because it makes me uneasy to think of them reading my steamier scenes, and not because they don't deserve it. They have offered me incredible support and always take interest in my writing, whether I want them to or not! (Just kidding). Mom and Dad, I love you, and thanks for being the best parents in the world. And please, for the love of all that is good, don't read this book!

Dedication

To Angie. I love you.

HOUR ZERO

At approximately seven o'clock on the evening of her twenty-eighth birthday, during an otherwise uneventful Friday night at the office, Dana Watts was confronted by the most perfect pair of naked female breasts she had ever seen. Given that her real-life exposure to naked female breasts had, until that moment, been limited to the odd glance in the locker room at the gym and, when she was twelve years old, a rather uncomfortable glimpse of her grandmother dressing in her bedroom with the door ajar, this was perhaps not saying a lot.

The breasts in question were attached to a half-naked stripper who landed on her lap and began gyrating in time with some godawful, bass-heavy music that blasted from an iPod now sitting on Dana's desk. Unable to move with the woman's weight across her thighs, uncertain about what to do with her hands, Dana could only sit and stare at the rosy-tipped breasts that swayed in front of her face.

They were perfect, and for a crazy moment she forgot about the proposal she was supposed to be drafting and considered reaching up to cup them in her hands. But Dana wasn't the irresponsible type, and she certainly wasn't the kind of woman who went around feeling up strippers. Humiliated by her impulse, she felt hot anger surge through her body. Her proposal was far more important than whatever cheap thrill this woman thought she was offering.

"What the hell do you think you're doing?" Dana snapped. "Stand up and turn off that music. Now."

The dark-haired stripper grinned, rocking against her body. "I'm your birthday present." She reached down and grasped Dana's hand, bringing it up to rest on one of her perfect breasts. "Enjoy me," she whispered hotly in her ear.

Dana's fingers curled automatically at the sensation of an erect nipple poking into the center of her palm. Exhaling through her nose, she repeated, "Turn off the music. Don't make me ask you again."

The stripper stared at her, still straddling her thighs. She raised an elegant eyebrow. "You don't seem totally disinterested."

Dana willed her face not to color in embarrassment. "Just get off my lap. Put your shirt on, for God's sake."

Her tone was harsher than she'd intended. Being so close to so much bare skin made her anxious, and she was determined to show control. Someone was responsible for this, some idiot coworker who would live to regret this stunt.

Thankfully, the stripper seemed to understand she wasn't kidding. She stood and backed away from the chair. As she bent to fish her T-shirt from the backpack she'd dropped on the floor, Dana tried not to let her gaze stray to the woman's bottom. She failed miserably.

The stripper grinned over her shoulder as she straightened up. "See something you like?"

"I'm just wondering how you made it in here without getting arrested for solicitation," Dana shot back as her unwelcome visitor pulled on a form-fitting T-shirt and torn, low-slung blue jeans. "You certainly look the part. Is the trashy outfit a stripper thing or just your own personal preference?"

In truth, the young woman looked lovely. The barest hint of black panties rose above the waistband of her jeans. In her hand was the lacy black bra she'd cast aside when she dropped onto Dana's lap. Her nipples strained against the cotton of her T-shirt.

"Scott was right," said the envoy from Slut City. "You do need to loosen up."

And suddenly it all makes sense. "Scott put you up to this," Dana said without humor. "Of course."

"Of course. But he didn't warn me you'd be such a bitch. What's your problem? Are you scared of naked women or something?"

Dana regarded the woman coolly. "Maybe I'm scared of what I might catch with you squirming around on my lap like that."

The stripper's eyes flashed. "Fuck you. I'm leaving. Happy

birthday, and go to hell." She snatched up her iPod from Dana's desk, shouldered her backpack, and half turned to stalk out of the office.

Dana stood up and grabbed her by the elbow. "I'll escort you out." She wasn't about to let a total stranger, an interloper in her domain, wander the hallways alone. *Then I'll call Scott and bitch at him for ruining a perfectly productive evening with his stupid little stunt.*

The woman pulled away, eyes burning. "Don't bother. I found my way in, so I'm sure I can manage to find my way out."

"It wasn't an offer," Dana said. "I'm taking you downstairs. I don't know how you managed to get into the building after hours, but you shouldn't even be here."

As she marched the stripper across the room, the woman complained, "You're a lot of fun. What's got you so uptight? Wait, let me guess—you haven't gotten laid in about five years?"

Dana didn't rise to the baiting, taking giant strides to the elevator down the hall from her office. The lights were dimmed in the hallway, a testament to her solitude in the building. Everyone else had left much earlier to begin their weekends at home. To Dana, home was intolerably boring compared to work. There was nowhere she would rather be than right here, at Boynton Software Solutions, indulging herself in her passion. Project management.

She stopped in front of the elevator and jabbed at the call button.

Incredibly, the stripper hadn't given up. Bumping Dana with a playful shoulder, she said, "If I gave you a pity fuck, do you think you could manage a smile?"

"Getting laid isn't as high a priority for me as it apparently is for you," Dana said. "What makes me happy is having a great job. You know, like the one you interrupted me doing tonight."

"Yeah, it looked fascinating."

Dana ignored the sarcastic comeback and stared up at the display. How long did it take for the car to crawl from the lobby to the twenty-ninth floor? Was it incredibly slow tonight, or was she just incredibly angry? Indulging herself in some tit for tat, she remarked, "I wouldn't expect a girl who takes off her clothes for money to understand the pleasure that comes from being successful."

"And I wouldn't expect a cold bitch like you to understand what's really important in life."

Dana snorted. "What? Having some cheap stripper shake her tits in my face?"

The elevator doors slid open in time to avoid further conversation. Dana stepped inside, dragging the woman with her, and pressed the button for the lobby.

As the doors slid shut in front of them, the stripper muttered, "You looked like you were enjoying my tits until you remembered that you might be stripped of your Ice Queen title."

Dana spun her head around, a denial on her lips, when the lights flickered and then blinked out, and the elevator shuddered to a halt. The sudden motion threw them both forward a step, and Dana brought her arms around the other woman instinctively, preventing her from tumbling to the ground. For a moment, the elevator was pitch black, then the dim emergency lights activated and flooded the car with gentle light. After a beat, they both looked at the elevator door and the rows of buttons next to it.

The woman in Dana's arms stared up at her with wide blue eyes. "No way," she whispered.

Shocked into action, Dana released her and took a step toward the door. She shook her head. "Everything's fine. We'll just push the emergency button." She examined the controls, searching for the one that would get them out of their unlikely prison the fastest.

"Are we...stuck in here?"

Dana shook her head. "No. There is no way I'm getting stuck in an elevator with a goddamn stripper when I'm in the middle of my goddamn proposal."

"Your proposal?" The stripper looked incredulous. "You're trapped in an elevator on your birthday, on Friday night, and you're worried about a proposal?"

Dana chewed on her lip, pushing each button on the panel in succession. None lit up, and none seemed to trigger an emergency fail-safe. "It's an important proposal."

"Oh, man. Stuck in an elevator, and it has to be with the most boring woman alive."

Having tried the last button, Dana slammed the heel of her hand against the elevator door. "Fuck! We can't actually be stuck in this thing."

"Someone will notice us, right? They'll get us out of here."

"Eventually, but everyone's already gone for the weekend." Dana couldn't believe she'd stepped away from her desk without her cell phone. They were probably going to be incarcerated here until Rocky, the security guard, arrived at seven or eight tomorrow morning.

"Eventually?" the stripper screeched. "No *fucking* way I'm going to sit in this elevator all night. With *you*."

Dana winced at the shrill put-down. "You think I'm happy? This never would have happened if you hadn't bothered me with your stupid lap dance—"

"Hey, I was just doing my *job*," the girl retorted. "You know, the one *your* friend hired me to do? If you're pissed off, take it out on him. Not me." She moved as far away from Dana as she could, facing the back of the elevator car and folding her arms across her chest. "Although I understand why he thought you needed it. You're just a barrel of laughs."

"Just great," Dana whispered to herself. "What a perfect birthday present. A bitchy little stripper all my own for the night. I don't know how I'll ever repay Scott for this one." Castration was a first thought, but she was open to more elaborate punishments.

"Wonderful," her angry companion muttered. "Fucking great."

"Exactly my thought," Dana said.

They stared at one another for a moment in perfect agreement. Dana assumed it would be one of very few such moments of accord.

Hour One—7:00 P.M.

H er name was Laurel.
"Yes, imagine that," she said after revealing this fact. "Strippers have names...kind of like real people."

Dana produced a humorless smile, finally looking over to her companion. The young woman sat with her knees pulled up to her chest, arms wrapped around her legs. She regarded Dana with stormy blue eyes.

"Listen, if we're going to be stuck in here together, do you think you could manage just a little bit of civility?"

"Let's make a deal, *Laurel*." Pretty name. It matched the pretty breasts. Frowning at her line of thought, Dana quickly continued, "You sit quietly on your side of this elevator and I'll do the same on mine. If we can manage that, I think we'll get along just fine."

Laurel eyed her with obvious disdain. "Seriously, what's your problem? I'm willing to start over if you are. Being trapped in here doesn't have to be as completely miserable as you seem to be determined to make it."

Tired of arguing—*with a goddamn stripper*—Dana didn't respond to the quiet words. The last thing she wanted to do was make nice with a woman Scott had hired for the express purpose of making a statement about her life. From the moment the surprise birthday humiliation burst into her office and filled the sterile room with music and intoxicating perfume, Dana had felt vulnerable and exposed. Being trapped in a small space with her seemed a particularly cruel punishment.

She raised her eyes to the dim emergency lights that illuminated the elevator car. Dared she hope she'd saved her document recently enough that this power outage hadn't wiped out hours of work? Leaning her head against the wall, she started piecing her proposal back together in her head. She was startled when Laurel spoke again.

"My cat Isis is going to kill me," she informed Dana. "I promised we were going to have bathtime tonight. She likes sitting on the edge of the tub and putting her nose in the bubbles. It usually irritates me, especially when she sneezes, but right now I'd give anything for bathtime."

Dana felt her lips twitching and tamped the reaction down fast. The mention of "bathtime" elicited images that made her frown. She wasn't going *there*. "Well, I'm sorry you're stuck with me instead."

Laurel's mouth stretched into a slow smile. Her white teeth and full pink lips distracted Dana so completely she forgot to maintain her cool disinterest. Despite herself, she returned the warm look. Then, just as quickly, she forced her mind back to her proposal, the one she'd lost because Scott decided to send Laurel-the-perfectly-breasted careening into her evening. Her dark mood returned, and with it, her desire to draw blood. Her eyes dropped to Laurel's hard nipples, outlined by the thin cotton of her T-shirt. The bra that was supposed to shield these distractions was still in Laurel's hand.

"Would you mind putting your bra on?" Dana asked in a rough voice. Flustered, she added, "I feel like I'm being stared at with those things pointing at me."

Laurel stretched out her legs and cocked her head. Suppressing what looked to be a smile of grand amusement, she said, "Whatever makes you happy, Dana." With that, she shuffled away from the wall and pulled her T-shirt off.

For the second time that night, Dana found herself trying hard not to stare goggle-eyed at the woman's bare breasts. Startled, she whipped her head around so that she wouldn't cave in to temptation. "What the hell are you doing?"

"Putting my bra back on, as requested." There was a smirk in her voice. "You're scared of naked women, aren't you?"

Dana glanced over to Laurel, trying hard not to flinch at the sight of her in the lacy black bra. Her breasts looked no less spectacular than they had while bare.

"I'm not 'scared' of naked women," she retorted in a remarkably even voice. "I imagine I'd have a hard time looking in the mirror every morning if I were."

Laurel moved her eyes over Dana in a leisurely appraisal. "For the record, I imagine very few people would have a hard time looking at you in the mirror every morning."

Why the hell would she say that? After a moment of internal debate, Dana voiced her suspicion. "Did Scott hire you to have sex with me?"

Blinking hard, Laurel said, "No." Quickly, and with visibly shaking hands, she pulled her shirt over her head and tugged it down over her torso. "I'm not a goddamn prostitute."

Dana gave a casual shrug. "Sorry to offend. I guess I couldn't tell for sure."

Laurel moved back to her spot against the wall. "You're right," she said in a flat voice. "Why don't we just sit quietly and wait to be rescued?"

Mission accomplished. Dana wondered why she felt so shitty about her personal attack. She stared distractedly at the numbered rows of buttons on the panel next to the elevator door. The woman was a stripper, for Christ's sake. She got naked for money. Where did she get off acting offended about anyone's assumption that she might do even more than that for a paycheck?

Dana was able to stay silent for roughly five minutes before the guilt overwhelmed her. "Look, I'm sorry. Okay, Laurel? I'm sorry."

Laurel shrugged. "For what?"

"For assuming that you might have sex for money. That was wrong, and I'm sorry I offended you." When there was no response, Dana released an explosive sigh. "You know, when you do stuff like put someone's hand on your breast—"

"I was trying to get you to loosen up." Laurel swung her cold gaze over to Dana. "You looked like you wanted to eat me alive but had no idea how to even start."

"I did not," Dana responded. "I was just wondering what the hell you were doing in my lap. I was too shocked to even react at first."

"Well, I'm sorry if I offended you. In fact, I'm sorry I ever took this stupid job." Laurel swiped the back of her hand over her cheek, sniffling.

Dana felt her stomach drop. "Are you crying?" She swallowed

against the lump of pure dread that was lodged in her throat. "Please don't tell me you're about to start crying."

"I'm not crying," Laurel responded, a little too quickly. She brushed the back of her hand over her eyes again, straightening up where she sat slumped against the wall. "I'm just great. Trapped in an elevator on a Friday night with nothing to do but get called a whore by a woman who can't stand me…nowhere near the cat, the book, and the bathtub I was dreaming about enjoying tonight. Why wouldn't I be just fucking fantastic?"

This pronouncement left Dana feeling, all of a sudden, like the biggest asshole on the planet. Great, she thought, running her fingers through her hair. Just great. At a loss, she tried hard to pry her foot from her mouth.

"I'm sorry, Laurel. Really." She tried to explain what had incited her cutting remark. "I just didn't know why you said what you did… you know, about looking at me in the mirror."

Laurel gazed at her for several seconds not saying a word. Finally, she murmured, "I said it because you're a physically attractive woman." She paused. "Despite your wholly unattractive personality."

Dana felt the quiet comment like a punch to the chest. "Oh." She didn't know what else to say. She looked down at her hands. *I love this girl. Forty-six minutes with her and I realize I'm the biggest jerk alive.*

"You're forgiven," Laurel said.

Tears of frustration pricked at Dana's eyes and she lowered her head to hide them from her companion. She wasn't the kind of woman who buckled under pressure.

She thought they weren't talking again until Laurel said, "You really thought your friend would pay someone to have sex with you?"

"I don't know."

"You don't seem the type to appreciate a gesture like that."

Dana looked up. "I'm not."

"Then why would a friend do something like that for you?" Laurel appeared to have a genuine interest in the answer, and Dana could detect no malice in her eyes.

She was briefly tempted to explore that question, but it had already been a long day. "I don't know," she said. "A guy thing, maybe."

Laurel nodded as if accepting this thin rationale. "Well, it's your birthday." With a smile, she asked, "Wasn't it a good day? I mean, other than the...strip-o-gram."

"No better than any other. I came, I worked, I got stuck in an elevator with a half-naked woman who makes me feel like an asshole."

"If you feel like an asshole, I'm sorry." Laurel seemed to be struck by a thought, her gaze sharpening. "Is this whole getting-stuck-in-an-elevator thing going to fuck up some big plans later tonight?"

Dana thought again of her proposal and sighed. The "urgent" project was supposed to keep her from thinking too much about her solitary, boring birthday. A strategy Laurel and Scott had very ably ruined.

"No," she murmured. "No big plans. I was thinking about maybe catching a movie tomorrow, but I'm going to have to re-create the proposal that got interrupted."

"What do you mean, re-create it?"

Dana raised her arm and gave an irritated wave at the emergency lights. "Power outage. I'm sure I hadn't saved the file in quite some time, *if* my computer even survives the whole thing."

"Oh," Laurel said. "Well, it's not really my fault, you know. But... I hope you don't have to redo everything." She waited for Dana to respond, and when she didn't, she asked, "What kind of proposal is it?"

Dana struggled to figure out how to make the task sound as important as she suggested. "It's for a software development project," she said. "We want to sell our client some additional functionality to a piece of custom software we wrote for them. I want to get it e-mailed by Monday morning."

Laurel blinked. "You write software?"

"No." Dana chuckled and shook her head. "I manage the programmers who write the software. They make the application work, and I make them work."

"Do you like it?"

"Yes, a lot."

"It sounds a little...boring. No offense, just not my thing."

Dana felt immediately defensive. "It's a good job. It challenges me." Unable to resist, she added, "Don't tell me you can say that about your career."

Laurel maintained a polite smile. "It's not my career, not that it's any of your business. And I guess the best thing about my job is all the great people I meet." She shot Dana a meaningful smirk. "Like you."

"And the opportunity to make money without relying on any real skill," Dana sniped back. God, why did she find it so easy to get into it with this woman? "Coasting through life, courtesy of your perfect breasts."

Laurel tilted her head to the side. "You think they're perfect?"

Dana blushed hard and sought to retract her careless revelation. "To tell you the truth, I really didn't pay much attention."

Laurel laughed out loud. "Uh-huh. That's why I still have scorch marks on my skin from where your eyes were burning into me."

"You're imagining things." Dana scowled.

"If you say so."

Refusing to admit to her intense fascination with the stripper's chest, Dana decided to pull out the big guns. "I'm not a lesbian."

Laurel's smile gave way to a look of shock. "What?"

Shifting in discomfort at Laurel's obvious surprise, Dana repeated, "I'm not a lesbian. Your breasts are irrelevant to me."

"Huh." Laurel frowned. "So why the hell did Scott hire me to dance for you?"

"Trust me," Dana said, "I plan on asking him that very question first thing tomorrow morning. As soon as we get out of here."

"So, do you have a boyfriend?" Laurel asked in a careful voice.

"No." Dana didn't elaborate. Eager to shift the attention away from herself, she asked, "Do you?"

Laurel broke into a wide grin, showing Dana her white teeth. "No. I *am* a lesbian."

Dana's throat went dry. "Oh." How was she constantly left speechless by this woman?

"Does that bother you?" Laurel asked.

Something in her knowing smile rankled Dana. She thought hard before answering, torn between revealing her turbulent emotions and keeping the peace. "No more than anything else about you bothers me."

Laurel snickered. "Don't worry, I won't hold your sexuality against you, either."

"I appreciate that." Dana managed a half-smile.

"See?" Laurel murmured. "I told you I wasn't such a bad conversationalist."

Dana tipped her head in acknowledgment. "Better than sitting in here in complete silence all night long, that's for sure."

"You never know. By tomorrow morning, we might actually be friends."

Dana rolled her eyes. "Don't get ahead of yourself. It's going to be a long night. Anything could happen."

At that, Laurel folded her arms over her stomach, hugging her body. Her expression seemed almost hopeful, and a little shy. "You're right. Absolutely anything could happen."

Dana could only wonder what the next twelve hours would bring. Hopefully no more tears.

HOUR THREE—9:00 P.M.

W hat are you doing?"
"Dreaming of escape." Dana studied the square metal hatch above their heads. "Think if I lifted you up there, you could pop that thing open?"

"No way," Laurel answered without hesitation. "Not a chance. You're not getting *this* Mrs. Rosen to climb up the Christmas tree."

Dana recognized the reference immediately. *The Poseidon Adventure*...one of her all-time favorites. Her estimation of Laurel increased a notch, almost against her will. Dropping her gaze, she felt a nervous little flip-flopping in her belly. She gave Laurel a teasing smile. "Where's your spirit of adventure?"

"Probably at home with my book, my cat, and my bathtub," Laurel said with an impatient snort. "I refuse to climb up there. We're not on a sinking ship. It won't hurt us to stay right where we are and wait for help."

"It hurts my productivity," Dana protested. Once again, she raised longing eyes to the ceiling.

"Listen, I'm not going to go all disaster movie with you for the sake of some stupid proposal," Laurel replied firmly. "I've always said that I would be the first character to die if I were in one of those films. I'm convinced of it, in fact. I'm just not that clever or tenacious...or lucky, and my life is more important than your getting to work another Friday night."

"Important to whom?" Dana muttered.

"Use this time to relax." Laurel's expression softened into a cajoling smile. "I promise to try and keep you entertained."

"Will this entertainment involve bad music and naked dancing?"

"Only if you ask nicely." She paused. "Technically, your half hour was up two hours ago."

Dana shook her head. The back of her neck felt hot with renewed embarrassment. "How much did that little performance set Scott back?"

Laurel clicked her tongue and gave Dana a look of mild disapproval. "Now, that's between Scott and me. If you want to know, you can ask him."

"I'll do that if we ever get out of here."

"I thought cell phones worked inside elevators," Laurel said. Hers lay on the floor between them, discarded when she couldn't get a signal. "Technology. I bet you feel naked without it right now, don't you?"

Dana managed a sheepish nod. "Yeah. I think it's like a security blanket for me at this point. I feel really…vulnerable without my computer."

"I'm the same way." Laurel held up her hands, shaking them in exaggerated trembling. "I'm already getting twitchy at the thought of not checking my e-mail for the next twelve hours."

"My inbox tends to slow down on the weekends." Dana allowed a self-deprecating grin. "You wouldn't believe how many people take a break from work on Saturday and Sunday."

"Well, I get some school-related e-mails, but most are personal, especially during the weekends. So I check all the time."

She never would've taken Laurel for a computer geek, Dana mused. E-mail and *The Poseidon Adventure*. She was full of surprises. "I don't do all that much personal e-mail. Just the usual family stuff to Mom and Dad."

"Where do they live?"

"Royal Oak."

"Do you have brothers and sisters?"

"One brother. Younger. Last time I checked, he's still practically living at home with my parents."

"I don't have any siblings, but I always thought that would have been fun," Laurel said. "I've got a few really good friends all over the world. Online friends, you know. I'm not—" Inexplicably, she blushed. "I'm not the kind of person who goes out a lot to the bars or anything.

My closest friends tend to be the ones I meet online. The friendship is more focused on communicating with each other rather than distracting ourselves with food and alcohol."

The realization that she'd stereotyped Laurel made Dana feel stupid with shame. She had no idea who this woman was, but she'd insulted her anyway. Wanting to make up for her insensitivity, she tried to take an interest in Laurel's online hobby. "So...where are some of the places your friends live?"

"Australia." Laurel seemed happy they were finally just talking like new acquaintances. "France. Oh, and sometimes I e-mail this really interesting woman in Portugal."

Dana tried to imagine becoming friendly with a virtual stranger, someone she had never seen before in real life. Hell, she could barely manage making friends face-to-face, let alone separated by miles of ocean. Scott was her friend because they had grown up together more than anything else.

"What do you talk about?" she asked.

"God, anything. What's going on in our lives. Our worries, our fears. Politics, religion, current events. Sex." Laurel paused to shoot her a wolfish grin. "Always sex."

Dana could feel the blush creep across her face, an unstoppable attack on her composure. Hesitating for only a moment, she asked, "Like...cybersex?"

Laurel laughed long and hard at the tentative question. "No, we just talk about what we enjoy, who we want, what we'd like to try. What we've fantasized about."

Dana felt incredibly uncomfortable with the direction the conversation had taken. Still, she couldn't resist one last question. "Have you ever had cybersex before?"

"Oh, sure," Laurel said, waving a dismissive hand. "On occasion. Usually when I'm feeling pretty desperate and masturbation alone just isn't going to cut it for me. It's okay, but not nearly as fun as the real thing. You know?" Almost as an afterthought, she said, "Have you tried it?"

Though there was no real reason for her to blush after Laurel's revelation, Dana's face was on fire. "Yeah. Once or twice."

"I had cybersex with a man once," Laurel said. "Just to see what it would be like. I'll tell you what, if men are half as bad in bed as this guy was with the keyboard, I'm confident that I'm not missing a damn thing."

Dana shrugged. "Probably not." She'd had one-time encounters with both men and women online. The men tended to bore her to death with their crude phrasing and rampant misspellings. Not to mention all the penis talk.

"So are they as bad in bed as they are online?" Laurel asked.

Dana thought about Jason Lewis, her first and only boyfriend. "Sometimes."

"You don't like talking about sex, do you?" Laurel's friendly gaze seemed full of regret, and perhaps a little pity.

Dana looked down at her lap, desperate for a way to send their conversation in a different direction and coming up totally blank. After a period of awkward silence, she asked, "Do you think we could change the subject?"

"Sure." Laurel stretched one long leg out, scooting away from the wall to poke at one of Dana's feet with the tip of her shoe. "Whatever's going to make you happy, birthday girl. So what do you want to talk about instead?"

Inevitably, Dana's mind refused to budge from thoughts of sex—ideally with Laurel. She imagined latching her lips onto one of the fat nipples she had seen earlier, sucking hard at the rosy pink flesh. *Jesus, get a grip.* She cleared her throat.

"What book were you going to read tonight?" She winced at the way her voice squeaked at the non sequitur. *In the bathtub. Naked.*

Laurel hid a toothy grin behind her hand. "Not a very good attempt at changing the topic, I'm afraid. It was a collection of lesbian erotica."

My God, she's sex obsessed. Dana shook her head. "So, I'm trapped in an elevator with a lesbian nymphomaniac."

"I can think of worse things to have happen on a Friday night," Laurel retorted. "And I wouldn't consider myself a nymphomaniac. Just in possession of a very healthy—though underutilized, not that it's any of your business—sex drive."

"Well, as long as you keep that healthy sex drive on *your* side of the elevator, we'll be fine." Dana regretted the words as soon as she saw the quiet hurt in Laurel's eyes. *Yes, Laurel, the moment you think I might be okay, I'll make damn sure you know I'm a jerk.*

"Don't flatter yourself," Laurel muttered.

Shit, Dana thought. She'd only wanted to steer the conversation away from sex, not alienate her only company for the long night. Struggling to push past her own verbal gaffe, she quickly plucked another topic out of her memories of their chat so far. "So you're in school?"

"Yes, at Michigan State."

"What are you studying?"

"Veterinary medicine. I'm graduating in six months."

That one stopped Dana cold. As much as she almost couldn't believe it, she was deeply impressed. And she felt very silly recalling her derogatory remarks to Laurel about not understanding what it felt like to be successful. "Wow. Uh, your cat Isis must be very proud of you, huh?"

Laurel's smile crinkled her nose in the most adorable way. "Except when I practice on her."

"Your parents must be proud, too." It was a blatant attempt to fish for more information, but Dana didn't care. She had a strange desire to find out which of her many assumptions were wrong.

Laurel lost her sunny expression, though the corners of her mouth remained turned up in a wistful smile. "My mother is very proud, yes."

Not your father? Dana didn't ask the obvious question, afraid to create awkwardness. Instead, she forced herself to say what was long overdue. "I owe you an apology, you know."

"I know," Laurel answered. "For what?"

Dana grumbled internally. A part of her was pleased, though. She almost liked that Laurel wouldn't let her get away with anything. "I apologize for the comments I made about the whole stripping thing. Assuming that it was your career and everything."

Laurel gave her a solemn nod. "Even if it was, I didn't deserve to be treated like that. I know plenty of girls who strip for a living and, believe it or not, they really are decent human beings."

"Point taken." Dana's head had started to ache, deep and steady. The pain was subtle, but she sensed that this one could escalate. "I was upset," she said, thoroughly chastened. "I was trying to hurt you."

"So you don't really think I'm just some cheap stripper?" Laurel's eyes twinkled.

"No." Dana stared down at the ugly patterned carpeting on the elevator floor. Remembering the perfect breasts she had insisted Laurel cover up, she added, "I would imagine that you're top of the line, actually."

"Nah," Laurel said with a dismissive wave of her hand. "It doesn't generally take much with men. Especially if I'm dancing for a woman. Guys love watching a woman give another woman a lap dance. They're easy."

Dana felt sick with embarrassment at the very thought. "Thank God I was alone in the office. I doubt the guys I work with would have considered it very 'hot' at all. Not with me involved."

After long moments of intense visual examination that left Dana squirming where she sat, Laurel said, "You're hard on yourself, aren't you? Probably all the time?"

Her voice was kind, but the question rattled Dana. Her head continued to ache. "You're the one who deemed me the most boring woman alive earlier, remember?"

Even in the dim light, she could see Laurel's face flush.

"I guess it's my turn to be sorry," Laurel said. "I don't happen to think that's true."

"Sometimes it is," Dana admitted.

"See? Too hard on yourself. You need to stop that."

Dana snorted. "I can't make any promises. You know what they say about old habits."

"For the rest of the night, at least?"

Laurel was so earnest in her request that Dana didn't have the heart to refuse. "Yes, ma'am."

"Mistress," Laurel corrected.

"Excuse me?"

"Ma'am makes me feel old. Mistress makes me feel like a kick-ass dominatrix or something."

Dana's instinct was to retreat, but instead she did something uncharacteristic. She played along. "So be it, Mistress."

One dark eyebrow lifted in amusement. "Much better."

Dana chuckled, then winced at her growing awareness of the pain in her skull. *Please, no,* she thought to herself. *Don't let this be a bad one.*

"Something wrong?" Laurel asked.

Dana concentrated hard on breathing, trying to stave off the massive headache that threatened. "Just a tension headache. I get them when I'm feeling anxious."

"Is there anything I can do to help? I wish I had some Tylenol."

"Just kill me."

"I don't want to do that," Laurel said. "I'm kind of starting to like you. Why don't you lie down? You can't be comfortable sitting all hunched over like that."

Dana gave the dingy carpeting a skeptical look. "I'm not lying down in here. It's filthy. And there's no room."

The pain in her head intensified, making her wince. Perfect. She was about to get the worst headache of her life while trapped in an elevator with a beautiful, nymphomaniac lesbian stripper who was almost a veterinarian. She groaned in self-disgust. What a loser.

Before Dana could protest, Laurel crawled over and wrapped an arm around her shoulders.

"What are you doing?" Dana's voice sounded loud and accusatory. Shock at Laurel's touch gave way to plain agony, and she grabbed her head with both hands.

Laurel pulled her closer. "Lie back on me. Put your head on my lap and just try to relax, okay?"

Gritting her teeth, Dana tried to jerk away. "I'm fine. Get back on your own side. You're making it worse."

"No, you're the one doing that. If you'd just lie down, you'd feel better."

Dana released an explosive sigh. Her head felt so heavy and achy that it was all she could do to keep it upright. Laurel wouldn't let go.

"Stop fighting me," she said, pulling Dana into her soft body.

A thrill of pleasure shot through Dana when her arm pressed into Laurel's generous breasts. She had to admit, her lap looked awfully inviting. Rather than struggle, she surprised herself by acquiescing. She shifted so that she could lay her head down on Laurel's thigh, stretching her legs across the length of the elevator car.

"Thank you," Laurel whispered.

Dana gazed up at the smooth skin of her cheeks, the elegant shape of her nose, and the deep, sincere blue of her eyes. Not good. She was never going to relax staring at this face. She turned onto her side, realizing only too late that she'd rolled the wrong way. Laurel's stomach was directly in front of her. She took shallow breaths, trying hard not to think about how close her face was to the space between Laurel's legs.

"Comfortable?" Laurel whispered. Her stomach moved beneath her snug T-shirt as she spoke.

"Oh, yes." Two hours ago, it would have seemed impossible to be so close to such a beautiful woman. Dana still had trouble believing the elevator nightmare was really happening. It was the kind of far-fetched plot twist that made her grimace when she was reading a book. She moaned as Laurel's hand found the tense, knotted muscles between her shoulder blades. "Oh, God, that feels good."

Laurel rubbed harder, hitting all the perfect spots, gradually relaxing Dana's tortured muscles. "You like that?" There was a quiet satisfaction in her voice.

"It feels amazing." Incredibly, Dana felt her muscles loosen, and the tension in her head began to dissipate. Whimpering, she said, "My lower back hurts, too."

Laurel chuckled and moved her hand down along the path of Dana's spine. "Was that a hint?"

Dana burrowed closer. As silly as she felt accepting the tender attention, she couldn't deny the effect it was having on her. The headache—so much worse than a normal episode—was fading away. A hot shower had nothing on Laurel's soothing hands. And the sensation of being touched after so long without was nothing short of overwhelming. She would never admit to craving human contact, but Laurel's long, deep massage made her more aware than ever of what she was missing. By not seeking relationships with other people, she thought she could avoid complications. Maybe that was valid. But the price seemed high, and she wondered if she'd been fooling herself, making justifications so she could avoid confronting the truth. Becoming a lonely, uptight workaholic was a pathetic way to deal with the fear of rejection.

"God, you're so stiff," Laurel said. "So tense. No wonder your head is killing you."

"I'm sure the whole 'trapped in an elevator' thing triggered it this time." And most likely the lap dance didn't help. She hadn't been that upset in a long time.

"You really get these headaches a lot?"

"Semiregularly," Dana whispered. "I'm a little high stress sometimes."

To her credit, Laurel didn't take that comment and run with it. "This is exactly why you need a Friday night off," she said.

Dana let the comment pass without argument. "Though preferably not inside a seven-foot by seven-foot space."

"True." Laurel raked her fingers through Dana's hair, scratching lightly across her scalp. The other hand continued to knead her lower back, no longer massaging as much as tracing distracted patterns. "How's your head now?"

Swimming. Dana resisted the urge to purr. She felt like a pile of jelly. "Maybe a little better."

"I can feel you starting to relax. See, it's not so bad just letting go of your tension. Everyone needs that."

Laurel had no idea just how badly she needed it. "Um, do you think you could keep going for a minute?"

"Oh, so you really like this?" Laurel's voice was warm. She kneaded Dana's lower back with renewed intensity.

Forgetting her pain completely, Dana struggled not to orgasm right then and there. "It's definitely...helping."

"Anything to help."

Laurel's hands were made of magic. Dana was so grateful for the quick relief of her pain and the pleasure of the massage that she didn't try to censor her words. "It feels so good to be touched."

She realized what she'd said, and how pathetic it sounded, when Laurel's fingers faltered for a moment. Dana shifted, so she could sit up, but Laurel pressed a hand against the middle of her spine, holding her in place.

"Don't leave," she said. "I'm enjoying this as much as you are. Takes my mind off being stuck in such a small space. Plus, I kind of like feeling as if I'm more than just a pain in your ass."

"Oh, you've always been more than just a pain in my ass," Dana mumbled. "A thorn in my side, a cramp in my style, a—"

"A song in your heart," Laurel interrupted. "Don't try and deny it. I'm a light in your life."

"Okay, so you're right," Dana said. "You're a diamond in my rough."

Laurel made a small, disapproving sound.

"No?" Dana looked up into Laurel's face, which loomed over hers.

"No. We were on a roll, but—"

"I ruined it, huh?"

They traded goofy grins.

"You know"—Dana broke their eye contact—"I'm feeling a lot better."

"I fixed you?" Laurel's sunny smile made her look young and impossibly pretty.

"I guess you did." Dana felt sheepish about their continued contact, hyperaware of the weight and warmth of Laurel's hand resting on her stomach. Now that her headache had passed, her bad case of nerves returned. Stiffening, she said, "I guess I should sit up now."

"If you insist."

Dana mourned the loss of those fingers from her hair, but gave Laurel a nonchalant grin that belied her inner turmoil. She settled against the wall, her shoulder brushing Laurel's. She rather enjoyed the warm infusion of heat where their bodies touched. Greedily, she didn't want to give up this innocent contact.

"Do you want me to get back on my own side now?" Laurel asked without enthusiasm.

"Nah." Dana managed an absent shrug, hoping like hell that Laurel couldn't hear her heart beating. "You can stay here, if you want."

"It *is* less lonely next to you. And not nearly so cold."

A manic giggle tickled the back of Dana's throat as Laurel leaned into her. This was flirting, wasn't it? She enjoyed the thought for a beat, then remembered something that wiped the giddy amusement away in an instant. *Shit. I have no fucking idea how to flirt.* In grand Dana Watts style, she managed a heavy-handed response that was nothing at all like what she really wanted to say. "Are you coming on to me?"

Laurel blinked rapidly. "Of course not. You're not a lesbian, remember?"

Oh, yeah. Summoning the courage, Dana asked something she suddenly needed to know. "Do you have a girlfriend?"

Laurel gave her a shy smile. "I told you I was single, remember?"

"You told me you didn't have a boyfriend, because you're a lesbian. You never told me you were single."

"Well, I'm single. Does that mean I'm allowed to flirt?"

Dana's heart thump-thumped. Face hot, she forced herself to continue the playful conversation. "I thought you weren't coming on to me."

"That was before I realized that you cared whether or not I had a girlfriend," Laurel said. "Now I've decided to admit that I *was* coming on to you. A little."

"I never said I *cared* whether or not you were single. I just wondered."

"Well, now you know."

"Now I do." Dana moved her gaze rapid-fire over every inch of the elevator car in a kind of desperation to figure out what to say next. She locked onto Laurel's backpack. "Do you have any snacks in your bag?"

Laurel gave her a knowing smile. "I might. Craving anything in particular?"

"How about a nice slice of angel food cake with chocolate whipped cream topping?"

"I don't know about that, but I'll see what I can do." Laurel reached across the elevator car for her backpack, her bottom thrusting into the air only inches away from Dana's arm.

She had a lovely shape, and it occurred to Dana just how easy it would be to give her ass a nice squeeze. She flinched in shock at her own thoughts. *Good. Now I'm on the verge of assaulting her.* Laurel had only allowed herself to be groped earlier because Scott had paid for her professional services. Dana moved her hand discreetly beneath her thigh, trapping it against the floor. *Don't go and make a fool of yourself now.*

Laurel sat back and extracted something from her backpack, asking, "Special K bar? I've only got one. It's peaches and berries."

Dana's stomach growled. "You'd be my hero if you split it with me. I skipped lunch, and hadn't gotten around to dinner yet."

"Take it. It's yours."

"I couldn't do that," Dana's hand twitched beneath her thigh, eager to snatch the bar. "I don't want to take your only piece of food."

"I didn't say it was the only thing I had. I've got some dessert that I thought we'd save for later."

Dana wasn't in the mood to be stoic. "Okay," she said, holding out her hand.

Laurel handed it over with an easy smile. "That's probably another reason you got a headache. You shouldn't be skipping meals."

Dana rolled her eyes and tore off the wrapper with gusto. She took a healthy bite and chewed, letting her eyes close at the pleasant flavor. "This is ambrosia," she moaned.

Laurel laughed. "Shit, if I'd known that all it would take was a back rub and a breakfast bar, I would've soothed the savage beast a couple of hours ago."

"With me, slow and easy is best. Dropping out of 'bitch mode' too fast causes whiplash, or so I'm told."

"Slow and easy, huh?" Laurel gave Dana a shit-eating grin. "I'll keep that in mind."

"You do that," Dana murmured, then blinked in shock. She was actually flirting back.

And if the look on Laurel's face was any indication, she was doing it well.

HOUR SIX—12:00 A.M.

"Why the hell do you have whipped cream in your bag?"

Laurel's face was a delightful shade of rosy pink. She broke their eye contact, gazing down at the floor. "It was..."

Dana got the feeling that she was being obtuse, but she honestly didn't understand Laurel's embarrassment. "For dessert?" she asked.

"For my breasts." Laurel reached into her backpack and pulled out a small box of birthday candles. "Happy birthday."

Dana handed the can of whipped cream back to Laurel. "You were going to let me—"

"Lick it off. Yes." Laurel shoved the can of whipped cream and the box of candles back into her bag, not meeting Dana's eyes. "You think I'm a complete slut, right?"

Strangely, that had been the last thought on Dana's mind. *No, I think you're a goddamn wet dream.* She was relieved that her birthday surprise had ended before she was confronted with cream-tipped nipples. Most people would probably take that opportunity and run with it, but she would have blown it. She *did* blow it.

"That doesn't make you uncomfortable?" she asked, shifting the focus away from her own responses. "Letting some stranger just...put her mouth on you?"

"It's not like a regular part of my act or anything." Laurel shifted away. It was only a few inches, but Dana felt the loss. "I just figured—a female client. I don't know, I thought it might be pretty hot."

She was clearly uncomfortable, and Dana wished she'd been more tactful. Trying to make her feel better, she said, "I love whipped cream. And I suspect that it's even better when served on perfect breasts."

Having placed her supposed heterosexuality in doubt, she expected a mocking reply, but Laurel gave her a shy smile that made the admission worthwhile.

"Thanks, Dana." She thrust her hand back into the depths of her bag and pulled out an object that made Dana moan in anticipation. Waving the Hershey's chocolate bar in front of Dana's face, she asked, "Hungry?"

When Dana reached out as if to grab the chocolate bar, Laurel snapped it away.

"You never said dessert would be conditional." Dana sighed.

"I'm sure you'll earn it. I'm easy to please."

"Oh, really?" Dana drawled. Damn, flirting was fun. "Easy to please? I guess I'll keep *that* in mind."

"You do that."

"Anything else? What other wonders do you have in there?"

Breaking into a wide grin, Laurel withdrew two books. The one she handed to Dana was slightly battered and obviously well loved. Dana was immediately riveted to the cover image of two beautiful women engaged in a sensual kiss. The title of the book was *Stories for the Long Night: A Collection of Lesbian Erotica*. Instantly turned on, she was unable to form a sentence. She reached for the other book.

"*Emergency Procedures for the Small Animal Veterinarian*," she read aloud. "A little light reading?"

"It's for one of the classes I took. It's actually a really good text." Laurel followed the books with a stethoscope, which she caressed with mock-seductive coyness. "How about this for excitement?"

"I guess we're covered if we want to play doctor later," Dana said, holding her gaze.

Laurel released a shaky breath. "Don't tease the lesbian. It's been…forever since I played a good game of doctor."

The desire in Laurel's voice was obvious. *Did I really do that?* Dana grinned, growing warm inside. "Don't get too excited," she said, giving Laurel a sidelong glance, "We have to finish this game first, at least."

Laurel set the stethoscope on the growing pile of stuff and hauled out a nylon bag. "Blanket in a bag. Essential for the student preferring to lunch by the river between classes."

"You can fit an actual blanket in that thing?"

"Yes. A warm gray fleece one. Maybe if you're really nice, I'll let you share it later. If you decide you need to nap or something." She peered into her bag. "That's about it. There's just my wallet."

Dana settled back against the wall, glancing at her wristwatch. "We're probably going to be stuck in here for at least another seven hours, so I'm thinking we could kill five or ten minutes with your wallet."

"I don't suppose you have a wallet so you can reciprocate with this little show and tell?"

Dana shook her head. "I'm afraid it's in my office." She delved into her pockets and pulled out the contents, reporting, "I've got half a roll of Life Savers, two quarters, the receipt from the muffin I bought on the way to work this morning, and some pocket lint."

"So I'm on my own here, with the whole 'share your life with a virtual stranger' thing?" Laurel didn't sound upset.

Dana flicked some lint in her direction. "You're feeling shy *now*? After straddling my lap and giving me an up-close-and-personal view of your perfect—"

"All right, all right." Laurel slapped Dana's arm playfully. "I guess I have no secrets now."

Dana shivered, feeling gooseflesh raise on her skin. "You're killing me. They're going to find a stripper and a dead project manager in here tomorrow morning, for sure."

Laurel burst into loud, braying laughter, which she quickly stifled with a hand over her mouth. At Dana's quizzical look, she leaned into her and gasped, "I'm just trying to figure you out."

She didn't say any more, and they fell into a silence that seemed to pulse with sexual energy. Laurel kept meeting her eyes shyly, then looking away, all the while wearing a grin that suggested she held some tasty secret. Dana could feel her own gaze straying to Laurel's face without her consent, and every time their eyes met, her heart would race. How would she ever make it through the night without making a complete fool of herself?

The best way, she decided, was to keep talking about Laurel's wallet.

Dana held out her hand. "Is your driver's license photo as awful as mine?"

Laurel handed over the plastic card. "You tell me."

Dana gazed down at Laurel's small image, which wasn't nearly as lovely as the real thing sitting next to her on the floor, but beautiful nonetheless. Not quite trusting herself to make a casual comment, she scanned the details instead. Laurel Jane Stanley. May 13, 1982. "Jesus, you're a baby."

Laurel snorted. "Since when is twenty-five a baby?"

"You were born in the eighties and you're graduating from veterinary school in six months?" Dana felt simultaneously impressed and completely foolish. *And here I pretty much called her an empty-headed bimbo earlier.*

Laurel shrugged. "I skipped a grade in elementary school. So how old are you, wise elder?"

"Twenty-eight." Dana said.

"You're ragging on me for being born in the eighties, but you're only three years older?"

"Those are three very important years." Dana's heart started beating crazily. It was so easy to talk to Laurel. To joke around, even. She couldn't remember the last time she had enjoyed anyone's company so much. That thought, to put it mildly, shocked her. All of a sudden, she couldn't think of a single word to say. She snapped her mouth closed and waited for Laurel to break the quiet.

Laurel seemed to sense her shift in mood, because her smile faded and for a few moments she stared at Dana, light color rising on her cheeks.

"So what do you think?" Laurel asked. "Is my photo as awful as yours?"

Dana willed her heartbeat to slow down. She stroked her thumb over the image. "No, you're gorgeous."

As she returned the license, her fingers brushed Laurel's and they both exhaled at the accidental contact. Completely undone, Dana said, "Thanks."

She'd never experienced a moment like that with another human being. It was an actual moment, she thought, no one could dispute that. She wondered how exactly one was supposed to go on after a moment like that.

Apparently Laurel knew. "I have a picture of my cat," she murmured, moving them past the fraught silence. "Do you want to see her?"

"This is Isis, right?" Dana asked as she was handed a photo of a black cat with a pantherlike face.

"Yes, tell me she doesn't look like a creature who should have been worshipped by the ancient Egyptians."

"Sneezing into your bubble bath is godlike?" Dana asked. *Bubble bath. Great. Right where I wanted my mind to wander.*

"Not that part," Laurel said. "She has six toes on every foot and a regal bearing."

"Very regal. And worshipped plenty by a modern American."

"That she is," Laurel agreed. "She's my baby." She exchanged the photo for another. "This is my mother."

Dana took in the image of a slight blond woman with an encouraging smile.

"She was my best friend," Laurel said. "She passed away last year."

Dana felt a lump in her throat. "Oh, Laurel, I'm so sorry."

Laurel shrugged. "So am I. She had cancer. It was pretty bad in the end, so in a way, it was time."

Dana handed the photo back to Laurel with silent reverence. "I still have both of my parents," she said after a moment. "I guess I still feel too young to lose them. Even though I'm not very close with them." She studied her companion, resisting the urge to stroke her chestnut hair. "Are you close with your father?"

Laurel's eyes darkened. "No." She tucked the picture of her mother away. "He left us when Mom got sick. I got to take care of her and he got a new, young wife who probably married him for the money he took with him."

Asshole. Dana experienced a surge of anger that felt out of proportion with her emotional involvement in the situation. "That was shitty of him."

"For sure," Laurel agreed. She spread the wallet open and showed Dana the contents. "Sixty-eight dollars." Dana watched in fascination as Laurel's lips quivered for a moment before she broke into a mischievous grin. "Got a dollar?"

Dana blushed as soon as she understood Laurel's joke, almost a full fifteen seconds after her companion put it out there. Sixty-nine. Great, just what she needed to think about. Managing a shy chuckle, Dana said, "Unfortunately, my wallet's in my office, remember?"

"Oh, yeah." Laurel cleared her throat and flipped slowly through the plastic sleeves in her wallet. "So I've got a credit card...my debit card...voter registration...my library card—"

"A library card? That's so...quaint."

"I'm bookish like that." Laurel offered a faux seductive eyelash flutter. "You know you think it's sexy."

"Oh, yes," Dana said. "Very sexy."

"I knew it." Laurel put her things away in her backpack, wearing a slight smile as she worked. She offered the lesbian erotica book to Dana before stowing it. "You sure you don't want a little light reading?"

Dana leaned across Laurel's lap and grabbed at the Hershey's bar on the floor. "I'd rather have the chocolate."

Laurel slapped her away and snatched up the candy. "Maybe after that game of truth or dare you promised me."

Her sweet, innocent smile was hard to resist. Dana knew her protest sounded feeble. "Promised? I'm pretty sure I never promised anything like that."

"Listen, do you want the chocolate or not?"

Dana released a long-suffering sigh. "Fine," she said. "After truth or dare."

HOUR SEVEN—1:00 A.M.

D oesn't anyone clean this building at night?" Laurel asked.
Crazed butterflies had taken up residence in the pit of her stomach at the prospect of ending their game and going to sleep. Her eyes felt heavy but her senses were restless. She and Dana had been circling around each other for the past hour, keeping their chit-chat superficial. Laurel had been tempted to dig deeper but Dana was skittish, and they had to endure another six or seven hours cooped up here.

"They're on a rotating schedule for Friday nights. Tonight they clean the carpets in the other wing."·

Laurel yawned. "Timing is everything."

Dana cleared her throat. "So may I ask you a question? A real question."

"As opposed to—"

"Beating around the bush."

Dana's eyes were close enough that Laurel could watch the faint pulse of the pupils in the emerald green irises. After hours trapped in the elevator, only a single lock of Dana's well-coiffed auburn hair was out of place. It fell across her cheek, and Laurel wanted more than anything to reach out and test its softness. There was something indescribably beautiful about Dana. She was the same height as Laurel, with a slight fullness to her face and body that was so sensual it made Laurel weak in the knees.

Good thing they were sitting down.

"Sure, you can ask me a question." Laurel knew what was coming. "What do you want to know?"

"I was just wondering, why stripping?"

"I actually prefer to call it dancing." She had her answer ready in advance. "The money is great and the hours are perfect, when it comes to juggling both work and school."

"But…" Dana still seemed to be coming to terms with her feelings on the subject.

"It's demeaning?" Laurel guessed. At Dana's nod, she shook her head. "I don't agree. I'm doing this of my own free will, I don't let anyone do anything I don't want them to do, and I've earned enough money to pay my way through college. Pretty soon I'll be *Doctor* Stanley, and I can't begrudge anything that helps me get there."

"I guess it just seems like… I don't know. You seem so smart."

"I am smart," Laurel said, and shrugged. "It's a job. I'm looking forward to quitting and being a vet, but it hasn't been that bad."

"How long have you been doing it?"

"About six years," Laurel said. For the first time since they'd begun this conversation, she gave Dana an embarrassed smile. "A long time, I guess."

"So do you usually do…private performances? Like tonight?"

Laurel shook her head. "No, actually, I work in a club. Tonight is kind of a new thing."

"How did Scott find you?" Dana asked.

"I started advertising in a lesbian magazine a couple of months ago. As a private dancer. Available to perform for other women."

Dana's gaze dropped to her lap. "You don't do private dances for men?"

"No, I dance for men at the club. I wouldn't feel comfortable doing a private show for a man."

"Have you had a lot of female clients?" Dana's voice sounded strained.

"You were the third," Laurel replied. "It was just supposed to be a side thing. A little extra money doing something a bit more…fun." She cleared her throat. Feeling a strange need to justify her new venture, she picked at the frayed edges of a hole in the thigh of her jeans. "I mean, I've danced for women at the club before. Women come in more than you might imagine. That's kind of why I decided to do this on the side."

Dana seemed intrigued, yet uneasy. "You don't like dancing for men?"

"Oh, I don't really mind." It was mostly true. Dancing for men was a means to an end, and most of the time, they were gentlemen. Laurel was long past second-guessing her decisions in this area. She had risen to the challenge when her mom got sick and her father left, and she was a stronger person for her experiences. "I mean, there are good customers and bad customers, you know? Some guys are all hands, or rude, or just generally unpleasant. But a lot of them are really sweet. I've got regulars who come in and just want to talk, to spend time with me."

"Does your club have rules about how customers treat you?"

Laurel could tell what she was thinking. She'd had similar views herself when she first thought about exotic dancing, picturing taking off her clothes for the eager patrons of a seedy strip club. "There are rules. We wear g-strings at all times. No touching. Or rather, we can touch them, but they have to keep their hands off us." She gave Dana a tender smile. "It's really not as horrible as I suspect you think it is. I do a lot of table dances. I don't much like doing lap dances for guys."

"But you're so good at them." Dana graced her with a rakish grin.

"It helps when your client is hot."

Dana's grin faltered slightly, and Laurel watched a wave of insecurity flash across her face. At the same time, she could see that Dana was struggling to regroup without letting on how the compliment affected her.

"Was it hard the first time? Getting naked, I mean? Dancing in front of so many people?"

"Oh, sure. I was almost as nervous the first time I danced as I was the first time I had sex."

Dana had nothing to say to that. Her cheeks were red.

"I cried afterward, too," Laurel confessed. "Once I got home. My mom was there waiting for me, and I just couldn't help but cry in her arms." She shrugged. "That was only a few months after Dad left, though, so I was still pretty overwhelmed by everything. My mom was great about the dancing. She knew I was doing it, I mean, and she understood why I felt like it was our best option."

"You have no idea how much I feel like an asshole by now," Dana commented in a quiet voice. "You were nineteen, alone with a sick mother, and paying your way through college. I'm not going to apologize again, because I know we've forgotten about it, but I want to say something. I think you're an incredibly together young woman. You sound like a good person."

"Thanks." Laurel had the impression that Dana's judgments were more about herself than Laurel. But it was still nice to hear her acknowledge she'd been wrong. "I have to admit, I thought you were an asshole for a little while there, but I don't anymore. I can see there's an incredibly funny, sweet woman inside of you."

"I'm glad you're convinced," Dana said. "Sometimes I wonder."

She sounded so cheerless, Laurel wasn't sure what to say. "You don't let very many people in, do you?"

"Pathetic, I know."

She looked so broken, Laurel moved to a safer topic. "Where did you go to school?"

"The University of Michigan," Dana said. "Ann Arbor. I graduated seven years ago. Bachelor's of Business Administration." She paused, then added, "With a concentration in computer information systems. It was a newer program at the time, but I was interested in the technological side of business. It appealed to me more than accounting, at least, and I'm good at it. My team always delivers excellent work, usually under budget."

"I imagine your parents are proud of you, too," Laurel said.

"They are. We don't talk all that often. They're much more involved with my younger brother. He's going to apply to law school, or so he says. I can't even imagine my baby brother as a lawyer."

"So why are your parents more involved with him?"

Dana pulled her knees up to her chest and rested the side of her face on them. "Because he wants that. He's still pretty attached, being younger and all. He practically lives there on weekends. I have my own life, and I like it that way. I'm more of a loner, I guess."

"I always hung out with my mom when she was alive," Laurel said. "My dad... I couldn't care less about having anything to do with him at this point. I admit I haven't quite forgiven him for what he did to us."

"I have great parents," Dana hastened to explain. "I just don't feel entirely comfortable around them."

"That's too bad," Laurel murmured. "I hope you're able to appreciate them fully while you have them." She hesitated. "I'm not trying to be morbid or anything. I'm just saying—"

"I understand." Dana's eyes glowed with sincerity. Their color was the green of rolling hills in springtime. "I always assume I'll have time to get closer to them, that it'll happen naturally. Maybe I need to remember that I should make more of an effort while it's still an option."

Laurel blinked back her emotion. "I think that's a great idea."

"So…did your mom know about your sexuality?"

"Oh, yeah. I told her when I was eighteen, right after she was diagnosed with cancer. I'd known for a couple of years at that point, but I wasn't out. Once I realized she was sick, I couldn't justify hiding it anymore."

"Was she okay about it?"

"She was surprised at first. At that point, though, I think that my being a lesbian was the least of her worries." Laurel remembered the scared, lost look her mother would sometimes get in her last months, when she thought no one was watching. Even now, thinking about that look, and knowing that so much of it was fear and grief over having to say good-bye, made Laurel's heart ache. "She even accused me of planning the timing of my little announcement perfectly. After finding out that she had breast cancer, she couldn't manage a bad reaction over something minor like her baby girl liking other girls."

Dana's chuckle sounded nervous more than amused. "So it was pretty painless? Coming out?"

"I cried that day, too, but all things considered, yeah. It was painless." Laurel didn't feel like going into detail. "So how about you? How did your parents react when you told them you were straight?"

Dana laughed. "Smart-ass."

"You like calling me that."

"You like being that," Dana shot back. "So, does your dad know, too?"

She couldn't get off the subject, Laurel thought. "He knows, and his opinion doesn't really matter to me."

"It must matter a little bit." Dana looked puzzled. "What your parents think always matters, at least a little."

"My father lost the privilege of having an opinion that mattered when he abandoned my mother at the time she needed him most," Laurel said. "My mom loved me and accepted me, and in the end, that's all that really matters." Wanting to move to a lighter topic, she asked brightly, "Ready for some more truth or dare now that I've discussed the three most terrifying moments of my life?"

"Maybe." Dana checked off her fingers. "Losing your virginity, working your first night in a strip club, and coming out to your mom. That's it?"

"I think that's more than enough. And now it's your turn."

"I'm getting tired."

"Oh, come on. Talking to me hasn't been that bad so far, right?"

"I don't think you've been asking the really hard questions." Dana's grin was nervous. "Or giving me dares."

"I promise to be nice." Laurel batted her eyelashes innocently.

"I'm worried about your definition of nice."

Something about Dana's shy anxiety made Laurel's entire body tingle. She seemed so sweet, almost demure, but Laurel sensed the sexy, playful woman beneath the reserved exterior. Surrendering to a sense of mischief, Laurel murmured throatily, "I've never had anyone complain about my definition of 'nice' before."

Dana stared at her with a mixture of excitement and fear. "Okay, let's play," she croaked.

❖

Dana didn't know how they'd reached this place. They were finally speaking to each other as though they had nothing to lose. She shook her head, torn between fierce excitement and utter fear.

"How many men have you slept with?" she asked.

She was instantly surprised by the proprietary feeling that flashed through her at the thought. She didn't want to imagine Laurel with some man. It was bad enough to picture her dancing for them. She tried to imagine Laurel grinding against another woman the way she had when she was on Dana's lap earlier. That idea offered no solace. *Get a grip*, she thought. Laurel was a beautiful young woman with perfect breasts and a brain to match, and *she* was a twenty-eight-year-old born-again virgin who could stand to lose fifteen pounds.

Laurel was looking at her strangely and Dana realized her breathing was audible. She coughed with embarrassment. Laurel reached over and patted her on the back a few times. The shock of her gentle touch was enough to start Dana breathing again, albeit shakily.

"Are you all right?" Laurel asked. "If you're tired we could try to sleep."

Like she could sleep with the concept of playing truth or dare with this woman floating around in her mind. Dana felt like she was under the microscope. The sensation unnerved her. "I'm fine," she lied.

Laurel remained silent for a few moments, and then answered the question. "None, actually. How about you?"

"One." She could see Laurel doing the math in her head. Twenty-eight years old. One man. Not very impressive for a heterosexual.

Relieved not to be pressed for follow-up information, she deflected the question back onto Laurel. "So how many women have you slept with?"

"Three," Laurel answered without hesitation.

Dana was surprised. She had expected the number to be higher. "Really?"

"Yes, really. Shocked?"

"No," Dana lied.

Laurel snorted. "Truth or dare, Ms. Watts?"

Dana tried to ignore the twinge in her clit at the way Laurel murmured "Ms. Watts." It sounded like something that came from the very best of her executive assistant fantasies, in which she ravished a sexy subordinate on the large oak desk in her office.

"Truth," Dana rasped.

"How old were you when you lost your virginity?"

"Is this going to be all about sex?" Dana complained. Not that she didn't expect it, but the whole "lie if it's embarrassing" plan seemed less and less feasible with those sweet blue eyes on her. "I told you I don't really like talking about this stuff."

Laurel stroked her fingertip across one of Dana's wrists, a fast, tender caress that came out of nowhere and ended after only a moment. She gave her an encouraging smile. "You never have to see me again after tonight. Why not give it a try? I promise to be nice."

Dana was frustrated by how hot her face became, and in an effort to overcome the burden of her own personality, she answered, "I was seventeen. He was my high school boyfriend. Jason." She forced herself to stop talking when she realized that she had far exceeded the question asked. *Jesus. Leave something for her to find out.*

"See? Nothing to be embarrassed about there."

Dana laughed. "You haven't heard the story yet. Truth or dare?"

"Oh, hell, truth again," Laurel said. "Hit me."

"How old were you?" Dana asked. "When you lost your virginity?"

"I was eighteen," Laurel said. "It was a one-time thing with my partner on the debate team during undergrad. We shared a hotel room during the final tournament that year…and a double bed."

I need to ask her to tell me that story for her next truth, Dana mused. "Ask me another question."

"Was it good?" Laurel asked. "With Jason?"

Dana wrinkled her nose. "We only did it twice."

"Not good enough to do it a third time?"

"Not really," Dana admitted.

Laurel looked as if she wanted to ask another question but nodded instead. "Why don't you give me a dare this time?"

Dana's heart stopped beating for half a second. Now was not a good time to remember that she didn't know how to play this game. Asking questions was easy; trying to come up with a dare that wouldn't be totally awkward for one or both of them was another story.

"Start with something easy," Laurel suggested. "Something silly."

Dana flashed on one of the only games of truth or dare she had ever played as a teenager, during Krista Donnelly's sixteenth birthday party. "I dare you to play the rest of the game braless."

Laurel beamed, pulling her arms into her shirt and starting the intricate process of unhooking her bra beneath her clothing. "I thought you felt like you were being stared at when I wasn't wearing it."

"Are you refusing to perform the dare?" Dana asked. "I'm pretty sure there are consequences for that kind of thing."

"I'm obviously not refusing, am I?" Laurel slid the lacy black bra from beneath the hem of her T-shirt and handed it to Dana draped across both hands. "I believe the rules state that you are now the proud owner of this for the duration of the game."

Dana checked out Laurel's unrestrained breasts. Her T-shirt hugged them in the most delicious way, and between that and the subtle scent of perfume from the bra in her hand, Dana felt absolutely giddy.

"So how about you?" Laurel asked. Her nipples grew hard beneath Dana's surreptitious gaze, but if she was aware of it, she didn't let on. Her pale yellow T-shirt left little to the imagination.

"Dare." Dana gave in to a rush of true courage.

"I dare you to give me a hug," Laurel said. "Both arms, at least thirty seconds long."

The dare knocked the wind out of Dana. *A hug?* She felt an embarrassing wetness between her legs. "A hug?"

Laurel nodded, getting up onto her knees. "I've been wanting to give you a hug. Now's my chance and I'm taking it."

"Playing dirty, huh?" Numb, Dana rose.

"Oh, you don't even know how dirty I can play." Laurel spread her arms in invitation. The motion caused her breasts to jut out against her T-shirt, throwing her erect nipples into stark relief beneath the thin cotton. "Come on."

It had been six months since Dana had hugged anyone, and then it had been her father. She was full of stiff uncertainty as she wrapped her arms around Laurel, holding her as if she were made of fine china. She felt clumsy, oafish, and self-conscious about the relative softness of her body pressed against the firm leanness of Laurel's.

"Relax," Laurel murmured into her ear. She brought a hand down to press against the small of Dana's back, holding her close, and moved the other up to cradle her neck and stroke her thumb over the nape. "This is nice, right?"

Dana shifted slightly, afraid of the way her heart was thundering against Laurel's chest. She tried to remember the count. Thirty seconds was taking a long time.

"Stop wishing it over," Laurel chided. She drew back, but kept her arms around Dana in a loose circle. "I hope it was okay. You just… looked like you needed a hug."

Pulling back with a nod, Dana wished she could have just stopped thinking and enjoyed it. Emotions close to the surface, she chose to plunge straight back into their game. Truth this time, she took the opportunity to hear about Laurel's first time with her debate partner. In return, she told Laurel about Jason. For the first time, she admitted how awful it was, and awkward.

Now Laurel truly knew more about her than anyone else.

Dana wanted to keep this going. "How many serious relationships have you had?"

"Only one," Laurel said. "Ash. I met her in school and we were together for about two and a half years. She just wasn't ready to commit, and it got to be too much for her to deal with. I was spending a lot of time taking care of Mom, driving her back and forth to the hospital for chemo..." She shrugged. "I wasn't ready to focus on a relationship, either. But I loved Ash, a lot. I was pretty devastated when it ended."

"I'm sorry," Dana said. Though she'd be lying if she pretended to regret that Laurel was single now. Giving herself a mental slap, Dana invited another truth.

Laurel's mouth took on an affectionate smile. "If you could change one thing about your life, what would it be?"

Dana barely had to think before answering. "To be less afraid." She looked down after she said the words, aware of how she sounded.

"Afraid of what?" Laurel kept her hands folded in her lap, but the compassion in her eyes reached out and wrapped Dana in a feeling of calm safety.

Dana shrugged, though she already knew the answer. "Being myself, I guess."

Laurel contended with that for a moment. Dana could see her mind working as they stared at one another. Neither said anything for a beat.

"Are you being yourself right now?" Laurel finally murmured.

"Right this second?" Dana hadn't felt normal since they'd gotten trapped in the elevator. *I might just tell you anything you ask right now.* "I guess so."

"Earlier?" Laurel asked.

Dana shook her head. "Not entirely."

Laurel reached out to rest her fingertips on Dana's knee. "Why do I get the feeling that those parts of you that I really like are the ones I've seen when you're being yourself?"

Heat flooded Dana's face. *I must look like the most awkward, blushing, inarticulate idiot in the world right now.*

"Will you do me a favor?" Laurel lifted her hand from Dana's knee. "Be yourself. That's who I want to be trapped in an elevator with tonight. The real Dana Watts, not just the woman you want me to think she is." At Dana's nervous nod, she asked, "Are you afraid?"

Of course, Dana raged inside. Her "for other people" voice, when it emerged, was a lot more subdued than her inner voice. "A little."

Laurel held her gaze. "Don't be afraid, okay? I really do like you. I'm having a good time tonight…strangely."

"So am I." There was no going back now. Dana knew Laurel didn't absolutely hate being stuck in here with her. Admitting the truth felt a lot like surrendering. "I have another question," she said.

"Ask anything you want."

Dana spoke from her heart. "What do you look for in a woman? I mean, what do you find attractive in a potential date?"

"What do I notice first?" Laurel was still staring at Dana's face. "Eyes," she said. "Freckles…are a plus. Lips. I like redheads…and brunettes."

Freckles are a plus? Dana thought, feeling every one of the brownish marks sprinkled across her burning cheeks. *Redheads?*

"I like smart women," Laurel continued. "Motivated women. A good sense of humor. Considerate. Sweet, at least with me. I really love a woman who loves sex. Both as something intimate to share, and also fun to do."

Dana listened with rapt attention. Smart: check. Motivated: check. That other stuff: not so sure.

"I'm looking for a woman who's interested in me. Just me. I want to find someone I can spend a lazy Sunday with at home, or sit down and have dinner after work, and talk about our day. Someone who makes going to the grocery store fun, just because I'm with her." Laurel stopped talking and raised a dark eyebrow at Dana. "Do you think I'm looking for too much?"

Dana shook her head. "You deserve to find what you want, and I think she's out there." *In fact, I'm so jealous of her that I'd wring the skinny bitch's neck in a heartbeat.*

Laurel's gaze seemed inwardly focused, and an odd uncertainty passed across her face. Hesitantly, she said, "Dana, I'm really sorry about what I said earlier. About getting laid, and how long it might have been. I was just pissed off at you. It was a stupid thing to say." She paused, her blue eyes troubled. "Has it really been eleven years since you were…with someone?"

"Yes." It was an embarrassing admission, one she'd never made to anyone out loud.

"Why?"

"I don't know," Dana said, and the truth was that in a way, she didn't. She assumed that no one would be interested. And given that her only experience had been an unsatisfying one, why put herself out there? Why open her heart for rejection?

After these last few hours with Laurel, that seemed a weak rationale for having shut herself off from the pleasure of connecting with another human being. She wanted to kick herself for wasting so much time being afraid. When had she last felt as happy as she did right now? To hell with it. Starting right now, she was determined to let go and enjoy this.

"I think it's high time we injected a little levity into this game," Laurel said. "Give me a dare."

Levity, right. Dana considered that for a moment, then broke into an evil grin. "Okay, then. I dare you to show me, over your clothes, how you masturbate." Her stomach turned over in pleasurable anticipation at the thought. "And…fake an orgasm at the end."

Laurel's eyes narrowed. "Oh, I see how it is. Getting down and dirty, are we? I'll remember that when it's my turn to dole out the dares."

Dana felt strangely excited by the promise. Sick to her stomach, but excited. "Less complaining, more complying."

Laurel unzipped her backpack, smiling as she withdrew her blanket in a bag. "Oh, a woman who knows how to give orders," she purred with a suggestive wink. "Yet another quality I look for."

Dana grinned like a fool. A blushing, sweating, so-wet-it-was-scary fool. "You need the blanket for this?"

"Well, I've got to lie down. And if I'm going to lie down in here, I'm using the blanket."

Dana licked her lips. "Gotcha."

Laurel spread the blanket out across most of the elevator car, leaving Dana sitting on one exposed strip of carpet.

Laurel crawled across the blanket on her hands and knees,

smoothing each corner. Then she stretched out onto her back with feline grace.

Dana had a perfect view of the lean perfection of Laurel's form. How a woman who looked like that could ever give her the time of day, she would never know.

With a shy giggle, Laurel spread her legs, planting one foot on the blanket and tipping her upraised knee to the side. "Well, I usually lie like this. And mostly, I use my hands. Sometimes if I'm really horny, I'll maybe use a…dildo, too."

Dana schooled her breathing, desperate not to pass out and miss what Laurel would do next.

Laurel started to giggle again, making her words harder to understand. "God, this is weird. You'd better hope I don't dare you to do something like this. I feel really… I don't know. You'd think I'd be used to performing for an audience by now, right?"

"This is more personal," Dana acknowledged. "Do you want to stop?" Inside, she chanted, *Please don't stop, please don't stop.*

Laurel shook her head. "I don't want it said that I'm the sort of woman who refuses a dare." She moved a hand down to rest on the crotch of her blue jeans. "I, uh. I like to use two fingers and, um…just rub my clit like this."

Amazed, Dana watched as Laurel began simulating the stroking of a lazy circle directly over the seam of her jeans. Unbelievable. She was actually pretending to masturbate. It took everything Dana had not to rub her hands together with glee.

"And I also like…" Rather than finish her sentence, Laurel let her free hand rest on her left breast. With Dana watching in fascination, she lifted her hand inches into the air, and then reached down to grasp her erect nipple between her fingertips.

This touch wasn't simulated, and it wrenched a groan from both women.

"Yeah," Dana croaked. "I get it." She shifted, more aware than ever of her own wetness. "So, uh, the orgasm."

"Ah, yes. The orgasm." Laurel continued to circle her fingers in the air over the seam of her jeans. Releasing her nipple, she laid her palm flat over the erect nub, cupping her breast through her T-shirt. She began to thrust her hips upward in sensual rhythm, as if meeting the stroking of her busy hand. She started a low moaning that sent shivers through Dana's body.

Mouth hanging open, Dana watched as Laurel put on the sexiest, most intense show she had ever seen. *This,* she managed to think, eyes glued to Laurel's flushed face and full, parted lips, *is worth the price of admission.*

"Oh, God, Dana," Laurel gasped, thrusting her hips again, this time actually causing her fingers to make contact with the seam of her jeans. She moaned, a genuine noise of surprised pleasure, and turned her head toward Dana. "I'm going to come, Dana. I'm going to make myself come."

How Dana wished that were true.

Laurel's hips and hand were in constant motion, and she kept her eyes locked on Dana's face as she played out her most private routine. Her moaning was loud and throaty, making Dana wonder if Laurel's lovers had realized how lucky they were to cause a sound like that.

Back arched, her hand pressed hard between her legs, Laurel cried out in ecstatic, simulated release. Her words were nonsensical, broken by gasps and whimpers, and they trailed off as she relaxed her body and came back to rest on the blanket. Her chest rose and fell rapidly, as though she were really struggling to recover from a shattering orgasm.

Exhaling, she turned her head and grinned at Dana. "How was that?"

"Thorough." Dana managed a nervous cough. "Good."

Laurel sat up and brought the hand she used for her little demonstration to her mouth. Winking, she parted her lips and pressed two fingers into her mouth, sucking on them as if licking them clean of juices.

Dana's pussy clenched at the sight, sending a jolt of pleasure skittering up her spine. She made a strangled noise at her surprise release, shocked to have experienced it without being touched.

Laurel's eyes flashed, like she knew what she had just caused. "Truth or dare?"

HOUR EIGHT—2:00 A.M.

D id that turn you on?" Laurel asked with an innocent air that made Dana forget about pretending otherwise.

"Yeah, how could it not?" she answered candidly. It felt risky but exciting to be the "real" Dana for a change.

"Your turn," Laurel said.

Dana thought for a moment. Ah, hell, what did she really want to know? With a tremor of anticipation, she asked, "What do you like? Sexually, I mean."

Laurel broke into a goofy grin. "It might be easier for me to tell you what I *don't* like."

Could she possibly be sexier? "We've got time on our hands," Dana said, surprised by the throaty invitation in her voice. "What do you *really* like? Your favorite things."

"I love going down on a woman. *Love* it."

Dana struggled to breathe, imagining an enthusiastic Laurel engaged in that particular act. *Between my legs.* She let herself enjoy the fantasy. "What do you like being done to you?" This could not be her, asking a stranger such intimate, explicit questions. She was almost too afraid to ask herself what she liked. Or needed.

Dana wasn't sure when exactly she'd decided to back away from the inevitability of being alone forever. After spending so long ignoring her own desires, settling for an active fantasy life instead of anything real, she was suddenly ready to take a chance on whatever might happen tonight. It was her birthday, and letting go was a gift to herself. She was trapped in an elevator with a gorgeous, free-spirited, brilliant woman, and she was happy, comfortable, and painfully turned on. All bets were off, and more than anything, she wanted to see where this would go.

"I like being licked, too," Laurel said. "Or are you looking for something kinkier?"

There's something kinkier? Never one to let an opportunity go to waste, Dana gave a vigorous nod. "Kinkier is good."

"I like"—Laurel stared at her with faint challenge—"being spanked."

Dana fought not to pass out right then and there. "Spanked?"

Laurel's slim, long-fingered hand skimmed over the top of the gray fleece blanket. She picked at one corner, fighting what looked to be an uncontrollable grin. "When I'm being fucked. Or just as foreplay, you know?"

Dana's nostrils flared in arousal. Something about that idea made it hard to breathe. "Spanked on your butt, you mean?"

"Not just my butt. I like…" She covered her face with one hand, giggling a little. "Why am I feeling so embarrassed to talk about this stuff right now?"

Screw embarrassed, Dana thought. *I need to hear this.* "Where else do you like being spanked?" She wished she had her Franklin planner, so she could take notes.

"My breasts." Laurel crossed her arms upward, holding herself. The gesture made her seem achingly vulnerable. "And my pussy," she murmured so quietly, Dana found herself leaning in closer to hear her.

Thank God she was sitting down. She felt light-headed. "So is that the extent of your kinky desires? Getting slapped around a little?"

Laurel uncrossed her arms, giving Dana a nice view of her hard, cotton-covered nipples. She ran a hand through her hair, a sheepish grin plastered across her face. "Well, I also like when a woman talks dirty to me while she's…you know."

"Spanking you." Dana released a low whistle. "You're a freak."

Laurel laughed. "I guess I am." She raised an eyebrow at Dana in challenge. "Does *that* turn you on?"

Dana coughed again. Damn, was she coming down with a cold or something? "I'm not answering that question."

"So you want a dare instead of truth?"

I walked right into that one. "Sure." She was letting go, after all.

Laurel leaned over and pulled her paperback erotica book from her backpack, holding it up with a smile. "I dare you to read two pages of my choosing. Out loud." Her smile grew. "To me."

"No problem." Dana wondered where her cool confidence was coming from. Now that she had given herself permission to play this out, the words just flowed from some unknown wellspring inside her.

With a mischievous smile, Laurel flipped through the pages of the book, skimming the text. "Start here," she said. "Page eighty-three."

Dana took the book and quickly scanned a few lines. Hot and heavy foreplay. Wonderful. "Got me right to the good part, didn't you?"

Laurel planted her hands behind her hips and leaned back, nipples still rock-hard against her pale yellow T-shirt. "You bet."

Slightly nervous, Dana began to read aloud.

"Raise your arms," Reed whispered behind me. I found her eyes in the mirror, excited beyond all reason. This was better than any fantasy I had ever had.

She paused deliberately. She wasn't sure how she would keep her voice steady through both pages, or how much longer she would be able to keep her intense need to kiss Laurel to herself.

"Keep reading," Laurel said.

I raised my arms into the air. Reed pulled my tank top up over my head, tossing it on the floor beside us. She stared at my bare breasts in the mirror for a moment before reaching around to cover one with each hand. She raised her eyes to meet mine again, and then bent down to nuzzle my neck.

"These are so beautiful," Reed murmured.

Dana paused, wiping her fingers across her forehead.

Across from her, Laurel said, "Go on."

The way her mouth moved made the words blur as Dana's tongue got in the way.

"Thanks," I whispered. "Your hands feel so good."

Reed nipped at my earlobe. "They'll feel even better in a minute," she said. Leaving my breasts with one last tug on each nipple, she slid her hands down my sides to rest on my

waist. She kept the fingers of her left hand curled around my
stomach while she moved her other hand up to press down
between my shoulder blades. "Over, baby."

    I swallowed as my throat went totally dry. It was as if
Reed had tapped into every fantasy I had ever had about her.
My legs shook as I obeyed her quiet command, bending over
to rest my arms on the bathroom counter next to the sink. I
kept my head up, looking into her eyes.

Dana was aware of the way Laurel shifted slightly and of a change
in the cadence of her breathing. Idly, she wondered if she had a spare
pair of panties in her office. She would need them when she got out of
here. She kept reading, making her voice low and soft in an effort to
disguise her own growing arousal.

    Without a word, Reed grabbed the waistband of my
pajama bottoms and tugged them down until they fell to pool
around my ankles. I was completely exposed, vulnerable,
dripping wet with excitement. My breathing picked up until I
was nearly panting.

    "Step out of them, sweet girl," Reed commanded.

    I did as she asked, still bent over the sink. As I watched,
she dropped her eyes and kicked out at my pajama bottoms,
sending them across the floor to the wall. When her eyes
moved again, it was to stare between my legs.

Dana stopped reading and eyed the half-page left to go. "This is
just cruel," she complained.

Laurel dismissed her with a complacent wave. "Keep going. It's
just getting good."

Dana exhaled shakily. The rest of the second page looked every bit
as bothersome as the first. And this time she couldn't hide her arousal.
Her voice shook as she read.

    "You're wet," Reed murmured. I gasped as strong
fingers reached down and grasped my buttocks, pulling me
apart and opening me to her heated gaze.

    "I was thinking about you," I whispered. I dropped my

head as two searching fingertips traced down over my labia, and then found my opening with unerring ease.

"I was thinking about you, too." Reed's voice was low and throaty, unlike I had ever heard it before. All of the restraint between us had vanished. In its place was raw hunger, driving both of our actions. "About this," Reed said, and then drove one finger inside me with excruciating slowness.

Dana blinked, staring at the end of the page. That was it? *Way to leave me hanging.*

"You can keep going, if you want to know what happens," Laurel said. "You looked like maybe you were getting into it."

"That's okay," Dana returned the book. After a moment of indecision, she leered at Laurel. "Maybe later."

Laurel's surprised delight made her glad she'd decided to be playful.

"All these dares are making me horny," Laurel said. "I'll have to go with truth for a while."

Dana released a shaky laugh. "Now you're just trying to make me blush."

"Maybe." Laurel lay back so she could prop herself up on her elbows, stretching out across the fleece blanket. "Is it working?"

Snorting in amusement, Dana shifted so that she could join her. "Is this seat taken?"

Laurel scooted over, patting the space next to her. "It's all yours."

"Cool." Dana settled down beside Laurel and gave her a sidelong grin. "So…when was the last time *you* had sex?"

"About eight months ago. I started seeing someone not long after Mom died. We slept together a few times, but…"

"But what?"

Laurel shrugged. "I was looking for comfort. She was looking for someone to fuck. Period."

"Oh," Dana said.

"I don't like just being a fuck." Cracking a small smile, Laurel added, "Don't get me wrong, she was good. Great, even. That whole dirty-talking thing…" She shivered and allowed a brief, naughty grin. "God, she was good at that."

"Oh." Dana wondered if she could make Laurel shiver like that with her words. Did she like being told she was a dirty girl? That it felt good to fuck her tight pussy? Blushing, she forced her attention back to what Laurel was saying.

"I can't deal with being one of many. I didn't even realize I was until I went over to her place one evening and found her with someone else. If she'd made it clear what the situation was, it would've been one thing. But she didn't, and that kind of surprise...it's no fun at all."

"Her loss," Dana muttered.

Laurel let out a surprised laugh. "I've had the same thought, more than once." She gave Dana an affectionate smile. "Truth or dare, my defender?"

"Truth again." Dana's insides warmed at being called Laurel's defender, even jokingly. "I'm ready."

Laurel's smile turned tender. "Have you ever been attracted to another woman?"

Dana swallowed. She had known this question was coming, had felt it deep in her bones, but plunged onward in the game anyway. *And I can't lie.* A sharp stab of fear made every muscle contract, and she wondered if the slight jolt was visible.

It must have been, because Laurel placed a hand on her thigh. "Don't be afraid. There's no reason to be, okay?"

Dana nodded. "Yes."

"Yes, okay? Or yes, you've been attracted to another woman?"

"Yes, I've been attracted to another woman." The admission made her hyperaware of their closeness. Laurel's thigh brushed against her own. The heat almost overwhelmed her. "I've been attracted...to other women."

Just when she thought she might implode with nerves, she was drawn into a tight hug against Laurel's warm body. Too emotional to push her away, Dana felt her eyes sting. Embarrassingly, she wept hot tears she couldn't hide. In a move that rendered her speechless, Laurel pressed a soft kiss to her neck.

"Was that the first time you told somebody?"

Dana nodded, swiping at her damp cheeks with the back of her hand.

"I've got to tell you, I'm glad," Laurel said. "When you told me you were straight, all I could think was that if that were true, what a waste."

"You don't have to say that."

Laurel caressed the side of Dana's face with her hand. "Of course I don't *have* to say it." Her blue eyes were sincere. "I mean it. You're a very attractive woman. I told you that before, and I didn't like you nearly as much then as I do now."

Red-faced, Dana managed a quiet, "Thank you." She concentrated on the coolness of Laurel's fingers against her heated skin. "I find you very attractive, too."

"Thank you."

Laurel's hand lingered. Dana wanted to clap her own over it to prevent its withdrawal. The feel of that warm palm pressed against her cheek made her yearn for so much more. Her control seemed tenuous at best, no match for the intimacy of Laurel's touch. She wanted to give in to the impulses that tugged her common sense away. No amount of rationalization worked. This was probably how people felt trapped together on a desert island, far from the real world and the rules they made for themselves. If she were honest she felt weirdly liberated, like she'd just exchanged a heavy suit of armor for a thin, shimmering skin.

She wondered if Laurel had fallen under the same spell or if she was simply being herself because she didn't have to have anyone's permission for that. Not even her own. Dana couldn't imagine being so unguarded.

"Did you really know that I was a lesbian?" Dana asked.

"I thought you looked like someone who appreciated other women. When I was on your lap, I felt thoroughly appreciated." She smiled. "You know, before I got thrown off."

Dana nodded. "Scott must have figured it out, too, huh?"

"Given that he hired me to dance for you, yeah, I think he probably knows. You never told him?" Laurel finally took back her hand, leaving Dana's cheek wishing for a return of that soft warmth.

Feeling bereft at the loss of contact, Dana said, "No. I…don't talk to him about stuff like that."

"Well, I guess he knows you better than you realized." Laurel hesitated a moment, then asked, "Do you still want to play?"

Dana gave her a brave nod. *No reason not to at this point.*

Laurel didn't waste any time. "What's one of your favorite sexual fantasies?" she asked directly. "Not necessarily something you'd do, but something you like thinking about?"

Dana pressed her palms to her face. "I'm never going to go back to normal, you know. This blushing thing? I'm starting to think it's permanent."

"Listen, woman, you watched me pretend to get myself off." Laurel gave her a playful shove. "Asking you about a harmless little fantasy is hardly unfair after that."

Dana released a long-suffering sigh, raising her eyes to the ceiling of the elevator. There were so many to choose from. Fantasy, and the Internet, had been her only sexual outlets for so long, it was hard to know where to start.

"I think about women, usually." She conceded Laurel's I-knew-it grin with a wry look. "Most of the time, actually."

"Specifics," Laurel coaxed with her hand. "Give me specifics."

Dana cleared her throat. "I meet a woman—I don't know where, that's not really important. She takes me back to her place. When we get there, she pulls out these leather cuffs and gives them to me. She asks me to restrain her. And fuck her."

Laurel sat forward in eager attention. Her eyes sparkled. "Then what?"

"I cuff her to the headboard. And then as she waits for me on the bed, I go to the drawer where she has the cuffs and some other... toys."

"Like?"

Embarrassed, Dana could only manage to grin. "Like a strap-on."

"Ah." Paying rapt attention, Laurel said, "What does the fantasy woman think about that?"

"Oh, did I forget that part?" Dana gave a wolfish smile. "She's blindfolded. She doesn't know until I'm on top of her. When she realizes, though, she's not complaining. First, I make her come with my mouth. Then—"

"You slide your cock into her." Laurel's voice was very soft. She almost seemed to be talking to herself.

Dana couldn't speak. It seemed as though Laurel found her strap-on fantasy as exciting as she did.

Laurel pressed a hand to her chest, forestalling more words. "You'd better stop. If you don't, I might just put on a show for real."

The threat did little to discourage Dana, but she wasn't sure she could keep going with Laurel's intense gaze on her. Feeling as though she were moving underwater, she managed a nod.

"Ask me something." Laurel's voice was husky.

"Okay." Dana asked a hard question that would probably come back to her. "What was your most embarrassing moment?"

Laurel's smile faltered. "Well, that's not a very fun one."

"Bad?"

"To me, yeah. It's pretty bad." She seemed hesitant to continue, and Dana felt the genuine shame this story triggered. "I was dancing one Friday night in my first year at vet school. A guy called me over to his table and when I got there, I realized one of his buddies was a graduate student instructor for a physiology class I was taking."

Dana winced. That was definitely embarrassing. She touched Laurel's arm. "What did you do?"

"I took one look at my instructor and told the group I was going to send over another girl, that I was going on break. The guy who asked me over asked if I would do a lap dance for the birthday boy, first. Of course, he just happened to be my instructor. And my instructor's buddy grabbed my ass, right in front of everyone." Laurel rushed to finish the story. "My favorite bouncer saw the guy groping me and it turned into this big scene. Anyway…that was really embarrassing."

Dana's chest felt tight. "Did your instructor ever say anything about it?"

"Not to my face. But he looked at me differently in class after that night. It really bothered me."

"I'm sorry."

"I was glad to get out of that class, believe me. Do you want to tell me your most embarrassing moment?" Laurel asked, as though she knew that Dana was expecting it.

"Probably about as much as you wanted to tell me yours."

"I wanted you to know that I trust you."

Dana felt her breathing quicken, and was glad not to be standing. The words made her feel weak. She wanted to show Laurel the same thing, that she trusted her. "Junior year of college, I fell in love with my best friend," she said before she could change her mind. "We'd been friends for a couple years, and I'd been wanting her most of that time."

"Was she the first woman you were attracted to?" Laurel asked.

"The first one in real life. I thought she was beautiful. She thought…well, I don't know what she thought. That I was a good friend, I guess."

"She was straight, right? Falling in love with a straight girl—always very embarrassing."

Dana wished it had been that simple. "No, that's the *really* humiliating part. She was out and proud, and very open about it. I was in awe of her." She took a deep breath, unable to believe that she was about to share this story. "One night we were watching a movie in my dorm room, sitting next to each other on my bed. It was totally innocent, and it was driving me crazy. I was so attracted to her, it hurt. Stupid me, I decided that I was going to let her know how I felt."

"It didn't go well." Laurel's face was drawn and nervous.

Dana stared down into her lap. "No. I just remember that at one point we were laughing at something in the movie, and I leaned over and tried to kiss her. And she pulled away before I could even get near." Dana was still mortified by the memory. "She told me I just wasn't her type, that she liked me as a friend, but—"

"That must have hurt."

Dana nodded at the understatement. "It hurt even worse when she stopped speaking to me after that night. Nothing too obvious, but suddenly she always seemed to be busy and we never seemed to be able to get together, until a few months later I never saw her anymore."

"Her loss."

Dana couldn't help but grin at Laurel's obviously genuine reaction. It inspired another confession. "After that, I decided to just concentrate on school. Once I graduated, I focused on work. Thinking about relationships, or meeting women, scares me. I don't want to go through that again."

"All because of one clueless college girl a long time ago?" Laurel's voice was tender, and a little sad.

Looking back, Dana was puzzled, too. Everyone had formative experiences in their teens, including humiliation and heartbreak. Somehow hers had assumed greater proportions than it should.

"I felt much more for her than my high school boyfriend in the year and a half we dated. That scared the hell out of me, I suppose," Dana admitted, as much to herself as to Laurel.

"Getting your heart broken sucks," Laurel said with an understanding smile. "But it would be a shame if you never put yourself out there again."

"It's been easier." Dana hated to admit to her cowardice. Now that she thought about it, she realized she'd missed out on the kinds of experiences that put college crushes in context. Hers had inhibited so much, her withdrawal had become a safe, comfortable habit.

"Don't you get lonely?" Laurel asked.

"Of course." Dana stared at Laurel's legs, feeling that loneliness acutely. "I cope. I buy embarrassing amounts of porn, read stories, talk to women online."

"Do any of them know your real name?"

"I don't talk to anyone regularly."

Laurel touched the side of Dana's face again. "Don't you want something more?"

Blinking back stinging tears, Dana said, "Of course. I want so much that I don't know how to get."

Laurel's gaze was full of something Dana had never seen directed at her before. "Do you think you would ever consider breaking your self-imposed isolation?"

"Yes," Dana whispered. For someone like Laurel, in a heartbeat. "Under extraordinary circumstances, maybe."

Laurel looked around the elevator car. "Think this qualifies as extraordinary?"

"Maybe," Dana said. "Why?"

"May I take you to dinner sometime?" Laurel asked. She played with a lock of Dana's hair as though satisfying some long-standing desire.

"You mean—"

"Like a date," Laurel finished.

Was this kind of like the pity fuck she was talking about earlier?

As if the worry and doubt were displayed clearly on Dana's forehead the moment they flashed through her mind, Laurel frowned. "Don't even go there. After the way we started out, do you really think

I would express an interest in getting to know you outside this elevator if I didn't really want to? You make me laugh, I like talking to you. I think we get along pretty well."

"We do," Dana said.

"So have dinner with me."

"I'm buying."

"Oh, no," Laurel countered. "I asked. I'm buying."

Dana wouldn't concede this one. If she was going on a date with a gorgeous woman, she was going to do it right.

As though sensing her resolve, Laurel said, "We've got plenty of time to debate who picks up the check. Why don't you make me perform a dare instead?" Something mischievous sparkled in her eyes. "It seems like the right time."

Dana wondered if Laurel hoped she was going to dare her for a kiss. If only she had the guts to just go for the gold like that, Dana mused. She thought about various acts she could make Laurel perform, until she came up with something nearly as good as the kiss she really wanted.

HOUR NINE—3:00 A.M.

T his is gonna be bad, isn't it?" Laurel asked.
"Oh, I think it's very good." Dana beamed. "I dare you to finish that dance you were giving me earlier."

"Oh, God. For real?"

"Fair is fair. Scott paid for it, after all."

"You don't think you got his money's worth out of me yet?"

Dana shook her head. "Nope. I got to see the perfect breasts, but you pulled those jeans back on before I had time to enjoy the rest of you. How can we say that my birthday is complete?" She gestured over at Laurel's iPod, which sat at the other side of the elevator car. "You've got the music. Piece of cake."

Laurel's face turned an interesting shade of red. "It won't be easy doing a lap dance while you're sitting on the floor." Leaning over to her backpack, she produced the can of whipped cream with a challenging grin. "Shall I use this, too?"

Dana licked her lips, feeling faint at the thought. "How about we save that for later?" *I'd rather kiss you first.*

"Okay." Laurel seemed to be warming to the idea. She set the can aside, stood up, and kicked her shoes off into the corner. "So you just want to sit there?"

Dana nodded happily. "And watch."

"And watch," Laurel murmured. "Right."

She picked up her iPod and made a quick adjustment to the volume as music blared. Immediately her hips began to sway with the beat, and she propped the iPod against the wall, hitched her T-shirt up to just below her breasts, and launched into a seductive dance. Just like that, she was all confidence.

The hem of her pale yellow T-shirt remained gripped in her hands, and she lifted and lowered it as she danced, sometimes revealing the undersides of her firm breasts, but never the dusky pink nipples Dana ached to see again. Now that she had given herself permission to enjoy it, Laurel's dancing was one of the sexiest things Dana had ever seen. Her palms were sweating.

"Do you always tease this much?" she asked.

"Always," Laurel answered, her voice honey-smooth.

She raised a suggestive eyebrow at Dana, then eased her T-shirt up and over her head. After tossing it on the floor, she ran one hand through her dark, tousled hair and grinned. This time, Dana let her gaze slide over Laurel's flesh with far more than a casual interest. She stared openly at the most perfect pair of naked female breasts she had ever seen in real life. *Happy birthday to me.* She grinned back.

"You like?" Laurel covered both breasts with her hands, cupping her flesh and giving it a seductive squeeze.

Dana managed a mindless nod, her eyes fixed on Laurel's hands.

"Want to see more?" Laurel rubbed her bare breasts together for a moment before sliding her hands down over her stomach to the button on the front of her blue jeans.

"Please," Dana rasped. *Thank you, Scott. You devious, underhanded,* wonderful *son of a bitch.*

With a slow smile, Laurel unbuttoned and unzipped her jeans with one hand, and then brought both to grip the waistband to start another slow tease. Down a little, up, down again, then up once more. Dana felt dizzy at the seductive promise in her gaze.

"Breathe, honey," Laurel murmured over the music.

Dana released one explosive breath, and could hardly draw the next. Her tongue seemed to be glued to the roof of her mouth as Laurel turned, offering a nice view of her jean-clad ass. Giggling, she lowered the waistband of her jeans, but this time kept going, pushing the denim over her hips and down her shapely thighs. She dropped her pants when she had them to her knees. Bent over at the waist, she presented Dana with the most perfect nearly naked female bottom she had ever seen in real life.

Those weren't the panties she recalled from her covert glance back in the office. She was wearing a g-string. Dana wondered if she'd somehow fallen asleep earlier in the evening, and was trapped in the most erotic porn movie dream she could imagine. Stuff like this just didn't happen to the Dana Watts who got up at the same time each morning to rush to work, then stayed until the lights were out everywhere in the Boynton Software Solutions building but at her workstation.

Laurel swayed back around, releasing a sweet peal of laughter. "Baby, your face."

"Baby, your *ass*," Dana groaned. "I'm speechless."

Laurel stepped closer so that Dana was staring right at the lacy black fabric covering the area between her legs. One hand tangled in Dana's hair, drawing her face closer. Dana closed her eyes and inhaled, enjoying the scent of Laurel's arousal. She couldn't believe her own boldness. Her lips twitched with the desire to lean forward and kiss that warm, fragrant space.

Laurel released Dana's head and sank down to the floor so she could straddle her thighs. Lap full of mostly naked stripper, Dana felt as though she were floating outside her body, looking down on the scene from above. She stretched out her legs and brought her hands up to rest against Laurel's lower back, steadying her as she continued to writhe to the music. Her skin was smooth and warm, every inch of her flesh begging to be touched.

Rocking with the music, she settled down so her pussy pressed against Dana's thigh, then leaned forward and breathed hot words into her ear. "I'm willing to bend the rules for you, Dana. You're allowed to touch me all you want."

Dana stared at Laurel's breasts, bouncing gently mere inches from her face. *I'm going to pass out for real this time.* Her heart pounded so hard she feared it rivaled the volume of the club music. She felt her hands trembling against Laurel's bare skin, the palms slick with nervous sweat. Her breathing disintegrated into nothing more than a frantic gasping for air, the sucking in of desperate mouthfuls of oxygen.

Laurel snaked her hand through Dana's hair again, guiding her face to the impossible softness of the space between her naked breasts. "Enjoy this, sweetheart."

Unable to refuse, Dana kept her face pressed into Laurel's ample cleavage and dropped her hands to rest on Laurel's buttocks. When Laurel groaned, she tightened her grip instinctively, squeezing the firm cheeks with her fingers.

With a soft cry, Laurel sank against her, cushioning Dana's cheek against the slope of her breast. Dana couldn't believe that this was her life, that her lips were parted only centimeters from an erect nipple and her hands were full of naked Laurel.

She blinked, staring in wonder at Laurel's pink skin and listening to the heartbeat thumping beneath her ear. In an instant, her feelings shifted from passionate to adoring, and she released Laurel's buttocks and slid her palms up the length of her back.

"This is so nice." Dana splayed out her fingers and held her closer.

Laurel returned the tender embrace, repeating, "Yes. So, so nice. Dana?"

"Yeah?"

"I dare you to let me kiss you."

Dana's heartbeat stuttered and she released an involuntary moan.

"Is that a yes?" Laurel asked in a breathless whisper.

"Yes," Dana said. She loosened her arms and looked up at Laurel with a nervous smile. "Do it."

Laurel smiled back. "I've been wanting to do this forever."

I guess it does feel like we've been in this elevator forever, Dana mused. She moaned as Laurel closed the distance between them, cupping her face and pressing her mouth to Dana's in a gentle kiss.

Laurel drew away far too soon, asking, "Good?"

Dana forced herself to start breathing again. "Your lips are so soft."

"So are yours. Want to do it again?"

Dana nodded. "Turn off that godawful music first."

Laughing, Laurel turned and reached awkwardly toward her iPod, half falling on the floor to reach it. Dana moved with her as she stretched out. With a desperate jab, she cut the bass-heavy music and they were left with the sounds of their mingled breathing, heavy and aroused.

"Where were we?" Laurel asked, crawling back into Dana's lap.

"Here." Dana reached up to thread her fingers through Laurel's chestnut hair. Their mouths came together harder this time, and immediately Laurel parted her lips to deepen the kiss. Instinctively, Dana did the same.

What ensued was the clumsiest, most teeth-clashing kiss Dana had ever had the misfortune to help create. As their mouths dueled in wet, awkward disharmony, Dana knew that it was she, with her lack of experience, who was responsible for the absolute messiness of their joining. "I'm sorry," she sputtered, pulling away. Her cheeks burned with shame. "That was awful. I'm sorry."

"Honey, don't you dare be sorry about that." Laurel's face shone with sympathetic affection. "Despite what they write in stories, first kisses are often less than perfect."

"You're being generous." Dana dropped her gaze to Laurel's chest. And her bare breasts. "I'd say that was about as far from perfect as a first kiss could get."

"That's what practicing is for, Dana. I'm up for it, if you are."

Sucking in a surprised lungful of air, Dana couldn't help but crack a smile. "Practicing?"

"Do you think I started out as a great kisser?" Laurel asked. "I had to be taught. I had to practice for years. This stuff takes work, woman."

"And you're volunteering to practice with me?"

"I'm insisting on it," Laurel said. Their next kiss was slower, Laurel approaching with soft lips and hot breath, pressing their mouths together with infinite tenderness. Dana didn't move, frozen with fear that she would turn this perfect moment sour. She felt Laurel smile against her lips. "Enough truth or dare." Her lips brushed against Dana's, sending an excited shiver skittering throughout her paralyzed body. "Let's play a new game."

"What game?" Dana whispered.

She felt the tip of Laurel's tongue slide across her upper lip, then retreat so she could whisper, "Kissing lessons."

Dana trembled against Laurel's supple body. "Sounds like fun."

"Oh, I think it will be. Want to go first?"

Nodding, Dana managed a shaky exhalation. "Yes."

"Let me use my tongue," Laurel whispered. "Just surrender to me for a few minutes, okay?"

She'll do all the work, Dana translated. She felt her entire body relax. Thank God. She tipped her head in agreement. "Do you think you could—"

"What, darling?" Laurel licked at Dana's lips again.

"Put your shirt back on?" Dana requested, breathless. "I think it'd help with the nervous thing."

Laurel's laugh caused her bare breasts to bounce gently in rhythm. "All right. Fair enough." She twisted away to pull on her T-shirt.

Dana felt mingled sorrow and relief when the pale yellow fabric once more covered those exceptional breasts. "Not that I don't absolutely love them, you understand," she murmured.

"I understand." Laurel smiled. "Should I put my jeans on, too?"

"No. I think kissing lessons will be better with those off."

Laurel brought her face close to Dana's again, nipping at her lower lip with gentle teeth. "It'll work out perfectly for lesson three: using your whole body to full effect." She swiped her tongue across Dana's mouth. "Let me inside, sweetheart."

Parting her lips in wordless surrender, Dana accepted the gentle invasion of Laurel's tongue with a grateful moan. She held still, letting Laurel explore her mouth with languid strokes, resisting the need to return her kiss with all the passionate urgency she felt. Instead, she concentrated on the taste of Laurel, on the feeling of her sharing herself so intimately, on the soft press of her lips and the silky wetness of her tongue.

Laurel pulled back with a contented whimper. "Oh, you show great promise," she said, her voice throaty with desire. "We're ready for lesson two, I think."

"Lesson two?"

"*Your* tongue," Laurel said. "Time for you to use it."

Dana stiffened a little. Time for a little more of her slapstick routine.

Laurel wrapped her arms around Dana's body and held her tight. "Go slow," she murmured. "Just explore. Play with me. Tease me and make me want you so bad I'll explode if I don't have you."

No problem. Dana released a low, needy moan and pressed her tongue into the wet warmth of Laurel's mouth. Laurel released her own noise of pure need, grabbing at Dana's back with both hands and clawing her way up Dana's shoulder blades with blunt fingernails. Dana did what came naturally. She traced the tip of her tongue over teeth and tongue and gums, seeking to memorize every inch of Laurel's mouth. She didn't hurry, didn't push; she simply reacted, trying to express everything she felt, and how much she wanted Laurel, without saying a word. Now well aware of what a great kiss felt like, she tried to mimic Laurel's technique, holding her steady as they began a slow exploration with their tongues.

Advance and retreat. That was the new game they played, each taking turns licking at the other's mouth, moving back and forth with unconscious ease. Dana concentrated wholly on their intricate dance, no other thought in her head but the give and take between them. Gone was the self-critical analysis that would normally have been occupying her mind at a time like this, and the doubt. In its place was pure instinct, driving her actions.

When they broke apart, both of them were gasping.

"I think you're winning this game." Laurel grinned.

"And we haven't even had lesson three yet." Dana gave a coy smile. "I remember hearing something about using our whole bodies to full effect."

Laurel pushed her down onto the floor, pressing her back to the gray fleece blanket. She manipulated Dana until she lay diagonally across the car, and then settled her body on top, slipping a firm thigh between Dana's legs.

"The best kisses are about much more than just your mouth," Laurel murmured. "I want to feel your hands on me, honey. And I'm going to touch you, too. All over."

"Anything, as long as I can keep kissing you." Dana lifted her hands to Laurel's ass. She traced her tongue over Laurel's smile and then broke into her own answering grin.

Laurel eased one hand behind Dana's neck, bending low over her so their lips continued to touch, and settled her other hand on Dana's upper chest. "I can't believe I'm making out with you. I've been lusting after you from the moment I walked into your office and saw the red hair and the power-dyke suit."

"You get off on that kind of thing?"

Laurel shivered, her eyes heavy-lidded. "You have no idea," she said. "It turns out you're pretty much exactly my type." She dipped her head down, pushing her tongue into Dana's mouth with a groan of pleasure.

Dana let herself be thoroughly kissed for a minute or so before breaking away with a soft chuckle. "I suggest you reserve judgment until after you see me naked."

She blushed the moment the words left her mouth. What a stupid thing to say.

"Don't be silly," Laurel said. "I'm looking forward to that moment, and I know I won't be disappointed. You've got curves in all the right places."

Dana nodded, biting her lip to hold back her emotion. "Kiss me some more," she whispered.

Laurel closed the scant distance between them in happy obedience. When her hand started sliding down over Dana's chest, Dana nearly came unglued. Her body jerked in shock at the passionate caress and she tore her mouth away from Laurel's, crying out in pleasure.

"Oh, honey," Laurel rumbled. "You are going to be so, so responsive, aren't you?"

"Embarrassingly so," Dana admitted.

She pulled Laurel hard against her thigh, relishing the intense heat between her legs.

Laurel groaned and rotated her hips, grinding her lower body into Dana's. "I need to check on something."

"Check on what?" Dana slipped a finger beneath the black string that ran between Laurel's firm cheeks. She let a fingertip stroke the top of Laurel's ass, inching downward to explore between her buttocks. To her extreme delight, she found slick wetness farther from the source than she was expecting. "Oh, my."

Laurel squirmed away, cheeks turning light pink. Unbuttoning Dana's silky white shirt with trembling hands, she said, "I want to look at your breasts. Is that all right?"

Despite the slight hesitation she felt at being exposed, Dana forced herself to relax. *Loosen up. She's been topless half the night, and now it's your turn.* "It's all right," she agreed in a whisper.

Laurel fumbled with the last buttons and pushed the blouse open, easing it over Dana's shoulders. She grinned down at the white bra she found beneath.

"The innocent look." She traced her fingertip along the edge of the left cup. "I like it."

"One of us has to look innocent."

Laurel found the closure of Dana's bra between her breasts. "Front clasp." She unhooked it with a deft hand. "Very nice."

"A stroke of dumb luck." Dana swallowed when Laurel pushed her bra apart with gentle hands. *Keep talking. Don't think about the fact that she's looking at your bare breasts right now.* "And to think I almost wore my chastity belt today."

Laurel chuckled but kept her eyes locked on Dana's chest. Her nipples were light pink, much paler than Laurel's, and harder than Dana had ever seen them before. She gasped, shocked at the sight of her body's reaction. A moment later, she winced in pleasure-pain as Laurel dragged the flat of her tongue up the underside of Dana's right breast, around her areola, and then flicked the tip over the hard point of Dana's nipple.

Dana released a ragged breath. "Do that some more," she begged.

Her legs fell open, hips thrusting upward, and a rush of hot wetness stained her panties. *That's it, they're ruined.* Not that it mattered. It was a small price to pay, favorite pair or not. Dana reached up and seized a handful of Laurel's hair, compelling her closer. Laurel wrapped her lips around the left nipple and batted at it with her tongue.

"Oh, fuck," Dana groaned. Laurel switched from the left breast to the right, trailing wet, sloppy kisses over Dana's skin. Back and forth, back and forth, she worshiped Dana's breasts.

Dana felt unworthy of such adoration and care, but greedy for it, all the same. She held Laurel's head to her breast, toes curling in ecstasy. "God, you make me feel like I'm gonna…"

Laurel drew back, releasing Dana's nipple with a soft, wet pop. She retreated slowly, staring at Dana with wide, unfocused eyes. "Honey, I'm sorry. Maybe we should…"

Oh, no. Dana's face flooded with heat when she realized Laurel was putting an end to their intimate encounter. "What?" she whispered. "You think we should stop?" She sat up on the blanket, pulling her shirt over her breasts and holding it closed with one hand.

"Not because I want to." Laurel gripped Dana's arm. "Believe me, I could have stayed there all night."

Dana could still smell Laurel's arousal where it was drying on her hand. "Then why do you want to stop?"

"Well, because I want…" Laurel paused, and then looked down at a spot between their bodies. "Or, rather, I don't want you to think that this is all that tonight was about."

"What do you mean?" Dana loosened her hold on her open shirt, feeling somewhat less on the defensive as she listened to Laurel's voice. *She's serious. She's telling the truth.*

"I don't want to be your memory of a crazy, spontaneous sexual encounter in an elevator on your birthday," Laurel said. "With a stripper." She worried at her lower lip with her teeth for a moment. "I do want to go out with you, Dana. I really like you and I want to date you."

Okay, stop panicking and start focusing on what she's telling you. "Do you really think I'm looking at it that way?" Dana asked. "As a crazy memory I'll have? A one-night stand?" She took Laurel's hand in both of her own. "Do you really think I would take a chance, after all these years, on something that didn't feel like more than that?"

Laurel shook her head. "No, I don't. But that's the other reason why we should stop. Dana, you've never even been with a woman before."

Dana released her hand. "If you're going to suggest that maybe I'm confused, or that this is just a stage—or a product of this situation—then you can just get over yourself. I've liked women for a lot longer than just tonight in this elevator, and if you think I'm—"

Laurel held up a hand to forestall Dana's words. "No, I'm not saying that. Just listen to me, and try to understand. If we're together, I'll be your first lover in over ten years. I'll also be the first woman."

"Trust me, I'm painfully aware of that fact."

"Dana, I want to hang around for a while." Laurel paused. "Do you understand how big a responsibility all of that is? I need you to know that I see it that way, and not just as a hot night with a beautiful woman."

Dana managed a shy grin. "You can't see it as both?"

Laurel laughed, her tension clearly easing. "I want our first time to be right," she said. "Not on the floor of some elevator stuck between the nineteenth and twentieth floors."

"What do you think will make our first time right?" Dana felt warmth spreading through her chest at Laurel's sincere words, even if she didn't necessarily agree. "Wine? Flowers? Candlelight and a soft bed?"

Laurel nodded. "All wonderful ideas that I will take into account when I'm planning the big seduction. In fact, I'm already thinking about what I'll make you for breakfast the next morning. Something hearty, I think, since you'll be a little sore and most definitely dehydrated."

"I really like pancakes," Dana offered. Her voice betrayed her resurging arousal, now that the fear of rejection was gone. "If you're looking for ideas."

"Okay, then. Orgasms and pancakes. Post third-date material, at least."

Dana shook her head. "It's never too soon for orgasms and pancakes."

"Dana, I—"

Dana pressed her fingertip between Laurel's lips the instant she started talking. The words stopped and a warm tongue was bathing her finger with gentle, lapping licks. "If you're not ready, I'm not going to push you," she said. "I just need you to know that I *am* ready. I appreciate your sense of honor, and what you're trying to show me. I think you're almost too good to be true, really. I just…" She paused, uncertain about how to express herself in this. If Laurel was the right one, it shouldn't matter how they started, or when. "This feels right to me."

"Right?" Laurel repeated.

"Tonight we got trapped in an elevator as two people who couldn't stand each other. I was a total bitch to you, yet for some reason you've become my friend."

Laurel nodded. "Meeting you has been amazing. I wanted to smack you just a few hours ago, and now I want to make you feel good so badly it aches."

Dana whimpered at Laurel's words. *Don't talk about your aching unless you're prepared for a lapful of project manager.*

"I feel like we're going to be really good friends." Laurel gave Dana an odd smile. "Fucked up, huh?"

"Totally fucked up," Dana said. Somehow, Laurel had completely gotten to her and "friendship" didn't begin to describe what she felt. She made Dana want to lay herself bare, even though it scared her to death. "I feel so open and exposed with you," she said. "And I trust you, and that isn't going to change whatever we do tonight. I know you mean every word you say about this being something more. I feel the same way."

"We're moving pretty fast," Laurel said. "I would hate for either of us to have regrets."

Was that what Laurel thought—that Dana had no experience and therefore no context for her desires? That if they acted on their instincts, Dana might have second thoughts afterward and run away from whatever was forming between them?

"I understand what you mean," she said. "But I already know I won't be able to walk away tomorrow as if nothing happened. It's strange, I've spent the last ten years avoiding situations that could make me vulnerable, and it hasn't made me happy. I need to do something different."

"I don't want to risk hurting you," Laurel said simply.

Dana gave the answer she was just starting to realize herself. "Sometimes you have to take risks to find happiness."

Something took hold of Laurel, transforming her expression into sheer radiance. "It means a lot to hear you say that. And to think, all it took was some naked breasts, a g-string, and a little making out."

"No." Dana brought Laurel's hand to her lips and planted a soft kiss on the back. "All it took was meeting you."

It took a few moments for Laurel to summon up the will to speak. She managed a quiet, joyful noise that got Dana grinning wide. "Damn, Watts. Not bad at all. I'm not sure I can believe that you haven't already charmed legions of women into your bed."

"I'm no good with legions," Dana said. "Lucky for me, though, I seem to do okay with you."

Swooning, Laurel covered her heart with the palm of her hand. "Stop it, woman. If you mix total adoration with the lust I'm feeling right now, I can't be held responsible for my actions."

"What?" Dana asked. "More kissing? Using our whole bodies to full effect?"

Dana's face was full of so much earnest longing, Laurel had to break their eye contact to keep control of herself. More than anything, she wanted to throw Dana down on the floor, tear off her suit, and make her moan. But she really liked Dana, so much it was beginning to frighten her, and she felt paralyzed by the fear of doing something to scare her away.

"Is it too soon for you?" Dana asked after a moment, her voice low. "I mean, for all I know, you probably like to date a girl for months before taking her to bed, right?"

"It depends on the girl." Laurel took Dana's hand, desperate to reestablish contact. That seemed safe enough. Dana sounded so concerned about what she was feeling that she couldn't help touching her. She thought about the best way to answer, and decided that humor might set them both at ease. "You seem pretty easy. I doubt it would take that long."

Dana pushed a hand through her hair, obviously unnerved that her desire was so obvious. She seemed lost in thought for a moment, before saying, "You're teasing me, aren't you?" Quirking her lips into a tiny smile, she added, "It seemed like you were pretty ready about ten minutes ago."

Laurel's mouth twitched. "Well, I have to admit that getting trapped in an elevator with a beautiful stranger overnight seems like an awfully big opportunity to waste. It almost seems wrong *not* to do it."

"And just think of the great story we'll have to tell our grandkids," Dana said.

Laurel burst into surprised giggles. Facetious or not, Dana had gotten her point across. This was not a one-night stand as far as either of them were concerned.

"Let me think about it, okay?" Laurel laid the palm of her hand on Dana's throat, wrapping gentle fingers around the curve of her neck. She leaned forward and gave Dana a slow, wet kiss. "Why don't we take a breather and get to know one another a little better first?"

Dana's small groan of disappointment almost undid Laurel. She couldn't imagine enduring ten years of sexual frustration, then being moments from the promise of release only to be told to take a breather. But Laurel needed to get her head together before making the decision to jump into a sexual relationship. She wasn't used to treating sex as a casual decision, and she sure as hell didn't want to start with someone who made her feel as happy as Dana seemed to.

"If that's what you want." Dana shifted to sit cross-legged once again. "Though I should tell you that after just a few hours together, you already know me better than anyone else in my life. Isn't that pathetic?"

"It's not pathetic," Laurel said. "It's flattering."

"No, it's pathetic." Dana fastened the front closure of her bra with a wistful resignation that tore at Laurel. "I've never reacted to anyone like I do to you. It's crazy. You're so easy to talk to."

"So are you," Laurel said, distracted as she watched Dana rebuttoning her shirt. "What are you doing?"

"Putting my shirt back on. I feel strange sitting here half-naked while we talk."

Laurel pouted. "So you're going to punish me by hiding those delicious breasts away?"

"Don't think of it as punishment. Besides, I'm not going to sit here topless while you have a T-shirt on."

Laurel looked down at her own chest. "The T-shirt is negotiable."

"Not unless you want to get ravished right here on the floor," Dana said.

"Right. So about getting to know you better—"

"Ask away." There was a defeated note in Dana's voice. "Hell, I have no secrets left. For whatever reason, it seems I'll tell you anything."

"What's your favorite meal?"

"Starting easy, huh?" Dana thought for a moment. "The 'Big Night Out' at the Melting Pot."

"Duly noted. That's where I'm taking you for dinner, by the way. When we go out."

"Cool. So how about you? What's your favorite?"

Moaning, Laurel answered without hesitation. "Sweet potatoes."

"Sweet potatoes aren't a meal."

Laurel laid a hand over her stomach, which growled in sudden protest. "Shit, I'm hungry. How about we split that chocolate bar now?"

"Brilliant idea," Dana said. "Your breasts made me forget all about dessert."

"You like to blame my breasts for everything, don't you?"

"Well, no. Your ass shares part of the blame. It's also fantastic."

Grinning, Laurel searched through her backpack. "You're so easy to please."

"You're modest." Dana ogled her ass unabashedly. "I go a little brain dead when I look at you."

Laurel laughed. "Well, that's nice." She found the Hershey's bar, unwrapped it, and broke it in two.

Accepting her half, Dana said, "If you're going to give me chocolate every time I tell you how much I love your body, I'll weigh eight hundred pounds in no time."

"Ooh." Laurel popped a square into her mouth. "And the girl just keeps the sweet talk coming."

Dana ate one of her own squares, moaning in pleasure at the flavor. "Anything for chocolate."

"Trust me, I'll keep that in mind."

Dana watched Laurel's lips as she chewed. "What's going to make you feel like you know me well enough to sleep with me?"

Laurel almost choked at the blunt question. "I've always appreciated a woman who can be direct. Could you wait till I'm not eating next time?"

"I'm sorry. You can't get me that worked up and expect me to just get all mellow at the drop of a hat."

"Oh, I don't really ever think I'll see you 'mellow,'" Laurel said. "I guess I just wasn't expecting sex-crazy, dripping-with-desire Dana."

Dana flushed deep pink. "Neither was I. Do you like her?"

"Very much." Laurel stared at Dana's face and then somewhere in the vicinity of her breasts. "Maybe too much."

"Why are you so diffident about this?" A trace of tension altered Dana's voice. "You seem pretty sexually open to me."

"I am." Laurel could read the confusion and disappointment in Dana's eyes. She'd sent mixed signals, Laurel realized. One moment stripping and coming on to her, the next backing off like *she* was the one on sexual training wheels. "I can only imagine what you must think."

"Does it really matter what I think? I practically called you a whore for doing your job."

"Yeah, it matters." Wanting to make her point more clearly, Laurel said, "If I didn't want to see you after tonight, it wouldn't matter at all. But tonight is just a beginning for us."

Dana smiled. Her face seemed unburdened suddenly. "I had no right to judge you earlier," she said. "I only did it because I was feeling bad about myself."

From Dana's tone Laurel guessed she'd been indulging in self-recrimination. Maybe she thought Laurel had backed off for fear of being seen as a slut after the fact. "Why would you feel so bad about yourself?" Laurel asked gently.

"Sometimes I feel like the biggest prude in the world, so naturally I set about trying to make you feel like the biggest slut. It's not what I think at all. I hope you can forgive me."

"I already did," Laurel said. "But thanks for saying it again, anyway." She thought for a moment as she savored one of her last pieces of chocolate. "Do something for me."

"Anything." There was no flirtatiousness in Dana's tone. She gazed into Laurel's eyes as though she wanted to see deep inside her.

"Let's just talk for a little while. Like we're on a date and we're just finding out about each other."

"A date. I like that idea." Dana smiled.

"Let's assume you're not working," Laurel said. "Tell me about your ideal Sunday, starting from the time you wake up in the morning. No work."

"Well, on Sunday mornings, I generally don't get out of bed until I've…spent a little time with myself." Dana attempted a nonchalant leer, which didn't quite come off. Her cheeks flushed and she immediately averted her gaze, looking slightly uncomfortable with the admission.

"A woman after my own heart," Laurel said. "A Sunday morning without a self-induced orgasm is like a day without sunshine."

Dana brightened and met Laurel's eyes. "After that, I like to take a long, hot bath. Usually a movie on the couch in the afternoon. Grocery shopping, if I need to go. Reading. Something nice and explicit, usually, lesbian in nature—"

"You shit," Laurel said, chuckling. "'I'm straight,' you tell me. I *knew* you weren't straight, but with the way you blushed when I started talking about lesbian erotica, you almost had me convinced. So shy, so *scandalized* by the idea of a little literary porn. Now I find out that you're a lesbian erotica connoisseur?"

Dana grinned. "Well, I don't usually have to read it out loud to an audience."

"But you're so good at it," Laurel said. "Okay, going back to your morning. Do you sleep naked?"

Dana's grin faltered slightly, becoming shy.

"I do," Laurel offered. "Naked as a jaybird."

"Naked as a jaybird?" Dana tipped her head back and released a loud guffaw. "Nice expression."

"Blame my mother. Now answer the question. Naked?"

Dana nodded. "Naked."

"Good," she said. "Do you make noise when you come? You know, when you're spending time with yourself?"

"Did we somehow stumble back into truth or dare without my knowing?" Dana asked.

"You don't have to answer if you don't want to. Of course, I was *hoping* I'd be able to confirm the answer for myself soon enough."

Dana shook her head, dropping her gaze to her lap. "Not usually," she said. "Sometimes I can't really help it, but most of the time, I'm quiet."

"I'll have to do something about that," Laurel said.

Dana reached out and took her hand. She stroked the slim fingers with her own, studying the intricate lines of Laurel's knuckles. "I think part of the reason I'm quiet is because I grew up in a house with my brother in the room on one side of me and my parents on the other side. Years of masturbating in secret taught me to come like a ninja, silent and stealthy. It's a hard habit to break."

"Come like a ninja? Oh my God, that's *priceless*—"

"It's true," Dana defended. "Plus, I think I sound *weird*, you know? All breathy and out of control." She shuddered. "Ugh."

Laurel chuckled. A sense of humor was a definite turn-on, and this wasn't helping cool her down. "Oh, Dana…*God*, I like you a lot."

Dana wore a stupid grin. "That's the idea."

"And by the way, I'll be the judge on how you sound when I make you come," Laurel said. "I doubt 'weird' will be the first adjective I'll choose."

"You're killing me here." Dana slumped onto Laurel's blanket, lying on her side, staring over at Laurel's knees, her arms curling around herself.

Laurel joined her, stretching out to lie with her head on her upturned palm, one elbow propping her. She stretched her other hand out toward Dana's stomach, stroking her lightly through her shirt.

"I'm sorry," she said. "I'm not doing a very good job getting us away from the whole sex thing, am I?"

"Understatement," Dana replied.

"I'm sorry." Laurel traced lazy circles around her belly button. "It's difficult. I'm trying so hard to be noble here, and responsible."

"I know." Dana's gaze slid over Laurel's face and down her throat. "It's impossible not to want you right now."

She leaned in, pressing a gentle kiss to the side of Laurel's neck. Laurel tilted her head to grant better access, gasping when Dana nipped at the soft skin of her throat. "It almost seems useless to try and resist what's happening here," Laurel whispered, to herself as much as Dana.

"Almost?" Dana pushed her hand beneath the hem of Laurel's T-shirt, skimming her palm up the curve of her waist. "Try completely useless."

"Goddamn it." Laurel rose up and leaned over Dana, licking at her bottom lip. "I'm supposed to be the voice of reason."

"Why?" Dana asked just as her hand found Laurel's bare breast beneath her shirt. She gave the firm flesh a gentle squeeze. "I don't need to be protected, Laurel. I need to be touched."

Laurel whimpered as her nipple was pinched. She pushed her tongue deep into Dana's mouth, kissing her long and hard. Like that, all of Laurel's resistance melted away. Who was she kidding? She wouldn't last even another half hour in this enclosed space without giving in to her need—to both their needs.

As they kissed, she maneuvered both Dana's hands to the floor above her head. Holding her flat on her back, both wrists captured in a firm grasp, she checked her face for nervousness, but found only excitement.

Feeling foggy with passion, Laurel nodded. "All right," she whispered. "Then let me love on you."

HOUR TEN—4:00 A.M.

D ana stared up into Laurel's intense blue eyes. She tested the grip on her wrists, gasping when Laurel tightened her hold.

"Will you let me?" Laurel murmured, and bent to suck Dana's bottom lip into her mouth. Holding it between her teeth, she mumbled, "Make love to you?"

Dana exhaled shakily, glad she was already on her back. Surely her legs had stopped working by now. "Wow, it sure didn't take long to convince you."

Laurel retreated, swiping her tongue across Dana's upper lip. "You're very persuasive." She released one of Dana's wrists and stroked the back of her hand over Dana's cheek. "I admit it, I'm powerless against those beautiful green eyes."

Dana smiled triumphantly. "I'm glad I was able to seduce you."

"I'm glad, too."

"I'm twenty-eight years old." Dana flexed her fingers beneath the hand that still held her wrist, inhaling at the sensation of being restrained. "It's high time I start making questionable decisions where sex is concerned."

Laurel chuckled, but her eyes were serious. "Do you think this is a questionable decision?"

Dana grinned. "No. But I know it's supposed to be one."

Biting her lip, Laurel returned her free hand to Dana's unrestrained wrist. "You promise this won't…I mean, that you won't —"

"I won't freak out," Dana interrupted. "And I'll still respect you in the morning."

"Well, then." Laurel pushed her hips against Dana's and ground their lower bodies together. "I guess there's really no reason for me not to tear your clothes off and make you a woman right here and now."

"I guess there's not," Dana agreed. "So commence with the tearing."

Laurel began to laugh but stopped after only an instant, narrowing her gaze at something in the upper corner of the elevator car. "Oh, shit."

Dana twisted her shoulders, craning to see what Laurel was staring at. "Oh, shit, what?"

"Um…do you think that camera is still working?"

Dana sat up fast, dislodging Laurel from her position atop her body. She planted her hand on the blanket so she could stare open-mouthed at the surveillance camera mounted next to the row of buttons over the elevator door. *How the holy hell did I not remember that thing?*

"Uh…" With a pounding heart, Dana went through a mental checklist. *Let's see: we've got me lying on the floor with my head in Laurel's lap, Laurel half-naked and dancing, me making out with another woman…and my bare breasts.* Her mind spun as she started thinking about how to convince Rocky the security guard to hand a potentially embarrassing tape over, sight unseen. "Oh, shit."

As if sensing Dana's rising distress, Laurel laid a calming hand on her arm. "It probably doesn't work. If the elevator isn't working, how could the camera work?"

The same way the emergency lights are working. With growing horror, Dana continued to gape at the camera lens that stared them down. "Oh, shit."

Laurel gave her arm a gentle squeeze. "No, it's okay. You have beautiful breasts."

Dana shot Laurel an incredulous look. "Do you really think that makes me feel better? I *work* here."

"People see my tits in my workplace all the time," Laurel said with a teasing smile. "No big deal."

Dana managed a half-laugh, half-groan, burying her face in her hands. "Oh my God." That sealed the deal. They couldn't have sex now. She could do a lot of things with Laurel, but starring in their own lesbian porn wasn't one of them. At least not on the first date.

"Oh!" Laurel exclaimed. "I know!"

Dana uncovered her eyes and watched Laurel root through her backpack. "Please tell me you've got a handy-dandy videotape-erasing machine in there that you forgot to show me earlier."

"Almost as good." Laurel withdrew the can of whipped cream and held it aloft, smiling big.

Dana shook her head in fierce refusal. "There's no way I'm licking that off your breasts now that we're reality show material."

Laurel scoffed as she stood up, and shook the can before uncapping it. "No, silly." She rose onto her tiptoes, aiming the nozzle of the can at the camera lens. "I'm eliminating the problem."

Bemused, Dana watched as Laurel covered the lens with thick, white whipped cream. Though some dripped onto the floor, most stayed and effectively blocked the view.

"Genius," Dana whispered. "Of course, that doesn't do much about what they already have."

Laurel dropped back onto the blanket next to Dana. "Let's worry about that when the time comes, okay? There's nothing we can do about it right now."

Reluctantly, Dana said, "Okay."

Laurel cleared her throat. "Now…I believe I was going to make love to you."

She sure knew how to make a girl feel better. Dana willed her paranoia away, trying to concentrate instead on the moment at hand. She lay back down and stretched her arms over her head. "Weren't we right about here?"

"Oh, yeah," Laurel purred. "Right about there." She tugged her T-shirt over her head without hesitation.

Dana gawped at Laurel's breasts, lowering one hand to swipe at her mouth, which hung open slightly. No matter how many times she saw them, they were no less spectacular. "Perfect."

Laurel began to unbutton Dana's shirt again, and this time her hands moved slowly, as though she were in no particular hurry at all. "I want to feel you against me."

Dana stayed silent as Laurel divested her of her shirt and bra, and watched her own chest rise and fall with excitement. Inside, she was total chaos. She had never been this aroused, every nerve ending on fire. Her heart hammered so hard in her chest that she was afraid all her body's energy was being diverted there and she would stop breathing. Laurel settled back on top of her with a languid groan.

"That's more like it," she said, and brought her hands up to tangle in Dana's hair. Her skin was silky smooth on Dana's naked chest.

"I'll say." Dana's heart pounded against Laurel's bare breasts.

"You feel wonderful," Laurel said. She bent and captured Dana's mouth in a slow, lazy kiss. Breaking away, she placed a hand over Dana's heart. "Breathe, honey."

Dana nodded and inhaled deeply. The scent of Laurel made her dizzier, so she exhaled, then cradled Laurel and held her close. "You feel wonderful, too," she murmured. She raised her head and traced her tongue over Laurel's lips until they parted and she was accepted inside.

It didn't take long for their lingering kisses and gentle touches to escalate into something more. Dana squeezed and stroked the bare skin of Laurel's bottom as Laurel rode the firmness of her raised thigh. She could feel Laurel's heart rate increase to rival her own as they kissed, hot and sloppy, both of them moaning and breathing heavily.

Dana slipped her finger beneath the string that stretched between Laurel's buttocks again, but rather than move away from the intimate touch this time, Laurel tore her mouth from Dana's. "Do you want to take it off?"

Dazed, Dana asked, "Take what off?"

"My g-string." Laurel wiggled her hips, grinning when Dana wrapped her legs around them. "It sure seems like maybe you want it off."

Dana gazed up at Laurel, feeling improbably shy given the position they were in. "I want it off."

Laurel extracted herself from Dana's full body embrace and got to her feet. "Take it off, then, baby. I want you to see me."

Dana got up, swallowing against a too-dry throat. *Thank you, universe.* She stared at the triangle of silky black material covering Laurel and inhaled deeply, licking her lips. "Do you promise to rouse me if I pass out? I want to finish this no matter what happens."

Laurel looked both pleased and concerned. "You're in danger of passing out?"

"Honestly, yes." Dana brought her hands to Laurel's hips, hooking her fingers in the waistband of her g-string. "I'm afraid it's either going to be that, or else I'll wake up from this dream just as it's getting good."

Laurel gave her hair a gentle tug. "You really couldn't be any sweeter."

Holding her breath, Dana eased Laurel's g-string over her hips, starting slow and exhaling shakily when she uncovered the neatly trimmed thatch of dark, curly hair between Laurel's legs. "Oh."

Laurel set her feet apart, encouraging Dana to pull the flimsy material down the length of her legs. Dana leaned back as Laurel kicked them to the side carelessly, then leaned forward again so she could stare at the obvious wetness in front of her face.

"I rather like you in this position," Laurel said. She moved her hand from Dana's hair to her face, tracing a gentle line down her cheek, then across her jaw. She loomed over Dana like a goddess to be worshiped. "It's quite…appealing."

Unable to stop herself, Dana leaned forward and nuzzled the damp hairs between Laurel's thighs with her nose and lips. Laurel was hot and slick, and so fragrant that Dana moaned in pleasure. "I agree," Dana mumbled, sliding her hands up to cup Laurel's buttocks. "Appealing."

"Whoa," Laurel said shakily. Grasping Dana's face with both hands, she moved her from her place between Laurel's legs. "We need to slow this down, just a little."

Gathering her courage, Dana poked out her tongue and swiped it over the soft skin of Laurel's inner thigh before she was drawn away by insistent hands. A sweetness lingered on her tongue, and she felt her own pussy get wet when she realized she was tasting Laurel. "Why do we need to slow this down?"

"Because you need to be naked, too." Laurel got to her knees and faced Dana. "I'm firm on that one."

Naked. Right. Dana ran her eyes over Laurel's body, trying hard not to feel inadequate in every way. "Naked. Right."

Laurel chuckled and tugged her closer so that their breasts smashed together. "You're gorgeous, Dana." Craning her neck, she peppered Dana's throat with tiny, nibbling kisses. "Absolutely gorgeous." She dropped a hand down to press against Dana's belly, still kissing.

Resisting the urge to suck her stomach in, Dana closed her eyes and tilted her head to give Laurel better access. Immediately Laurel latched onto Dana's pulse point and sucked hard enough to send a jolt of pleasure thundering throughout Dana's body. "I just hope…"

"Hope what?" Laurel asked, never breaking the contact of her mouth with Dana's skin.

Dana dropped her hand between their bodies and skimmed her palm over the trimmed thatch of hair between Laurel's legs. Laurel sucked in an unsteady breath and finally stopped her kisses, leaning her forehead against Dana's shoulder.

"I hope you're okay with a more untamed look," Dana whispered. She cupped Laurel in her hand and gave her a gentle squeeze, punctuating her point. *If only I'd known I was going to get trapped in an elevator with the woman of my dreams today, I would've started a new grooming regimen.*

Laurel giggled, a sound that was breathy with arousal. "I'm more than okay with it." She slipped her hand between Dana's legs and palmed her through her pants. "I'm ravenous."

Dana closed her eyes as she struggled to contend with the overwhelming sensation of being touched so intimately. Even through clothing, it was the single most electrifying caress she had ever received.

Laurel moved her hand to the button of Dana's pants. "May I?"

When she could make her mouth work again, Dana said, "Yes."

Laurel brought her other hand down and fumbled with Dana's pants. The slight trembling of her fingers surprised Dana, and she asked, "Are you nervous?"

"Incredibly," Laurel murmured. She managed to get the button undone, and eased the zipper down slowly. "Aren't you?"

Dana took stock. Somehow it helped tremendously to know that Laurel was nervous, too. That it was normal, and not just because she was socially inept. "Not as much as I was."

"Good," Laurel said. She pressed one palm against Dana's lower back and moved the other hand to rest on Dana's stomach.

Dana was ready to take back her confident words the moment Laurel slid a hand over her abdomen and into her unbuttoned pants. Before she could register what was happening, Laurel's hand was cradling her, and careful fingertips slid through the abundant wetness that had gathered.

"Oh, Dana." Laurel's voice sounded strained. "You're soaking wet."

Dana's cheeks burned. There was no way that much wetness was normal. "For hours now, honestly."

"My poor girl," Laurel cooed, and removed her hand so she could tug Dana's pants down over her hips. "Let me take care of that." She put a gentle hand on Dana's shoulder and pushed. "Lie down for me."

Dana collapsed onto her back with a relieved sigh. She had been having trouble staying upright on weak, trembling knees.

"Lift," Laurel urged with a soft pat on her hip. When Dana planted her feet and raised her hips into the air, Laurel tugged her pants down. Tossing them to the side, she traced the waistband of Dana's panties with one fingertip. "These are ruined, aren't they?"

Dana squirmed beneath Laurel's touch, all too aware of the wetness that stained her panties and painted her inner thighs. "Until I can do some industrial-strength laundry, yes. Completely."

"Shame." Laurel rubbed her palm over the crotch of the cotton panties. "They're so cute on you."

"Favorite pair," Dana admitted.

"Mine, too. So far." Laurel eyed them seriously. "Even so, they've got to go."

Dana took a deep breath. Of course. That was the way these things worked. She agreed with a reluctant nod. "All right."

Laurel stretched out beside Dana, moving her hand to rest on her soft abdomen. "You've got the sweetest tummy," she said. Stroking the skin around her belly button with feather-light touches, Laurel added, "I love your body."

Dana stared down at herself with critical detachment. For the first time, she felt a certain warm glow at the sight of her full breasts and all her curves—especially with Laurel's hand on her. She grinned, emboldened by Laurel's obvious appreciation. "It's...all right."

Laurel slipped her hand beneath the waistband of Dana's panties, running searching fingertips through the wet, curly hairs. "You feel more than all right to me."

Dana stared at the shape of Laurel's hand moving beneath her panties with disbelieving eyes. When she felt her swollen clitoris brushed by a slippery fingertip, she arched her back and cried out.

Laurel brought her mouth close to Dana's ear. "So, so responsive."

Dana tightened her fists at her sides. Her hips ground out desperate circles beneath Laurel's hand, needy for more. "Take them off," Dana hissed.

"Take what off?" Laurel eased into a teasing grin. "You want me to have better access?"

Dana's ability to participate in witty banter was rapidly deteriorating. Along with her autonomic functions. She tried to control her breathing as Laurel pressed the length of her fingers over her labia, then rubbed up and down along the slippery flesh. "I want…uh…yes," she ground out.

Laurel removed her hand, leaving Dana cold and wanting with her absence. She tugged on Dana's panties with both hands, and Dana lifted her hips automatically, allowing Laurel to undress her.

"You're lovely," Laurel purred. She stared between Dana's legs and rubbed her palm over the thick patch of dark hair there. "I'm trying to decide what to do first," she mumbled, darting her gaze between Dana's breasts and her pussy. "It's not as easy as it may seem."

Dana's nipples tightened at the sensation of Laurel's hand between her legs, and at the sound of her throaty voice. "Kiss me," she suggested in a whisper. She reached between her own legs with trembling fingers, taking Laurel's hand and bringing it to her lips. "Start by kissing me."

Laurel replaced her fingers with her mouth, giving Dana a kiss that made her toes curl. Dana spread her legs and allowed Laurel to settle between them, groaning at the feeling of Laurel's naked skin on hers. It was almost too much to process: Laurel's erect nipples rubbing against her own, the short, wiry hairs between Laurel's legs tangling with Dana's own damp curls, the pleasant weight of a lean female body atop hers.

This is the best birthday I've ever had.

Laurel ended their kiss by sliding her mouth down over Dana's chin to her neck, nibbling and licking her skin every inch of the way. "You're so soft," Laurel murmured as she trailed wet kisses down to the slope of Dana's breast. "Feel so good." She licked a trail down to Dana's erect nipple. "I never want you in clothes again," she said, then took Dana's nipple between her teeth briefly before releasing it and laving it with the flat of her tongue.

Dana laughed, a breathy noise that sounded more like a muffled gasp than the expression of unrestrained joy that it was. Laurel's mouth eased into a smile around her nipple, for a moment still licking, then sucking hard. Dana watched, still fascinated by the reality of being touched by another woman.

Laurel released her nipple and kissed over to its twin, lavishing the same kind of attention on her other breast. Dana writhed and moaned beneath her touch, amazed by her complete lack of self-consciousness when it came to reacting out loud to Laurel's caresses.

Laurel's thigh pressed into the copious wetness between her legs, forcing a strangled plea. "Laurel, please. Please."

Laurel lifted her head with a grin. "Well, it didn't take me long to make you beg."

Shameless, Dana tried to catch her breath. "I'm more than willing…" She cried out when Laurel seized a nipple between her fingertips and tugged. "To…to beg."

Laurel kissed her mouth, murmuring, "That won't be necessary." She disentangled herself from Dana, then began a slow descent of Dana's body, trailing hot, nipping kisses along the way. The next thing Dana knew, her pale thighs were lifted over Laurel's slim shoulders.

"What are you doing?" she whispered in shock.

It was perfectly clear what Laurel was doing, of course. Dana had watched enough porn and read enough stories to have no doubt. She just couldn't quite believe it was happening to her. She scooted back a little to make more room and Laurel settled more fully between her thighs. She licked her lips as if in anticipation of a great meal, staring at Dana's pussy with hunger in her eyes.

"I'm going to taste you," she said quietly. She bent and kissed Dana's inner thigh, and when she drew back, Dana could see her shiny juices coating Laurel's full lips. Laurel poked her tongue out and swiped at her lower lip, eyes drooping closed in obvious appreciation. "Delicious."

Dana didn't answer, too concerned with the incredible teasing between her legs. Laurel moved her mouth across her inner thighs, delivering gentle nibbles along the creases on either side of her aching pussy. She smiled up at Dana with flashing blue eyes as she worked, poking her tongue out every now and again to swipe at sensitive skin.

Dana schooled her breathing. She didn't know if she would survive the night.

Laurel hummed as she pressed her lips against the tuft of hair shielding Dana's throbbing clit, providing just enough pressure to make her gasp and arch her back in anticipation. Dana threaded her hands in Laurel's thick chestnut hair, thighs trembling at what was about to happen.

Laurel lay her hand on Dana's stomach and met her eyes. "How are you doing, sweetheart?"

Dana nodded fast, opening and closing her mouth a few times without managing to actually form any words. She tightened her fingers in Laurel's hair, then groaned when Laurel planted another kiss on her soaked curls.

"Are you ready?" Laurel's eyes were bright and alive, full of obvious pleasure.

Dana opened her mouth to answer in the affirmative, but all she could manage was a quiet moan that turned into a gasp when Laurel bent slightly to blow a stream of air over her overheated pussy. The breeze raised her nipples into even harder points, wrenching a pained grimace from her.

"Please, kiss me," Dana pleaded. There was no hesitation. She was beyond being afraid to ask for what she wanted.

Laurel planted another gentle kiss between Dana's legs, pressing her nose into her curly hairs. Retreating, but keeping her lips mere inches from where Dana needed her most, she mumbled, "Like that?"

Almost against her will, Dana raised her hips to try to force more contact. "Kiss me…harder."

Laurel lowered her mouth and pressed firm lips to the same spot, teasing Dana's clit with the promise of her attention, but the kiss was still muffled by hairs that absorbed the caress. "Harder like that?" she asked.

Dana tightened her hand in Laurel's hair again, resisting the urge to force her face between her legs. "God, Laurel, please—"

Laurel moved her hands so she could spread Dana open, exposing her wet, swollen need, and lowered her face to trace the tip of her tongue along her labia. Dana cried out in surprise at the exquisite sensation.

Laurel lifted her face. "Like that?"

Dana nodded, frantic for more. "I've never...I've never felt anything like—" She tugged on Laurel's hair, urging her back. "Please...please."

Laurel dragged the flat of her tongue up the length of Dana's sex, unleashing a whole new wave of wetness that Dana was sure Laurel had to feel on her chin. Drawing away for only an instant, Laurel said, "You're so beautiful, Dana. Thank you for this."

And then she settled in to feast.

Dana's mouth fell open and stayed that way, fists tightening and toes curling, when Laurel covered the engorged flesh of her pussy with her whole mouth. Her body tensed at the intimate kiss, so much more intense and all consuming than she had imagined it would be. Her hands loosened in Laurel's hair; she was boneless beneath the tender assault, and she lacked the strength to exert her will in any way.

She surrendered to Laurel, body and soul. She became more vulnerable than she had ever been before, and infatuated with the heady bliss of giving herself over to Laurel completely. Moaning, she was all instinct and no thought at all.

Laurel's tongue played Dana with casual skill, lapping up and down her ridged flesh and slick wetness. It teased lower, circling Dana's tight opening, pressing inside only slightly before withdrawing with a sensuous wiggle. Laurel kept her palms pressed against Dana's inner thighs, holding her open, and she moved her head up and down, back and forth, as she worked her over with lips and tongue.

Dana cradled Laurel's head with both hands, cursing her thighs for trembling uncontrollably with the pleasure of it all. Laurel wrapped her arms around her thighs and held on, moaning loudly when Dana pumped tentative hips into her face, seeking release. Laurel allowed Dana to thrust into her mouth as she licked and sucked her pussy.

"Yes, Laurel, yes...yes," Dana gasped. She planted her feet on the blanket, seeking leverage as she continued to move her hips in rhythm with Laurel. "Yes, please, yes."

Laurel opened her mouth wide, sliding her tongue in large circles over Dana's throbbing clit.

The pleasure was so intense that Dana's body almost didn't seem to know where to go with it, how to break through that final barrier to mindless release. She hovered on the precipice for what felt like hours, eyes squeezed tightly shut as she sought that last caress that would push her over the edge.

She found it when Laurel brought one hand up and pinched her nipple hard, rolling it between her thumb and forefinger, still licking, then sliding her lips up and down the length of Dana's distended clit.

Dana cried out and arched her back, holding Laurel's head tightly to her, still pumping and thrusting. She was not at all silent when she came. She wailed and keened incoherent pleasure as the orgasm ripped through her body. She endured the rush of sensation as long as she could, desperate to experience every last bit of it, but finally had to push Laurel away with shaking hands.

"Wait," Dana sobbed. "Wait, I…" She remained limp in Laurel's arms until the oral assault ceased, hot tears streaming down her cheeks. Her eyes burned with emotion brought on by all the feelings Laurel stirred in her, and crying was the only way to relieve some of the pressure inside. "My God, I—"

Laurel kissed her way up Dana's abdomen, over her belly, and brought both hands up to curl over Dana's shoulders in a tender embrace. Her mouth left a wet trail along Dana's ribs, her right breast, her shoulder and neck and chin. Laurel pressed her slick tongue into Dana's mouth, sharing a flavor Dana had only hesitantly sampled before that moment. She tasted delicious on Laurel's mouth.

Laurel cradled Dana in her arms, kissing her for long moments before withdrawing with a tender smile. "That was amazing," she whispered, brushing the back of her hand over Dana's tear-dampened cheek. "Dana, honey, you were wonderful."

Dana clung to Laurel's shoulders, burying her face in her soft, warm neck as she continued to cry. Laurel eased her arms around Dana's back, holding her close. She whispered into Dana's ear.

"I'm so glad I met you tonight. So, so glad you gave me a chance, that this stupid elevator got stuck. It felt so good to touch you, to taste you. I'm not sure I've ever gotten so turned on tasting a woman before."

Dana's tears slowed at Laurel's quiet words, then stopped altogether. She tightened her arms around Laurel, cleaving to her supple body as her heart rate began to slow.

"Thank you," Dana mumbled against Laurel's neck. "That was… that was…"

"It was," Laurel agreed, rubbing her hands over Dana's shoulder blades. "You taste so sweet." She paused, then dropped a light kiss on Dana's lips. "Are you okay?"

"I'm crying," Dana murmured, bringing one hand to her face and swiping at the drying tears. "I don't know why I'm crying."

Laurel relaxed into a cocky leer. "Because I'm *so* good. That's why."

Leave it to Laurel to make me feel okay about even this display of emotion. Dana brushed dark hair away from Laurel's face. "You're right, that must be it."

Laurel shifted so she could stretch out beside her. She kept one arm curled under Dana's back and reached down with her other hand to stroke the oversensitized flesh of her abdomen.

Dana sucked in a startled breath. "What are you doing?"

"Getting ready to make you come again." Laurel dropped her hand between Dana's legs, slipping her fingers down to find Dana's swollen clit. "If I'm going to make love to you, I'm going to do it right."

Dana's breathing grew ragged again. *Ah, yes. The difference between sex that involves a man and that which doesn't. Instant replay.* She took stock of her body, trying to decide whether she could withstand another shattering orgasm.

"I promise to leave you in one piece," Laurel murmured. She nipped at her earlobe, rubbing her fingertips over Dana's labia. "But you're not done yet. I need more."

Dana wasn't about to argue. She let her legs fall open for Laurel's hand and braced herself for more. "You can have whatever you want."

Laurel brought the tip of one finger down to probe at Dana's opening, tracing gentle circles around the impossible wetness that coated her. "May I go inside?"

Dana didn't hesitate. "Yes," she whispered, then exhaled as she schooled herself to relax. *It'll feel good,* she told herself, trying hard to let go of the memory of the last time someone had been inside her body. *Laurel will make this feel good.*

Laurel pushed the slippery length of her finger inside Dana with a soft groan, the penetration filling but not stretching, gentle and controlled. Dana closed her eyes and whimpered at the feeling of surrounding Laurel with her pulsing flesh.

"Feel good?" Laurel whispered. She drew her finger back an inch or so, then thrust it in deeper. She kissed Dana's temple, poking her tongue out to trace her hairline. "You're so nice and tight around me, Dana."

Dana opened her eyes and held Laurel's intense gaze. She blinked, overcome and wanting more. Raising her hips to meet one of Laurel's slow thrusts, she whimpered, "Don't stop."

"Oh, I'm not going to stop." Laurel's thrusts remained steady, moving deep inside Dana's pussy. "I won't stop until you come all over my hand."

Dana bit her lip so hard that she was sure she was drawing blood. She tightened one fist on the blanket and moved her other arm further around Laurel's shoulders. Breathing heavily, she spoke in time with Laurel's deliberate strokes. "Try...another...finger."

Laurel pulled back to the entrance, then pressed inside with more. She slid in deep, moving so slowly that Dana could feel every millimeter of torturous progress as blunt fingertips scraped against her inner walls. Dana cried out, spreading her legs as wide as they would go, desperate to be taken.

"Still feel good?" Laurel whispered, giving her a brief kiss on the mouth. Her hand maintained its steady motion between Dana's thighs, long fingers sliding in and out of her pussy, still excruciatingly slow.

Dana gritted her teeth, nostrils flaring as she struggled with her rising need. "F-faster."

Laurel's fingers picked up speed, angling upward to rub at Dana's inner walls firmly. "Like that?" When Dana closed her eyes, hesitating and breathing hard, Laurel whispered hotly into her ear. "I like hearing what you want. I like knowing that this feels good for you. Talk to me."

Dana tried to contend with her hazy thoughts, uncertain that she even remembered how to speak. She licked her lips, then cried out when Laurel began stroking a spot that made Dana ache with desire. "Yes, like that."

"Are you going to come for me?"

Dana released a loud yelp of pleasure when the pad of Laurel's thumb came to rest on her clit, and rocked her hips to meet the firm thrusting of Laurel's fingers. "Yes!" she cried out, though she couldn't remember the question she was answering.

"Come for me, Dana," Laurel whispered into her ear. Her hand moved in perfect rhythm, fingers penetrating, thumb rubbing, robbing Dana of all coherent thought.

Dana gave voice to her release in a litany of gasping, loud words, curses, tearful gratitude, and reverent recitations of Laurel's name. Laurel tightened her arm around Dana's back as she came, pumping her fingers until Dana slammed her thighs closed on her arm. Stilling her motion, she kept her fingers buried deep as Dana regained her breath and shuddered at the aftershocks that racked her whole body.

"You're hot," Laurel murmured, and wiggled the tips of her fingers where they rested inside. "And you make me feel like some kind of sex goddess, coming like that."

Dana groaned, grasping Laurel's wrist in her hand. Extracting her carefully, she croaked, "That was all you, darling. You earned it."

Laurel wiped her wet hand on the blanket then tugged her into a tight embrace. "So that was better than what's-his-name?"

Dana snorted. "Who's what's-his-name?"

Laurel sighed, tracing careless patterns over Dana's stomach and chest with the tips of her fingers. "Do you want to go out for our date on Sunday night?"

Dana smiled, understanding the non sequitur perfectly. "I'll pick you up?"

"Perfect," Laurel said, and rested her cheek on Dana's breast. "Ready for a nap?"

Dana blinked in surprise. "Nap? Are you nuts? I want to…" She hesitated, trying to choose the appropriate word. "Touch you."

Laurel picked her head up and batted her eyelashes at Dana. "You want to…what?" she asked with an air of mischief, as though she knew what Dana had almost said.

Dana felt her heartbeat pick up. "I want to…fuck you. And lick you."

Laurel exhaled shakily. "Maybe I'm not so tired after all."

Hour Eleven—5:00 A.M.

You know you're going to have to help me if I do this completely wrong, right?"

Laurel laughed as Dana sat up and straddled Laurel's hips, settling on top of her. "I doubt you'll do anything completely wrong," she murmured. "You don't seem totally ignorant about sex to me."

"But I am totally ignorant about making love to a beautiful woman." Dana traced her fingertips along Laurel's defined collarbone. "You didn't mind what I said before…about fucking you, did you?"

Laurel tilted her head. "Mind?"

"Well, I guess it's not a very tender word, right?" Dana shrugged, feeling sillier as she kept talking. "I mean, I know you're pretty open about this stuff, but—"

"Honey, we're having sex, not performing a religious ceremony," Laurel said. "It's supposed to be fun. I like tender, but making love doesn't always have to be romantic and slow and mushy."

Sweet relief filled Dana's chest. All right, so she hadn't committed a faux pas. Yet. She lowered her body and bent her head, kissing Laurel's erect nipple. "Okay," she mumbled, sucking the hard flesh between her lips and testing it with her teeth.

Laurel hissed in pleasure. "I told you I like dirty talking," she reminded in a breathy voice. "Among other less than tender attention."

Dana released Laurel's nipple so she could interrupt. "That's right, you're a kinky little thing, aren't you?" She licked around Laurel's areola, breathing harder. She hoped it wouldn't take her too long to get comfortable enough with Laurel to take advantage of that particular fantasy.

Laurel pushed her fingers into Dana's hair, holding her head against her breast. "I'm up for pretty much anything, Dana, if you want it."

I'm going to have to get Scott something really excellent for Christmas this year. Dana switched breasts, taking the other nipple between her teeth and circling it with the tip of her tongue. *Something that really reflects my deep, undying love for him, that magnificent bastard.*

Dana drew back and took a deep breath. "I want to taste you."

"Yes," Laurel moaned. She spread her legs wide so that Dana's hips settled into the space. "I was tested after my last partner," she said, avoiding Dana's eyes. "There hasn't been anyone else since."

Dana blinked, not having even thought to ask the question. She could feel her rounded belly growing wet with Laurel's desire. The sensation made her impatient, barely able to concentrate on Laurel's earnest words.

"In case you were worried about it," Laurel explained in an uncertain voice.

Dana's mind cleared just enough for her to recall one of the first things she'd said to Laurel. *Maybe I'm scared of what I might catch with you squirming around on my lap like that.* "I wasn't worried."

Laurel smiled. "I want to feel your mouth on me."

Dana shivered in anticipation. She licked her lips, almost unable to believe that she was about to fulfill one of her greatest fantasies. *I'm going to go down on this gorgeous woman. It's a birthday miracle.* She gazed upon the length of Laurel's body, admiring lean curves as she assessed the situation.

"Do you think you could get over my face?" Dana asked, breaking into a shy smile at the question. "If I lie on my back?"

Laurel groaned and sat up, reversing their positions with ease. Dana found herself on her back once again, gasping as a knee was planted on either side of her head and Laurel's pussy opened above her, deep pink and glistening with wetness, her engorged clit so swollen it was almost red.

"Remember what I said about rousing me. I really do want to finish this." Dana gripped Laurel's hips with shaking hands. "Please."

Laurel giggled and slid her hand down between her own legs. She spread herself open, then pushed two fingers on either side of her aroused clit. "We could start with something a little less intense." She rubbed herself with slow-moving strokes.

Dana bit down hard on her lower lip as her clit pulsed in pleasure at the sight of Laurel touching herself. "Oh, no," she said. "I like intense. Intense is very, very good." She lifted her head and swiped at Laurel's index finger with her tongue, whimpering in surprise at the delicious flavor of her juices.

Laurel moved her hand, leaving her swollen need exposed. "God, Dana—"

Dana reached for Laurel's hips, bringing her pussy lower. "My turn," she whispered, and extended her tongue to take a leisurely lick of the hot, wet flesh.

She forgot to worry about not knowing what to do the instant she felt Laurel's slippery labia against her tongue and began to envelop her large clit. She stopped thinking altogether, and rumbled in ecstasy as she explored every inch of Laurel's most intimate place with her whole mouth.

Laurel's thighs trembled and she weaved back and forth as Dana sucked eagerly. "Oh, fuck, yeah…"

Dana moaned at the sound of Laurel's growled words. She tasted so unbelievable, so sweet; Dana wondered if all women tasted this good, or just Laurel. She tugged harder on Laurel's hips, compelling her down more firmly on her face. She could bear the weight—wanted it, in fact—and she craved the sensation of being totally overwhelmed by Laurel's smell and taste.

"You're so…good." Laurel toppled forward, her hands connecting with the elevator wall. Propping herself above Dana, she moaned and squirmed as Dana's attack on her pussy continued.

Dana rolled her eyes back as far as she could, staring up past Laurel's belly, trying to catch a glimpse of her face. She wanted to watch exactly what she was doing to Laurel, to see if this felt as good to her as Laurel's tongue had felt to Dana. That she could reduce another woman to a trembling, whimpering mess left her feeling more powerful than she knew possible.

Laurel's whole body quivered in sync with the uncontrolled shaking of her thighs. She rocked her hips back and forth over Dana's face, smearing slick juices over her lips and chin and nose. One hand dropped from the wall to Dana's head, the fingers threading through her hair.

Dana tried to hold Laurel still as she focused on the hard ridge of nerves whose worship produced even more of the slick wetness she savored. She swirled the tip of her tongue back and forth over Laurel's hard clit, chasing it around with firm strokes. Every so often she would move her whole mouth lower, thrusting into the tight opening she found there, pulling Laurel hard against her as she penetrated her with a stiff tongue.

"Christ, woman," Laurel whimpered, now more subdued within her grip. "You're...it's...yes, baby, suck me..."

Dana heard small, frantic noises and the thighs beside her head began to tremble more violently. She slid her hands from Laurel's hips to her buttocks, gripping hard and spreading the cheeks apart. Laurel stiffened and cried out, sending a rush of hot, salty wetness to soak Dana's lips, cheeks, and chin. Thrilled by what she could cause simply by following her instincts, Dana held her tight, trying to draw out as much pleasure as she could. She relaxed her grip only when Laurel began sobbing for her to stop.

"Oh, all right," she mumbled. "You can rest for a minute." She scooted out from beneath Laurel and sat up, chuckling.

Laurel simply collapsed onto the blanket and lay motionless on her belly, hair spread wildly around her head. She was panting, her arms stretched out and her round bottom providing a tempting sight. Dana crawled up the length of Laurel's body, peppering her shoulders and spine with soft kisses. She struggled for words, not certain how she could verbalize what she was feeling.

After a few moments, she said, "That was fucking incredible."

Laurel's shoulders shook with quiet laughter. "It was," she mumbled into the blanket. "I can't move."

Dana kissed the back of Laurel's neck, grinding her pussy into the naked bottom beneath her. "Oh, you don't need to move. I think you're fine just where you are."

Laurel groaned and pushed back, turning her face to the side. "You've done this before," she accused. "There's no way you're just that good."

Beaming, Dana rested her cheek against Laurel's soft hair. "I guess I'm just that good."

"I guess you are."

"Do I get to try for a second one, too?" Having brought Laurel to orgasm once, Dana found herself full of heady confidence. She was ready for more.

Laurel exhaled shakily. "It's got to be almost five thirty in the morning. You're trying to kill me."

"I don't want to kill you." Dana moved her hand from the dip at the base of Laurel's spine to the backs of her thighs, pushing her fingers into the juncture until she found wetness. "I just want to fuck you."

Laurel seemed to gather herself then. She attempted to push herself up to kneeling, but Dana quickly placed her free hand down firmly between Laurel's shoulders to prevent her. "Stay right where you are," she said.

Laurel shuddered. "If this is you as a beginner, I fear for my physical well-being."

"I've had a lot of time to dream," Dana said. "And watch, and read."

Laurel moved her knees apart so she was spread open. "I'm impressed. And I hope this means you're over being nervous. You have no reason to doubt yourself, trust me."

She did trust Laurel, absolutely. And miraculously, she found her nervousness had all but disappeared. "How can I be nervous when I've got you wet and open and on your belly in front of me?"

She got to her knees behind Laurel and rested a hand on her bottom. Feeling almost cocky, she drew back after several slow caresses and delivered a sharp slap, causing Laurel to jerk in surprise. "In fact, I'm almost ready to get kinky with you."

"God, and it's not even *my* birthday." Laurel dissolved into giggles.

Dana gripped Laurel's ass and spread her open, lowering her face to the pink folds she revealed and lapping at them with her tongue. When Laurel released a throaty moan, she replaced her mouth with her fingers.

"I bet you love getting taken like this," she murmured, tracing the edges of Laurel's labia with her fingertips. Swallowing a momentary worry about her technique, she continued to stroke her. "Do you love being taken like this?"

Laurel nodded fast, rocking back on her knees to meet the motion of Dana's fingers. "Yes," she choked out.

"I knew it." Hesitantly, Dana pressed a finger between Laurel's folds and searched for her opening. *I hope I know how to go inside of her from this angle. I hope I don't hurt her.* When she located the promising entrance she sought, she slipped her finger gradually inside.

Laurel released a quiet grunt of pleasure. "God, Dana."

"You want me in here?" Dana whispered. How the hell did she get so bold?

With a throaty moan, Laurel pressed back against Dana's finger. "You're getting very…forceful," she whispered, moving still more, urging her deeper inside.

"You make me want to be." Dana felt a welling of emotion she could not control. Laurel made her feel like she could be, or do, anything. She wiggled her fingertip into her opening, then withdrew. "Tell me what you want."

"I want to feel you inside me." Laurel's words were slightly muffled by the blanket. "I want you to keep talking."

Emboldened, Dana leaned close and took Laurel's earlobe between her teeth. She pressed her fingertip against Laurel, playing with the tight ring of flesh. She stroked her idly for a few seconds, then probed at her again with a trembling finger. *Calm down, Dana.* She exhaled through her nostrils, stroking Laurel's wetness as she worked to relax. *Calm down and make this so good for her.*

"How many fingers do you want?" she whispered into Laurel's ear. She rubbed gentle circles around her opening with two fingertips. "Tell me."

Laurel thrust her bottom higher. "Two," she whimpered. "Give me two."

Dana grinned at the feeling of power that surged through her body. *She's really turned on.* Eager to feel Laurel from the inside, she pressed onward, stopping when she slid in to her first knuckles. "Two?" She curled her fingers slightly and withdrew, rubbing slick inner walls as she retreated. "You want two fingers inside your pussy?"

Dana was drawing on every porn movie she had ever seen at

this point, every piece of erotic lesbian literature, and she knew from Laurel's tortured moan that she was hitting the mark.

Laurel's breathing grew increasingly labored. "Please," she begged, pushing back before Dana began moving with her. "Fuck me, Dana, please."

With a sense of victory unrivaled by any good grade in school or achievement in business, Dana thrust her index and middle fingers deep inside, groaning in unison with Laurel as she buried herself completely within the snug space. She closed her eyes for a few seconds, losing herself in the myriad of new sensations: the heat surrounding her fingers, the subtle pulsing she could feel throughout her whole hand, the wetness that soaked her palm and trickled down her wrist.

"You feel incredible," she breathed. "Laurel, you're so sexy."

She stared down, transfixed by the sight of her fingers disappearing inside Laurel. *I can't believe I'm really inside you.*

Prone on the floor in total submission, Laurel released a pained whimper and rocked faster and harder on Dana's hand, reminding her that she should really finish what she started. As Dana switched to deeper thrusts, they fell into an escalating rhythm that made her ache for her own release.

"Yes," Laurel hissed, moving her hand between her own legs to start stroking her clit.

Dana grinned. "Oh, yeah, you like this a lot, don't you?" She gave Laurel a couple of extra-hard thrusts, taking a cue from Laurel's frantic response that she was nowhere near her limit. "Don't you?"

Laurel nodded her head, face buried in one arm. "I love it," she said. "You feel so good." Her hand worked furiously between her legs.

Staring down at Laurel's wanton movements, Dana had a flash of inspiration. She stopped moving her arm, but kept her fingers deep inside. "Fuck me," she said. "Fuck my fingers."

Laurel cried out in startled arousal, and, after only a brief hesitation, began rocking in earnest, forcing Dana's fingers deep before pulling away so that only the tips remained inside, then pushing back so she was buried once again.

Dana wondered if it was possible for her to come again without being touched. Her clit twitched, aching with a deep pleasure-pain that took her breath away. She watched Laurel maintain an unashamed rhythm with her body, freely using Dana to push herself closer to climax. "God, you're hot," she growled.

Unable to resist, she began thrusting once again, this time letting her thumb rest against the puckered ring of Laurel's anus. She didn't attempt to penetrate, instead applying teasing pressure to the tiny pink opening. Laurel rewarded her with a strangled whimper.

"I want to make you come," Dana said.

Panting, Laurel gasped, "I'm almost...there."

Her hand worked at her clit, rubbing frantic circles as Dana moved within her. Dana began stroking tiny circles with her thumb, caressing the sensitive skin of Laurel's anus, while she kept up a steady rhythm of thrusts into her drenched pussy.

"Maybe one day I'll teach you to fuck my ass," Laurel gasped out. Her pussy contracted around Dana's fingers as she spoke, growing even slicker. "Would you like that?"

"Yes," Dana said without hesitation. She wiggled the pad of her thumb on Laurel's anus, and inhaled sharply when the very tip was drawn inside. Desire surged through her veins, and she increased the speed and power of her thrusting fingers, fucking Laurel's pussy as hard as she dared.

Laurel's hand was a blur between her legs. "Fuck, yeah."

"You like it hard," Dana said. Not a question, a statement.

"Oh, yeah, Dana, oh, yeah." Laurel's sweet voice was choked with joyous release.

Her entire body tensed, and for a moment, the only movement was Dana's hand pounding between her legs and her own fingers rubbing desperate circles on her clit. Her pussy spasmed around Dana's fingers, releasing a hot gush of wetness that trickled down Dana's wrist. She made a noise that set off an answering spasm between Dana's thighs.

Dana marveled at the way she could feel Laurel tighten and convulse as her orgasm hit. She felt like her hand was in the middle of some miracle, some powerful force of nature. With her eyes clamped shut, she tried to memorize every last detail of the hot, pulsing, wet pleasure she had caused.

"Stop, I can't take any more," Laurel pleaded, looking back over her shoulder.

Dana had already slowed to a gentle pumping, and now withdrew carefully. In silent reverence, she pressed her wet hand to the swollen flesh between Laurel's legs and crawled up to lie beside her.

"Are you okay?" she mumbled against the sweat-slicked skin of Laurel's shoulder.

Laurel nodded. Her cheeks were flushed and damp tendrils of dark hair stuck to her forehead. "Recovering," she croaked. "You're a rare find, you know that?"

Dana grinned. "What do you mean?"

"You've got a natural gift. I think I've just snagged myself an excellent lover before anyone else discovered that fact. Including you."

Although Dana couldn't detect anything but sincerity in the words, her earlier confidence seemed to be melting under the intensity of Laurel's gaze. Staring into eyes full of tender emotion, she felt incredibly lucky but equally uncertain. It didn't seem possible that Laurel was just being nice, but she checked in anyway. "It was really okay? After the whole kissing fiasco, I started to think—"

"You analyze too much." Laurel clucked her tongue. "It was more than okay, and you know it."

"That was so much more than I ever imagined it would be."

"Me, too." Laurel leaned forward and gave Dana a slow kiss. "You're exquisite. I'm keeping you."

Dana had to restrain herself from beating on her chest. She couldn't stop the wide grin that captured her mouth, though, or the pride she knew was shining in her eyes. "Remember, I'm going to need plenty more practice."

Laurel laughed. "We've unleashed a monster, haven't we?"

"I think so." Dana drew her into a warm embrace. "That was so much fun."

"Worth the risk?" Laurel's expression was serious.

"Oh, yeah. And then some."

"I agree." Laurel yawned all of a sudden.

"Nap time?" Dana asked, stroking her fingertips over Laurel's bare back. Though she didn't want to stop touching her for even a moment, she said, "We should put some clothes on. I refuse to let Rocky surprise us with a rescue while I'm lying naked on the elevator floor."

"Good call." Laurel disentangled herself and sat up on the blanket.

"I'm not sure how well I'll be able to sleep in here, but I'd hate to snore right through this elevator taking us down to the lobby."

Dana frowned as they both put on their bras and Laurel's perfect breasts disappeared from view. Laurel snatched up Dana's panties from on top of her backpack, twirling the cotton garment around on her finger with a playful smile.

Dana grimaced. "I can't put those back on. They're soaking wet."

Laurel picked up her g-string from the floor. "Mine, too. I'll just put them in here." She stuffed both pairs of underwear inside her backpack. Winking at Dana, she added, "Maybe I'll keep yours as a souvenir."

Dana snorted in embarrassed pleasure as she buttoned her blouse. "Only if you'll give me visitation rights. That is my favorite pair, after all." Especially now.

"Of course. Whenever you want."

Dana stood so she could pull her pants back on. "What I really want is a shower." Her stomach growled, signaling another need. "And breakfast."

"I hear you." After fastening her own jeans, Laurel took a step toward Dana. "First a hug and that nap we were talking about. That's if I can stop myself from looking at you for more than a minute."

Dana didn't hesitate to step into Laurel's arms. She loved the feel of Laurel's heart thumping against her own. "You know, I feel really happy right now."

Laurel beamed. "So do I."

Dana tried hard to wipe the goofy grin off her face. "Rocky's going to take about five seconds to guess exactly what happened in here, you know."

"Rocky's the security guard, right?" At Dana's nod, Laurel shrugged. "There's nothing we can do. This elevator smells like sex."

"And I'll be smiling like an idiot when the doors open."

"Not a usual thing for you?" Laurel asked innocently.

"Oh, no. You seem to inspire it in me."

Laurel snuggled up against Dana's body. "Lucky me."

"Lucky me," Dana countered.

They shook out the blanket and lay down on it, nuzzling close, face to face. Watching Laurel's sleepy blue eyes get heavier and feeling her breathing slow down, Dana felt that swell of pride again. *Damn, I knocked her out.*

Laurel pressed her face into Dana's breast. "See you when we wake up."

"Yes, see you soon," Dana said quietly.

She didn't know if Laurel heard her or if she was already asleep. All she heard was a little snorting noise and a soft sigh. Silky chestnut hair brushed her chin and she tightened her hold, trying to make Laurel as comfortable as possible. Staring down at her, she thought, *I really, really like this woman.*

HOUR THIRTEEN—7:00 A.M.

Dana drifted in and out of consciousness for quite some time before awakening fully. She couldn't say she felt refreshed, and she knew she hadn't slept for long on the hard floor. The discomfort and the unfamiliar warmth of Laurel in her arms conspired to end her nap not long after it began. Laurel's head rested heavily on her chest, her arm still thrown over Dana's waist. Her breasts pressed into Dana's side, triggering a flash of memory of their lovemaking.

Dana craned so she could deposit a soft kiss on top of Laurel's head. She inhaled the sweet fragrance of her shampoo mingled with sweat.

"Can't sleep?" Laurel mumbled.

Dana jerked a little at the sound of her voice, startled that she was awake. She gave her a gentle hug. "No, sorry if I woke you."

Laurel lifted her head from Dana's breast, blinking up at her with tired eyes. "You didn't," she said. "Sorry I just passed out on you like that. That took a lot out of me."

"We'll be rescued soon." Dana glanced at her wristwatch. It was seven. Rocky was no doubt on his way in to work. "Even if this was a comfortable bed, I don't know if I could have slept. I think I'm still a little excited."

Laurel eased into a tender grin. "About making love?"

"About everything. I can't stop thinking. And I'm not used to being so close to someone else. I just want to touch you all the time."

Laurel stroked Dana's cheek with the back of her hand, leaning closer to give her a brief kiss. "I understand."

"Do you? Is that how you feel, too?" Dana covered Laurel's delicate ear with her hand. She was so soft.

"I do," Laurel said. "I'm excited, too."

"I can't believe we've only been in here for twelve hours," Dana whispered. "I feel like a completely different person."

"You're the same person. Just…braver."

"No, I'm different." Dana moved forward, taking Laurel's lips in a slightly longer, deeper kiss. She wanted to stay in that kiss forever. Laurel felt like a miracle, turning her life upside down overnight. Already the idea of going back to her old habits made her feel sick to her stomach. "I'm better for having met you."

Laurel initiated yet another kiss, and this one lasted for a couple of minutes. She ended it with a contented groan, leaning back to smile at Dana. "So, what are your plans for after we get out of here?"

"This morning?" *I hoped they would include you.* Uncertain, she hedged. "What are yours?"

Laurel looked down at Dana's chest. "Think you'll be working on that proposal of yours?"

"What proposal?"

Instantly, Laurel's tension eased and she released a hearty laugh. She looked up at Dana with sparkling eyes. "Damn, that 'important proposal' sure got downgraded fast."

"Oh, yeah, *that* proposal." At this point, the work she had been doing when Laurel burst into her office the night before was meaningless. Or at the very least, it wasn't on her agenda for the rest of the day. She grinned at Laurel. "The proposal can definitely wait."

"Changing our priorities, are we?" Laurel's face shone with quiet pleasure.

Dana gave her a serious nod. "I think something just became more important than project management."

Laurel's smile rendered every moment Dana had ever lived before that one deficient, because they hadn't included that look of pure joy on the face of a lover. Stunned, she took Laurel's hand and was almost afraid to let go. Fear cast doubt on all she was feeling. Somehow it didn't seem possible that they could abandon this magical bubble suspended between floors that would soon hum with everyday normality, and not leave everything behind. Her eyes met Laurel's, seeking something other than the passion and tenderness she saw.

"You're not feeling overwhelmed?" Laurel asked.

Dana shook her head, reluctant to spoil the mood with her concerns. Perhaps she was just a natural born pessimist. As the morning closed in on them, with all it would bring, she started thinking like the project manager she was. How would this work? They were two very different people. Laurel was outgoing and warm and worked as a dancer in men's clubs. Was that something Dana could cope with if they began a relationship? It was one thing to be nonjudgmental about how strangers made their living, but a girlfriend? Dana had to be honest with herself. The idea made her very uncomfortable.

Laurel touched her arm. "Are you?"

"Overwhelmed? Yes, a little, but in the best way possible," Dana said. "It was high time I took a good, hard look at my priorities."

That was the truth. Whatever happened when they left this haven, she would never feel the same way about her life.

Laurel gave her a serious nod. "And sex is more important than proposals on that reorganized list."

Dana chuckled. "Well, sex *is* more important than proposals. But spending time with you is more important than sex."

"Great answer."

"Thanks, I figured that sort of answer was a surefire way to get laid again before too long."

Laurel laughed out loud, delivering a playful smack to Dana's arm. "You shit." When her laughter died down, she said, "For the record, you don't need any clever answers to get laid again. Bring those hands, that tongue, and your beautiful body, and you'll have to fight me off whenever you want."

Dana tightened her arms around Laurel. The promises came so easily while they were sitting here in the extended afterglow of their lovemaking. She wondered how they would stand up to the harsh light of day. "So about this morning, did you have something in mind?"

Laurel nodded. "I was wondering if you'd be interested in joining me for the breakfast and shower you were talking about earlier."

Like she even had to ask. "Of course I would," she answered.

Laurel beamed. "Cool. Which do you want to do first?"

Dana wrinkled her nose, answering without hesitation. "Shower."

"You, me, a shower... I can't guarantee that we'll make it to breakfast."

Dana's stomach growled. She laid one hand over her belly, acutely feeling her lack of nutrition over the past twenty-four hours. "Oh, we'll get breakfast. One way or the other." She leaned forward and nipped at Laurel's bottom lip. "Even if I have to eat it off your naked body."

Laurel snickered. "Now there's an idea."

"I'm full of them." She flashed Laurel a less-than-modest smile.

"You're full of *something*." The genuine affection in Laurel's eyes sent a rush of warmth through Dana's belly. "And on that subject"— Laurel stroked her abdomen gingerly—"I *have* to pee."

In a Pavlovian response to the mere suggestion, Dana felt an answering ache low in her belly. "Uh-oh."

"You, too?"

"Of course." Dana curled her body into an uncomfortable ball. "Why did you have to remind me?"

"Misery loves company." Laurel turned on her side again, mirroring Dana's position. "I'm dehydrated. You must be feeling it, too."

Dana's mouth transformed into an arid desert at Laurel's observation. She smacked her lips together, attempting to swallow. My God, how long was it since she'd had something to drink? And after all that fluid she'd lost earlier with Laurel. Her throat felt exceedingly rough.

"Stop," she begged. "Let me just float in this blissfully ignorant postcoital euphoria a little longer."

"Sorry." Laurel suppressed her mirth, wincing and crossing both arms over her stomach. "Oh, God, don't make me laugh. Please."

"You're loopy," Dana commented, admiring the lean body that convulsed with laughter. "Is this how you get when you're overtired?"

Laurel wiped at her watery eyes with the back of her hands. "A combination of exhaustion and deep sexual satisfaction."

"It's darling," Dana said. "Goofball."

Bright light clicked on overheard, causing Dana to squint and blink in surprise.

Laurel sat up, staring at the ceiling with red-rimmed eyes. "Oh my God, is the electricity back on?"

Dana looked at the display above the elevator door, at the rows of buttons to the side. "I don't know."

Laurel released another bleat of stifled laughter. "I'm sorry," she gasped. "Your face."

Shoulders shaking, she finally scooted over and leaned against Dana's body for support. "Oh, help me. I'm gonna pee my pants."

She was adorable overtired and sexually satisfied. Dana nudged her away. "Don't come any closer. I don't need to be near you for that one."

They both fell silent when the elevator lurched slightly and started moving. Panic seized Dana's stomach.

"Oh my God." She scrambled to her feet, offering her hand to Laurel. "We've got to clean this place up. At least a little."

"I'm never going to get this blanket back in that stupid little bag before we get to the lobby," Laurel complained.

"Just stuff it in your backpack." Dana grabbed one corner of the blanket, and they gathered it into a relatively neat bundle. She left Laurel to tuck the blanket away and bent to survey the rest of the floor. "What else do we have in here? That lesbian erotica book isn't lying around, is it?"

"No, and I didn't leave my g-string stuck to the wall, either."

Dana's cheeks flooded with heat as she inhaled the scent that clung to her. "I smell like pussy," she hissed. "Laurel, I *reek* of your pussy."

"Yours, too." Laurel zipped up her backpack and slung it over her shoulder. "Enjoy it." She lifted her right hand to her nose and inhaled deeply, breaking into a wide smile. "I am."

Dana couldn't help but smile. "I don't know how I'm going to face Rocky. I must look like shit." She glanced up at the display over the elevator door, noting that they were already at the twelfth floor.

"You look beautiful." Laurel hesitated only an instant, and then added, "I can't wait to have you again."

Dana's heart started pounding so hard that she was sure Rocky would hear it the instant the elevator doors slid open. If the smell of sex didn't knock him over first. "Laurel!" she said. "Behave."

Laurel wore a serene smile as she bent to pick up her iPod. "Nonchalant, baby. Act nonchalant."

Yeah, right. Dana hooked her finger in the collar of her shirt, pulling the material away from her neck. "Nonchalant," she repeated. "Sure. Not a problem."

"May I hold your hand?" Laurel asked in a sweet voice.

"Not when it smells like pussy." *Second floor.* "Now come on, act natural."

Another moment, and the elevator doors slid open to reveal a twentysomething young man with acne scars and a football-player build wearing a dark blue rent-a-cop uniform. He blinked at the sight of them. His nose twitched a moment later.

He looked from Dana to Laurel. In fact, his eyes lingered on Laurel's chest. He glanced hastily back at Dana. "You okay, Ms. Watts?"

"Yes, we're fine, thanks, Rocky."

"How long have you been stuck in there?"

Dana's mind went totally blank. *It's written all over our faces, isn't it?* She tried to grin at Rocky and found that she was already smiling. "Since around seven o'clock yesterday evening." She glanced at her wristwatch. 7:56 a.m. Just about thirteen hours.

Rocky's eyes darted over Dana's shoulder, searching the elevator car behind them. "I'm glad I found the two of you. The camera in there doesn't appear to be functioning properly. I figured I should come check it out…"

Dana cleared her throat, face flooding with heat. How the hell could she explain a camera lens covered in whipped cream? She dropped her gaze to her feet, wishing the elevator would swallow her up.

"I'm sorry, Rocky." Laurel gave the young man a charming smile. "I had a little accident with the camera. I don't think I caused any permanent damage."

Rocky gave a friendly grin. "It's no problem, miss. I'm just glad you're okay." He looked back to Dana, upper lip trembling for an instant. "And doing well," he added.

"Um…I need to go back up to my office so I can grab my purse," Dana said.

"Oh." Laurel looked from Rocky to Dana. "Well, I guess I'll go with you." She succumbed to a shy smile. "Keep you company."

Dana was disheartened to see him struggling to suppress a laugh. "Sounds good."

"All right, ladies." Rocky stepped back from the elevator door with a smug grin plastered on his face. "You two have a safe ride up. And an uneventful trip down."

For a moment, Dana thought she saw genuine empathy in his eyes. Warmth and kindness and a camaraderie borne of daily exchanges of "good morning" and the trading of casual nods as she left work each evening all shone in his knowing gaze. For a moment, she was sure he was going to have mercy on her.

"What'll you give me for the tape?" he asked without a blink.

Dana sighed, leaning against the elevator doorframe and giving Rocky a weary look. Opportunistic bastard. "Fifty dollars and a letter of commendation to the building manager?"

"Throw in one of those muffins you carry in every morning for the next week or so, and you've got a deal."

Dana slapped the button for her floor. "Have it waiting when I get downstairs."

"You bet," Rocky said as the door began to slide closed. "And I *won't* watch it. I swear."

Nonchalant, Dana reminded herself. "There's nothing on it, anyway," she called out, but the door was already closed. Faced only with her own reflection in the elevator door, she dropped her face into her hands and groaned.

Laurel gave her a quick hug. "I thought that went well."

Dana shook her head, inhaling deeply. Christ, she needed to wash her hands. How distracting. "I don't think we were very nonchalant," she muttered.

The Monday After

For the first time in her life, Dana couldn't keep her mind on work. The important proposal that was supposed to fill last Friday night remained half written on her computer screen, and for the past twenty minutes she'd been deleting and retyping the same sentence. The memory of her weekend with Laurel floated insistently through her brain, shutting out all customary activity. She just couldn't make this software development project matter.

Friday night in the elevator had been an epiphany, and the rest of the weekend had more than fulfilled the promise of that first night. Saturday flew by in a blur of lovemaking, laughter, and intimate conversation that bled over into Sunday morning, then threatened to stretch late into the afternoon. When she and Laurel finally said good-bye, it was only because they were both so weak and exhausted from having almost nonstop sex that they'd agreed time apart was necessary for the good of their health.

Sunday evening was heart wrenching. When Laurel walked out of Dana's apartment, the magic seemed to leave as well. The strange enchantment she wove that made the rest of the world irrelevant was gone. Since that moment, Dana had grown more and more uncertain about everything—their amazing connection, the passion they'd shared, and even her instinctive trust of Laurel.

Perhaps brain chemistry and pheromones had clouded her mind. In a lust-induced haze, anyone could fool herself into imagining love at first sight, or at least the chance of a relationship that extended beyond one intense weekend. Dana's hand twitched on her computer mouse, and she once again read the sentence that she was obsessively rewording. Everything told her to pick up the phone and call Laurel, but fear held her back. The weekend had been incredible; would trying to turn it into something more ruin everything?

She couldn't tell if that last kiss at her door was one in a string of kisses that would lead her and Laurel into a shared future, or if it was simply a sweet good-bye. Dana was sure no one wanted a perfect fling to end. Part of the charm of a passionate encounter like hers with Laurel was probably the fact that it was only short-lived. Reality would never impact.

She touched the phone, then withdrew her hand, unwilling to make the call that would confirm her worst fears. The smart choice was to wait for Laurel to call her. If she didn't call, then Dana would know the verdict and graciously withdraw. She was big enough to accept the gift she'd been granted and not demand more than Laurel could give.

Her desk phone rang, and Dana startled at the sound, sending the cursor flying across her monitor with a jerk of her hand.

"Hello?" Her voice shook so much, she knew she sounded like someone else. Swallowing, she tried to produce the coolly efficient greeting she normally gave when picking up her work line. "This is Dana Watts."

"Hey, birthday girl." The masculine voice on the other end sent a flash of disappointment through her, but she had to smile despite herself. "Still speaking to me?"

So it had only taken Scott two and a half days to work up the courage to call and see how pissed off she was about his strip-o-gram. He sounded nervous, and Dana decided to let him sweat it out a bit. "Why wouldn't I be speaking to you?"

She heard him hesitate, no doubt wondering if his birthday present had shown up on the right night. She played it cool, letting him work up the courage to ask. It was the least he deserved for catching her so off guard on Friday.

"Did you get my present?" His voice mixed concern and hope. "Or had you already gone home?"

"Having second thoughts about the strip-o-gram, are we?" Dana glanced at her office door, double-checking that it was firmly closed. The last thing she wanted was for anyone to overhear her talking about strippers.

"You did get it."

"I did." A smile came to her face unbidden. She had promised herself she would thank Scott for bringing Laurel into her life, so she did. "Thanks."

"Really?" She could hear him start to relax. "So you, uh, enjoyed her?"

"All night long."

Scott hesitated. She could practically hear the gears turning in his head. "Excuse me?"

"You heard correctly."

"She told you I only paid for a half hour, right?" He sounded bewildered.

"The power went out and we got stuck in the elevator as I was escorting her from the building," Dana said. "I was pretty angry with you for the first hour or two, I'll admit. But I got over it."

"You did?"

Dana could hear the caution in Scott's voice. He obviously didn't know where this was going, and was remaining guarded. She was surprised she was telling him this much about what happened, but she couldn't stop herself. It felt good to confide in a friend. "She's a really nice girl."

"She...is?"

"Her name is Laurel. She's about to graduate from veterinary school."

Scott laughed, sounding uncertain. "You really got trapped in an elevator with the stripper?"

"Trust me, neither of us was happy about it at first." Dana burned to tell him everything, if only because she could hardly believe it herself. But she hesitated to give him details, afraid that it would somehow tarnish what had been the most amazing night of her life. "It turned out to be a pretty good birthday, believe it or not."

"*Really?*" Scott asked, approaching a leering tone. Apparently he was feeling more comfortable now that he knew she wasn't out for his blood. "Did you finally give in to your Sapphic tendencies?"

Dana struggled not to overreact to the teasing comment. She couldn't believe he was asking her flat-out if she was a lesbian, but at the same time, she knew he didn't believe anything had really happened that night.

"Actually, she knocked me down a peg or two, which I probably needed."

"I can't believe it," Scott said. "So are you guys, like, friends now?"

Were they friends? After only one weekend, Laurel felt like the best friend Dana had ever had. She also felt like an obsession. Dana ached to touch her again, she needed to taste her skin just one more time. But what did Laurel want? No matter how sincere her promises of "next time" had been each time they made love, there was no way of knowing how she felt, now that they had spent some time apart. For all Dana knew, Laurel was even now realizing what a bore she really was. Dana wasn't sure she would blame her.

"Yeah," she finally decided, "we're friends."

"Well, shit," Scott said. "Happy birthday."

"Indeed." Dana glanced at her computer screen, rubbing her temple tiredly. She didn't want to talk about Laurel anymore. She wanted to get this proposal done, to get back to some semblance of normalcy. "Hey, I've got a proposal here that should've been done yesterday. I'll call you later."

They said their good-byes and Dana hung up the phone with a relieved sigh. Her hand lingered on the handset for a moment, and she eyed the number pad warily. She would give anything for it to be Saturday night again. To be buried deep inside Laurel, thrusting hard, feeling firm thighs wrapped around her hips. Now, in the cool light of Monday afternoon, it seemed unlikely that she would ever experience that sensation again.

They were such different people. Pursuing Laurel would be irresponsible, and foolish. No matter what they'd said in the elevator and later during the hours that followed their release, the truth was that they'd shared one crazy weekend and nothing more. Dana took her hand off the phone.

"One crazy weekend, and nothing more," she whispered, trying to solidify the reality check.

What had happened between them was one of the best things Dana had ever known. But it was time to get back to real life, and maybe that was a good thing. She didn't know how to be in a relationship. If that's what Laurel wanted, she would be disappointed. And what if nothing they did could ever live up to their first beautiful weekend? Would the memory eventually sour? Dana didn't think she could stand it if that happened.

Her desk phone rang again, startling her so badly that she cried out and brought her hand to her chest. Her heart hammered madly beneath her palm. No doubt it was only a client, but even though she had just talked herself out of expecting to ever hear from Laurel again, she found herself hoping. Gripping the edge of her desk in a desperate bid to stay tethered to reality, she answered the phone with a breathless "Hello?"

"Hey." It was Laurel, and she sounded sexy as hell. "Busy tomorrow?"

Dana collapsed back into her chair, exhausted with relief. "I've got a proposal to write, but it can wait. What are you offering?"

THE DATE

L aurel flitted around her apartment nervously, feeling more like a teenager trying to get ready for the prom than the cool, confident woman she prided herself on being. She was still in her bra and panties, having tried on and discarded at least a half dozen outfits in the past thirty minutes. Isis sat on the bed, full of feline gravitas, watching her descend into full panic mode. The thought of seeing Dana again had her mood swinging crazily from sharp anticipation to gut-twisting fear that their time together was a fluke.

Their weekend had been perfect. Hands-down, without-a-doubt perfect. If she could, Laurel would have chosen never to leave Dana's apartment, to stay forever in the fantasy world they'd created. For an entire weekend, only the two of them existed. The sex was a revelation; the companionship even more so.

But now they were back to the real world, and Laurel had no idea if they could pick up where they left off. She stopped in front of the mirror on her closet and looked at the anxiety written all over her face. Nothing so wonderful could last. After two relationships, one of them serious enough to have left her brokenhearted when it failed, Laurel knew one, inalienable fact: Life was bigger than one night in an elevator car, and it never hesitated to pull the rug out from under you.

Sighing, she tried on another pair of jeans. "What's wrong with me?" she asked Isis. "And here I was worried that Dana would freak out."

The black cat lifted her head and yawned.

"Just goes to show you how much I know." Laurel looked back at the mirror. "You think she'll like my ass in these jeans?"

Of course Dana would like her ass. That wasn't really the question. What Laurel really wanted to know was whether Dana would like her enough to overcome her solitary tendencies on a longer-term basis. And if the answer was yes, was she ready for another relationship herself? Unable to resume the search for the right top before she had a good heart-to-heart, Laurel stepped away from the mirror and plopped onto the mattress next to her beloved feline.

"When we were in that elevator, I was just sure that everything would work out," she said, giving Isis a tender stroke. "I could see she was scared, but I thought—well, of course she was scared. She was practically a virgin."

Laurel closed her eyes, smiling as she played back images from Saturday night, their first in a real bed. Somehow, impossibly, Dana was the best lover she'd ever had.

"I swear," she murmured. "If I hadn't known it was almost her first time, her performance never would have clued me in." Isis meowed, and Laurel took that as a sign of protest. "I know, I know. More information than you needed."

She scratched Isis's head and stood to return to her closet. Gazing at her assortment of tops, Laurel selected another to try on. This one was a favorite, hugging her breasts in a way that made her feel like she could conquer the world. When Dana saw her, they would probably be lucky to make it to the restaurant. The thought made her knees go weak. Feeling unsteady, she immediately returned to her spot on the bed.

What the hell was she doing? Laurel dropped her face into her hands and exhaled. She was in the middle of her last clinical rotation, only months away from graduation. Her dream of helping animals was finally coming to fruition. And now, after all the years of struggling, dancing to pay her bills, studying whenever she could grab a moment alone, she had managed to launch herself headfirst into something that threatened to sweep her away entirely.

What if it didn't work out? Was she strong enough to deal with another heartbreak, with everything else she had going on? Did she want to invite complications by falling for Dana?

"I wasn't supposed to be the one who gets scared," Laurel whispered, as though reminding herself. "I told her I wanted to be more than her memory of a spontaneous sexual encounter, and I meant it. Why am I doing this now?"

It was a silly question. She was scared because she was absolutely positive that she could fall in love with Dana, given half the chance. And when she already felt the way she did, after only one weekend, she wasn't sure she wanted to risk the inevitable heartache if this didn't work out. There was a reason she hadn't been out looking for a relationship right now, and it was because she didn't want to be stupid just when her life was really starting. Other people had let her down often enough that she had to be able to rely on herself.

"But I told Dana to be brave, so I have to do the same, right?" Laurel searched Isis's wide golden eyes, looking for the answer. "I'm the one who called her. I can't just run away now." She tried to imagine what Dana would think if she backed off now, and cringed. "No, I like her too damn much to do that."

Isis blinked, offering little in the way of advice.

"Right," Laurel said, and exhaled in a burst of air. "So here's the plan. We're not going to have sex tonight."

Isis flopped onto her side and stretched out languidly. Laurel chuckled and rubbed her belly.

"I can resist, I swear."

If sex was all this thing with Dana was about, then she needed to know now. A connection that was purely physical was probably not worth the distraction level right now. But if it was more, if there was a possibility that this could turn into something as serious as she thought it might, there was no way she could let herself do anything but close her eyes, take a deep breath, and plunge in.

The truth was, she craved a real relationship with all the trimmings. She wanted the romance, the urgent desire, as well as the comfort of the unconditional friendship she imagined the right woman had to offer. If there was any chance that Dana was the woman of her dreams, she couldn't afford to let her go.

"Tonight's a test," she said. "We'll go out to dinner, talk, and see what this feels like in the real world, without letting sex confuse the issue. If, after this date, I still feel like I'm drowning every time I think about her, well—" She exhaled. "Then I guess I'm just going to have to suck it up and let myself fall in love."

With that, she stood up and walked back to her closet. It was a good plan. Sticking to it would be the hard part. Images of all the ways they had made each other come kept flashing through her brain, and she worried that the mere sight of Dana would make her lose control.

At the bottom of her underwear drawer, she found the rattiest pair of panties she owned. Baggy and with an unflattering cut, they were reserved for days when she felt bloated or when she let the laundry go far too long. Laurel slipped out of her jeans, tugged off the silky blue panties she felt sure Dana would love, and replaced them with the granny panties. She checked herself in the mirror, grinning in satisfaction at the hole in the fabric over her left hip.

"Just a little insurance," Laurel told Isis. "There's no way I would *ever* let Dana see me in these."

❖

By the time they were halfway through dinner, Laurel wasn't nearly as certain that Operation Granny Panties was going to work. From the moment she'd opened her apartment door to find Dana holding a bouquet of purple irises to right now, watching her chase around a lost mushroom in their fondue pot of coq au vin, her willpower had been constantly undermined. With every word, every look, and every funny, sweet moment, she could see why she was so damn attracted to Dana in the first place.

It wasn't just her thick auburn hair, her porcelain skin, or even the supple curves that made Laurel's mouth water. It was a thousand intangible things, from her wicked sense of humor to the way she rushed ahead to open doors for her. Laurel was a sucker for the freckles sprinkled across her face, the keen intelligence in her eyes, and the way Dana hung on every word she said. Laurel felt the same desire, wanting nothing more than to keep talking with her forever.

Chewing a bite of ravioli, Dana lifted her gaze and gave her a shy smile. She was wearing a deep green blouse that showed off the barest hint of cleavage, a fashion choice that Laurel knew had taken a great deal of courage. Try as she might, she couldn't keep her eyes off Dana's chest, imagining what lay beneath the sleek fabric. She flashed on Dana in a lacy black bra and felt her heart rate increase.

Maybe she could endure the humiliation of letting Dana see her ugly, oversized panties, after all.

"Laurel?"

Laurel tore her eyes away from Dana's breasts, dragging her gaze up to the full lips that repeated her name. "Yes? Sorry."

"Like what you see?"

Laurel grinned. "Busted." She used her fondue fork to spear a piece of chicken. "I told myself I was going to be good, but...you're looking gorgeous tonight."

"Thanks," Dana whispered, and glanced down at the table shyly. "It might be a bit late to try and preserve my virtue, though."

"That's an understatement," Laurel murmured.

Their eyes met and Laurel knew instinctively that they were both remembering the passion they had shared the last time they were together. She tried to rein in her hormones.

"I want tonight to be about something other than sex," she said. "So I promised myself I'd be good."

Dana looked mildly perplexed. She settled back into her seat, as though preparing for a serious conversation. "Any particular reason? I mean, beyond not wanting to scandalize everyone in the restaurant?"

Laurel hesitated, unsure how to explain her logic out loud. She knew this conversation would have to happen, but now that the moment had come, she wasn't sure she was strong enough to resist temptation. Did the no-sex decision even make any sense? They'd already had sex, for hours on end, so what would one more night hurt? Immediately she shook the thought off, remembering that she needed to be strong no matter how difficult it might be. She was more experienced than Dana. It was up to her to show some common sense or they could both have regrets.

"I want you so badly I can hardly see straight," she said quietly. "It's like I can't think about anything else, and that's...not good."

"It's not?" Dana asked, with an expression somewhere between flattered and crestfallen. "What's not good about wanting me?"

Laurel opened her mouth to respond, but found that she didn't know how to say this without risking Dana's feelings. She searched for the right words, then finally admitted, "You make me want to throw caution to the wind."

"I thought that was your motto." Dana took a drink. Rather than seeming upset by Laurel's show of honesty, she almost appeared to relax. "Throw caution to the wind, live bravely."

"Yes. Well." Laurel paused to gather her thoughts. She had never been so tentative with a woman before. But had she ever felt this strongly? Dana was her opposite in so many ways, and yet there was something about her reserved, controlled exterior that drove Laurel wild.

"I've been a little nervous, too," Dana said casually, biting a piece of pasta off her fork. "I had just about written the weekend off as a one-time thing when you called."

Laurel blinked rapidly. It was one thing to try and put the brakes on her own feelings, but hearing that Dana had done the same made her a little uneasy. "Would you have called me if I didn't call you?"

"Uh…" Dana looked down at the table, avoiding her gaze. "I don't know. Maybe. Probably. After a while."

"I think it's good we're talking about this. It sounds like we've both had a lot on our minds."

Dana met her eyes. "I'm really happy to see you again."

"Me, too." Laurel reached across the table and took Dana's hand. The idea that Dana might never have called made her chest ache with an almost unbearable sadness. It felt a lot like a preview of the heartbreak this relationship could cause if it didn't work out. Struggling with how to explain what she was feeling, she hedged, "I really, really like you."

Something about the tone of Laurel's voice must have sounded ominous, because Dana's eyes filled, and her face took on a look of pure sorrow. "Wait. Are you…is this…?"

She thought she was being dumped, Laurel realized. And the last thing Laurel wanted was for this to end tonight. Dread seized her throat and she shook her head wildly, giving Dana's hand a squeeze. "No. I'm just trying to explain what's going on with me."

"Don't scare me like that," Dana said, and slid her hand up to Laurel's wrist. "God, you just scared the hell out of me."

"Really?" Laurel found Dana's reaction almost comforting. Was it possible she felt just as strongly as Laurel did?

"Really," Dana said. "Last weekend was magical. The thought of never experiencing that again is too much to bear."

"I know," Laurel said. "I feel the same way."

"I'll admit, I wasn't sure if we really intended to try and keep this going." Dana stroked her finger across Laurel's wrist, sending a shiver of pleasure straight between her legs. "We both talked about needing this experience to be more than just a crazy one-time thing, but it was easy to say that in a bubble."

"You're right," Laurel said again. "I meant it, though."

Dana gave her wrist a gentle squeeze. "So did I. I just hope you're not disappointed once you get to know me better."

"That's one reason I told myself I wasn't going to sleep with you tonight," Laurel said. She wanted Dana to understand that there was a rationale behind her self-discipline. "I thought it would be good for us to make sure that this is more than just a sexual thing."

"It's more than just a sexual thing." Dana's words were sincere, and her eyes burned with an intensity that Laurel had never seen before. "To me, at least."

"For me, too," Laurel murmured. She didn't need to finish their date to know that. Everything about Dana made her feel breathless, and alive. Being able to admit her fears, and having Dana address them directly, was exactly what she needed. "Getting ready tonight, I realized that you're going to have the power to really break my heart. When I commit to something, I put everything I have into it. That includes relationships."

Dana swallowed visibly. "I've never been in a relationship before."

"I know, and I'm so sorry to dump all this on you. But like I said, I really like you. Pretty presumptuous for a first date, right?"

"I think the elevator was our first date, technically. Maybe even our first three." Dana's eyes crinkled a bit at the corners when she smiled. The teasing quality it lent to her face was utterly charming. "And I don't think it's presumptuous to assume that this could turn into a relationship."

"Yeah?"

"Don't get me wrong, the sex is incredible." Dana's gaze was full of desire, and Laurel felt herself drawn in. "But that's not nearly all that I want from you. I have to admit, it makes me feel so much better, seeing this side of you."

Laurel felt a surge of emotional release, a lifting of the burden of second-guessing where both of them stood. "Yeah?"

"I feel like it puts us on equal ground," Dana said. "We're both scared to death, and excited as hell. You're feeling just as vulnerable as I am." She took Laurel's hand again and raised it to her lips to kiss the knuckles. "I'm not the only one risking my feelings on this."

"No, you're not."

"Thank you for telling me what you've been thinking. I'm willing to do whatever it takes to make you feel comfortable."

"Even if that means not sleeping together tonight?"

"Of course." Dana's shrug wasn't entirely convincing. "You're the nymphomaniac, remember?"

Laughing, Laurel recalled the times she'd almost fallen asleep in Dana's bed during the weekend, only to be woken by a desperate hand on her thigh, or a tongue sliding across her sweat-slicked skin. "As a matter of fact, that's not what I recall." She raised an eyebrow and stared pointedly at Dana, trying to communicate what she was thinking about.

Dana blushed, folding up her napkin and setting it on the table. "Granted, I hope this won't be a *long* moratorium on sex."

"It won't." Laurel took Dana's hand again, enjoying the warm softness of her skin. "Trust me, I'll be lucky to make it through tonight."

❖

Later in bed, Laurel was sure she was the stupidest person alive. Dana could be next to her right now, on top of her, inside her. But after a heated, groping kiss at her apartment door, Laurel had watched her walk away, against every instinct she possessed. All because she needed to prove to herself that she could.

And what revelation had this plunge into abstinence brought her?

That she wanted Dana and she would be damned if she didn't see this through. Even if there was a chance of heartache, she would never forgive herself if she didn't even try. Every moment she'd spent with Dana was so much better than the ones that made up every day. Yes, it was scary to imagine getting involved, but she was already invested.

Walking away now wouldn't prevent heartache, it would just guarantee it.

Laurel shifted onto her back, closing her eyes at the way the sheets caressed her oversensitized flesh. She was naked, as she always was when she went to bed, but she was starting to debate putting a T-shirt on, if only to give her hormones a break. Staring across the table at Dana all night, then having just a taste of her during their makeout session at her door, left her wet and ready and entirely unable to sleep.

"Fuck," Laurel whispered, and turned onto her side. She slipped a hand between her thighs and exhaled slowly. Maybe she could ease her own suffering and find some relief. "I'm an idiot sometimes."

From somewhere in the dark bedroom, Isis chirped out a quiet meow.

Laurel began to laugh, aware of how pathetic she was at that moment. She rolled onto her stomach, lifting her hips slightly, and closed her eyes. Imagining Dana kneeling behind her, she slid a hand under her stomach, then between her legs. She stroked herself gently, exhaling at the wetness that coated her swollen labia.

"Dana," she whispered, keeping alive the fantasy that her lover was watching her touch herself. The idea of letting Dana see her like this unleashed a fresh flood of hot wetness, and she swirled around her opening for a moment before pushing inside.

Ding.

Laurel jumped at the noise from her laptop, which sat on her nightstand. That was her e-mail alert noise, and she had left the volume up specifically because she'd given Dana her e-mail address at dinner. She glanced at the glowing red numbers on her alarm clock and rolled onto her side again. It was almost one in the morning. Would Dana really still be awake?

Laurel knew she wouldn't be able to sleep unless she checked. She grabbed her laptop, bringing up the display with a swipe of her finger across the touch pad. Her heart started thumping when she saw the sender's name on her lone unread e-mail.

Dana Watts. The subject of the e-mail read *Is this as hard for you?*

Taking a steadying breath, Laurel clicked on the message.

Laurel,

Please tell me that falling asleep after a kiss like that is just as difficult for you as it is for me. Every time I close my eyes, I remember how you looked the last time I was inside you. I need to see you tomorrow, and this time, I'm not letting you go to bed alone.

Dana

TOMORROW

I think we should wait," Laurel said. Her eyes glinted as they moved from Dana's mouth to her breast. But she sounded very serious.

"I don't think so," Dana said. Dinner had been eaten, they were finally back at Laurel's apartment, and Dana wasn't sure she could wait any longer to touch her again. "Did you forget? I'm not letting you go to bed alone."

"Really?" Laurel dragged her gaze along the length of Dana's body, stopping to linger on her thighs.

"I've never been so serious about anything," Dana said, distracted by the naked lust on Laurel's face. "Ever."

"Trust me, it's not that I don't…appreciate your position." Laurel stared hard at Dana's lap, then casually drew her tongue across her lower lip. If she was trying to drive Dana crazy, she was doing one hell of a job.

"I have a lot of positions you can appreciate," Dana said. Overwhelmed by the intense arousal she was feeling, she couldn't help but fall back on humor. "Remember?"

Laurel shifted imperceptibly closer on the couch, gazing at her with heavy-lidded eyes. "I'm just not sure if it's a good idea," she drawled, then lowered her gaze to her fingers, apparently distracted by a hangnail. "Sleeping together so soon."

Dana exhaled slowly, trying to calm her racing heart. She had never been so physically attracted to someone in her life, and Laurel was oozing sex tonight. Her rich chestnut hair fell in waves just past her shoulders, and her olive skin begged to be caressed. She wore a form-fitting T-shirt that clung to her breasts like a lover and showed off the lean definition of her arms. She smelled lovely, in a way that was uniquely Laurel.

It was painful to be so close to her and not touch.

"Why wouldn't sleeping together be a good idea?" Dana asked. After a moment of hesitation, she reached out and took Laurel's hand. She tried to keep the contact as chaste as possible, even as her fingers burned to grab Laurel's shoulder and haul her over for a long, hard kiss. "I thought it went well last time."

Laurel laughed, showing off her gorgeous white smile. Dana swallowed past the lump in her throat, remembering the delicious scrape of those teeth on her breasts. Her nipples tightened to the point of mild pain, and she had to tear her gaze away from Laurel's mouth.

"You're right," Laurel murmured, sending a shiver through Dana's body. "It went *very* well."

The words dripped with seduction, but Laurel made no move to close the distance between them. Dana sought her eyes, trying to decide if Laurel was really saying no. Her words didn't match her actions, and Dana found herself uncertain about how to react. She wanted nothing more than to push Laurel down onto the couch, wrench her T-shirt up over her breasts, and take a nipple in her mouth while sliding her hand into the low-cut jeans Laurel wore so well. She snapped back to attention at Laurel's next words.

"I'm just not sure it's the best move. You know, letting ourselves get swept away by our hormones so early in our relationship." As she spoke, she traced a fingernail along Dana's wrist, raising goose bumps in her wake.

Shuddering from the white-hot desire that lanced through her, Dana choked out, "Oh, really?"

With a sincere nod, Laurel tickled a path up the inside of Dana's arm. "I just don't want us to make a mistake."

Laurel's eyes were the color of the deep, tempestuous sea, and they flashed with unmistakable need. Her chest rose and fell quickly, even as her voice remained steady. The protests she raised didn't agree with what her body was telling Dana. And that was all Dana needed to know.

Emboldened, she decided to test the waters. "Maybe you're right." She leaned slightly away. "I don't want to move you too fast."

Laurel's face betrayed nothing, but she smoothed a trembling hand over her hair and glanced away. "Thank you."

"The last thing I want to do is make you uncomfortable."

Laurel exhaled, giving her a tight nod. She smiled, but it didn't reach her eyes.

Feeling a surge of confidence, Dana put a hand on Laurel's knee. "But you're not really uncomfortable, are you?"

Laurel's throat worked, and her eyes sparkled. "I don't know," she said quietly. "What do you think?"

Leaning in close, Dana inhaled the fresh scent of Laurel's lush hair. "I think you're a tease."

Laurel shivered and said nothing.

"Are you teasing me, Laurel?" Dana asked. She closed the scant distance between them and let her lips touch Laurel's neck, giving her a feather-soft kiss. "Does it make you hot to get me all worked up like this?"

"I'm just trying to…be responsible." Laurel's voice was weaker now, as though she could barely get the words out.

"What would you do if I stood up right now and walked out the door? Is that what you really want?" She listened to Laurel's breathing hitch, and moaned quietly at the answering flood of wetness between her own legs. "I don't think it is."

"I never said I wanted you to leave."

Dana could hear the desire in Laurel's voice now, and brought her mouth to brush against Laurel's earlobe. "No, you don't want me to leave. Because your pussy is wet, isn't it? Like mine."

"Dana—"

"You're so wet you can hardly stand it, right? Wanting me. Needing me."

Even as she whispered into Laurel's ear, Dana wondered at her newfound confidence. She sensed the nature of Laurel's game, and it brought out a side of her that she had never known existed. Lust coursed through her veins, and she balled her free hand into a fist to try and control herself. Everything in her screamed to take Laurel, to claim control of this encounter.

"It's not about not wanting you," Laurel said. She seemed to be having trouble talking now, stumbling a bit over her words.

"What's it about, then?"

Laurel offered no answer, not when the scent of her arousal hung in the air. Dana inhaled deeply, feeling her mouth stretch into a predatory smile.

"I came over here tonight with every intention of fucking you," Dana breathed into Laurel's throat. She kissed a jumping pulse point, then sank her teeth into warm flesh. "And I'm not leaving until I feel you wrapped around my fingers again."

Something in Laurel seemed to break, and she brought a hand up to clutch at Dana's shoulder, digging in with her fingers. "Then fuck me."

Granted permission, Dana let herself lose control. She caught the back of Laurel's head in her hand, crushing her lips to Laurel's mouth. Laurel returned her kiss, frantically, and brought her hands up to grasp Dana's shirt.

Tearing away from the kiss, Dana growled, "I hope you want it fast and hard."

She shoved Laurel back onto the couch, pinning her to the cushions. All restraint gone now, she pulled Laurel's T-shirt and bra up to her neck, exposing her breasts. She found a rock-hard nipple and bit down.

Laurel threw her head back and grunted. Her hips crashed into Dana's, as though directly connected to the nerve endings in her breast. Dana ground her pelvis into Laurel's, then slipped a hand between their bodies to jerk open the button on Laurel's jeans. Roughly, she shoved them down to Laurel's thighs, taking her panties with them.

"I can smell you," Dana said. "Tell me you want to get fucked."

At first Laurel said nothing. Dana drew her fingers down over her abdomen, through soaked curls. She forced her way between Laurel's thighs with a groan of pure need. Wetness coated her fingers, stoking her desire.

Seizing Laurel's clit firmly, she said, "Ask me to take you. Ask me to make you come all over my hand."

Chest heaving, Laurel spread her legs wide. "Take me. Fuck me, Dana. Please."

Dana positioned her fingers at Laurel's opening. With a wild cry, she drove her fingers inside. Laurel was just as tight and hot as she remembered. Maybe even better than she remembered. Dana was in no mood to draw this out; they had all night. She used her whole arm for leverage, pounding into Laurel so hard that Laurel's body jerked with every stroke.

"Yes," Laurel gasped, using her hips to fuck back against her hand. "Fuck my pussy. Take it. Take my fucking pussy."

Dana gritted her teeth as Laurel tightened and swelled around her. She kept up her battering thrusts and slid her mouth over to Laurel's other breast.

Laurel released a guttural noise, stiffened, and squirted hot liquid into Dana's hand. "Oh fuck," she cried out, grinding her hips into Dana as she came. Tears streamed from her eyes, but Dana didn't worry. She could read the satisfaction on Laurel's face.

And for the first time in almost a week, Dana felt like she could breathe.

A WEEK LATER

With a belly full of pancakes and her hair still damp from her second shower of the day, Dana lay on a queen-sized bed in Laurel's little apartment in Royal Oak, thighs spread wide, watching Laurel lick her pussy like it was her one mission in life. Sparkling blue eyes stared up at her every so often, usually in conjunction with a quiet moan of pleasure from her feasting lover. The late morning sun crept into the room through gaps in the blinds, painting warm stripes across their bodies and picking out strands of copper in Laurel's chestnut-colored hair.

Dana arched her back and clutched at the bedsheets. "Fuck," she gasped. "You're going to make me come, if you're not careful."

Laurel drew back and revealed a smile that was shiny with Dana's juices. "Not yet," she murmured. "First I want to lick you until you scream."

"Why so mean?" Dana said, groaning.

Laurel lowered her face and dragged her tongue up the length of Dana's sex. She pulled back with her tongue still extended, showing Dana the shiny string of wetness that still connected them. "You like it when I'm mean," she murmured, and resumed licking in earnest.

Next to a VHS tape labeled *Elevator Two—Surveillance* that sat on the nightstand beside Laurel's bed, Dana's cell phone came alive. Set on a ring-and-vibrate combination, it was a buzzing, beeping distraction that proved impossible to ignore.

"Goddamn it," Dana growled. The phone was vibrating its way toward the edge of the nightstand.

Laurel lifted her head. "Just ignore it."

Dana gave Laurel a playful smile and pushed her face back between her legs. "Did I say you could stop?"

The cell phone continued to ring. Incessant...obnoxious... distracting... Dana snatched it up and gasped "Hello?" without looking at the display. Laurel chose that exact moment to slide a finger inside her pussy, beginning a slow thrusting in time with the sucking of her mouth.

"Dana?" A pause, and then, "Are you okay?"

"Scott." Dana bit back another gasp as Laurel began rubbing a particularly sensitive spot somewhere inside. "Yes, okay. I am." She tugged on Laurel's hair and tried to back up a little, but the headboard kept her in place, and at Laurel's mercy.

"You're talking like Yoda," Scott said with cautious amusement, no doubt waiting for her to snap at him for the teasing. But post-Laurel Dana was far more mellow than the Dana of old. And extremely preoccupied.

"I'm fine," she managed.

She slid her hand down the curve of Laurel's jaw, feeling it working beneath her fingers, and attempted to pry her lover's mouth away from her clit. She couldn't hold a conversation like this. She couldn't even hold a thought in her head.

Laurel giggled into Dana's wetness, making her toes curl at the unusual sensation.

Scott said something else, she had no idea what. She struggled to think. "Listen, um... could we do this another time?"

Scott didn't speak for a few moments, leaving her free to concentrate on the sensual treatment she was receiving. She jerked in surprise when he finally said, "But the Web site launches tomorrow. When do you want to talk about this?"

Dana bit her lip, stifling a cry of pleasure as Laurel flicked her tongue fast over her distended clit. "I have to hang up, Scott. Let's talk later."

"Too busy to talk shop? Shall I send a medic?"

Dana's toes curled as she tried desperately to stave off what promised to be a crippling orgasm. "That might not be a bad idea." She groaned in disappointment when Laurel pulled away from her pussy and gestured for the cell phone with her free hand. One finger on the other hand remained buried deep inside Dana.

"Really?" Scott asked. "I was just kidding, but—"

The cell phone slid from her hand, extracted by Laurel. Shooting Dana a mischievous smile, she asked, "Scott?" Her voice was low and husky, and it sent chills up Dana's spine.

She was too happy with her life to give the fact that her lover was talking to Scott a second thought. Her lover. Dana grinned and threw her arm over her eyes, content to enjoy a moment of respite. Maybe she could cool down and draw this out a little longer.

Laurel chuckled at something Scott said. "Hey, this is Laurel." After a moment she amended, "Venus. This is Venus, the girl you hired to dance for Dana?"

Dana shifted, feeling every inch of the finger that still rested inside her. Venus. That was kind of sexy.

"Yeah, how are you doing?" Laurel asked. She giggled, then said, "At first, yeah. Not now."

Dana tilted her head, wishing she could listen in on the phone call. What could Scott possibly be thinking? Almost immediately, she accepted the obvious. He had known she liked women, without her ever having trusted him enough to tell him. He knew damn well what was going on.

"Listen, this really isn't a very good time for Dana to talk. We're...a little busy." Impatient for the phone conversation to end, Dana reached between her thighs and gripped Laurel's wrist. She began moving Laurel's hand herself, thrusting inside her own pussy with deep, long strokes. Dana peeked out from beneath her arm and watched Laurel grin.

"Oh, and Scott?" Laurel met Dana's gaze tenderly. "We need to set up a time to meet so I can return the money you paid me."

Dana's chest grew heavy with pleasure. She continued to work Laurel's hand between her legs, feeling a need that was only partially about sexual release. The connection she felt with Laurel existed on so many levels and transcended anything she had ever imagined. Laurel shot her a mischievous look, raising her eyebrow. Suspecting what was about to happen, Dana nodded. Why not?

Laurel snorted, a silly noise that sent a wash of affection through Dana's body. "Yeah, I'm sure. I don't want to feel like I got paid for what I'm doing to Dana right now."

Oh, to see the look on Scott's face. Dana was surprised to find herself pleased by the disclosure, and incredibly turned on. She had been wanting to shout this from the rooftops. Telling Scott was a great start.

"He says congratulations," Laurel said.

"I say I'll call him back later. And thanks."

"Hear that?" Laurel said to Scott. "Thank you. You, too. Bye." She clicked the phone off and handed it to Dana. "There you go. Distraction eliminated."

"You naughty little thing." Dana took the phone from Laurel, powered it down, and tossed it back onto the nightstand. "I ought to spank you for that."

Laurel grinned and lowered her face until the wet curls between Dana's thighs brushed against her chin. "Not until I make you scream."

A MONTH LATER

L aurel stood in the front foyer of Dana's parents' house as her lover extricated them from their inaugural evening as a couple with her family. Dinner had been eaten, conversation had grown forced, and Laurel was ready to escape.

"Thank you both for coming," Dana's father said. Zach Watts was a tall man with a reserved bearing that made him look mildly in pain.

"Thanks for inviting us." Dana gave her mother a quick, awkward hug. "Dinner was great, Mom."

"I'm glad you enjoyed it." Vicki Watts flashed a cautious smile full of hope at Laurel. She was a plump woman with shoulder-length auburn hair. Just like Dana's.

"It was wonderful, Mrs. Watts."

Zach Watts wore a wide, nervous grin as his gaze shifted between Dana and Laurel. "It was so nice to meet you, young lady."

"Yeah, it was," Trevor agreed from the door frame of the living room. "It's great to finally meet Dana's *girlfriend*."

He gave Laurel a lazy grin, and she wondered if she'd imagined his emphasis on the word "girlfriend." For Dana's family, her involvement with *anyone* was obviously a novel concept, let alone her involvement with someone of the same sex. Laurel withstood another lingering appraisal from his hungry eyes. If he were not Dana's younger brother she would probably have cut him down with a withering remark that called his manhood into question.

All night she'd felt on display, and she could sense Dana's unease that they were both under a microscope. Laurel wasn't surprised by the intense scrutiny and she didn't feel that the Watts family had a negative view of her, or of Dana. It had to be strange for them to see their daughter in a completely different light.

Laurel grinned around at the three of them, trying to muster up the confidence she'd always had onstage. *Dazzle 'em, sexpot.* "We'll have to do this again before too long."

She meant it. She could see why Dana would want to avoid awkward family occasions, but Laurel suspected that the Watts would chill out if she and Dana visited with them regularly.

Zach beamed at her. "You're right, we will." He pulled a tense Dana into a tight hug. "How about it, pumpkin pie?"

Laurel fought not to giggle at the nickname, or at the way Dana's cheeks flooded bright red.

As Dana backed out of his arms, she said, "Sounds good to me, Dad."

She took Laurel's hand but they didn't get more than two paces toward the front door before Trevor approached Dana with a mischievous smirk. Pulling her into a hard hug, throwing her off balance for a moment, he growled. "Nice to see you again, sis." He took a step back and moved as if to haul Laurel into a similar embrace.

Oh, you'd love that, wouldn't you, pal? Laurel resisted the urge to shrink away. She breathed a sigh of relief when she felt Dana's arm around her waist. Trevor gave Dana a knowing look and leaned close to her ear, murmuring, "Don't do anything I wouldn't do."

"Too late," Dana whispered, low enough that her parents couldn't hear. She stepped past her brother and wished everyone good night.

"Thank you again, Mrs. Watts," Laurel said as she and Dana made it through the front door.

"Call me Vicki, okay?"

Her smile was genuinely warm, but Laurel detected a lingering anxiety. She sensed Vicki Watts was as relieved as Dana that the evening was ending. "See you again soon, Vicki," she said and felt Dana tense slightly.

Zach showed them out, and he and Vicki stood side by side at the front door to watch them walk to Dana's car.

When Laurel climbed into the passenger seat, Dana greeted her with a tired sigh. "So how bad was it?"

"Well, I'm still crazy about you. So I guess it wasn't too bad."

"And my brother?" Dana gave Laurel a wry smile as they fastened their seat belts. "I'm sorry he's such a…guy."

Aware that Dana's parents were still watching them, Laurel managed not to lean over and kiss her right there. "He's fine," she said. "The novelty will wear off soon, don't worry."

"It'd better." Dana started the car with a grumpy snort. "I wanted to slug him about forty-eight times tonight."

"But I only caught him staring at my tits forty-six times."

Dana growled and backed out of the driveway.

"I'm kidding." Laurel curled her fingers around the back of Dana's neck, giving her a tender squeeze. "It was thirty-eight times."

"Laurel—"

"Men look at my tits all the time." And they paid for the opportunity, a fact she didn't state, knowing Dana preferred not to be reminded. Trevor might have been a little creepy, but there was nothing sinister about his roving eyes. He was just a prisoner of his hormones like any other twenty-three-year-old male.

"Are you trying to make me feel better?"

"Is it working?" Laurel asked.

"Not at all. I'm jealous."

There, Dana thought. She'd admitted it. All night she had been struggling with irrational feelings of jealousy each time she caught Trevor ogling Laurel. She knew Trevor was just being a pain-in-the-ass younger brother, no doubt just trying to get under her skin. And it worked, but to an extent that shocked Dana. When she thought about Trevor or any other man staring at Laurel like she was some kind of sex object, it made her blood boil. God, she really wished Laurel wasn't still dancing at that club.

Smiling, Laurel leaned over to rest her head on Dana's shoulder. The fire in Dana's voice surprised her, and she sensed the emotion she saw was about more than just Trevor. Dana really was jealous, and over such a silly thing. Though Dana was always careful with her words, Laurel knew she hated thinking about men paying to see her body. Normally that kind of protectiveness would rankle her, but she found that with Dana, it had the strange effect of turning her on. To know that Dana felt so strongly about her was a powerful aphrodisiac, and also a comfort.

She stared at the passing houses, at the neighborhood where her lover had grown up. The thought made her feel warm inside. "Your parents are nice," she said.

"I think they really liked you," Dana commented.

"Yeah?"

"Oh, yeah," Dana said. She took one hand off the steering wheel and rested it on Laurel's thigh. "I know it may have been hard to tell, with those frozen smiles on their faces."

"They weren't that bad," Laurel protested. "I was really impressed, actually. They were surprisingly cool given that you just came out to them, you know? I could tell they were really trying."

"Well, even beyond the fact that you're basically the most incredible person in the world—"

"That goes without saying," Laurel interrupted. She sat up and flashed her teeth at Dana, who gave her an indulgent nod.

"Honestly, I think my parents are so happy that I finally brought someone home, the fact that it's a woman hardly bothers them." Dana stared out the windshield, gazing at the traffic as they merged onto the freeway. "They probably thought I was going to be alone for the rest of my life."

Laurel's heart pounded as she turned the words over. So many possibilities danced through her head. Dana seldom spoke about the future, and when she did she seemed cagey. Laurel had no trouble picturing them together for the rest of her life, but Dana didn't seem to think much further than the next time they would make love. Yet her comment raised Laurel's hopes. Maybe she was starting to give her deepest dreams room, and maybe they included Laurel. She forced herself to calm down, reminding herself that she was content to move at Dana's pace. Clearing her throat, she said, "I can't imagine they thought you would never have a partner. They must know what an incredible woman you are."

"Not like you do, believe me."

"I'm glad they liked me, though," Laurel said. "I like them, too." She paused. "And I *really* like their daughter."

"Lucky her."

"Damn right. Don't you forget it."

"You won't let me, darling," Dana murmured. She reached out

and ran her finger along Laurel's jawline. "Like I could forget, anyway, when I think about how wonderful my life has become every single day."

Laurel leaned against Dana's side, cuddling up close. "Damn, you are *so* good."

"Thanks." Dana planted a kiss on the top of Laurel's head. "Your place or mine tonight, honey?"

Laurel sighed. "Mine, I think. Isis gets grumpy when I stay away too long."

"We don't want Isis to get grumpy," Dana said.

Laurel pressed her face into Dana's neck and inhaled. "She's used to having me around the apartment all day. If I don't spend time with her this weekend, she'll probably pack her bags and move out."

"Poor baby," Dana murmured. "I can't blame her, though. I know I miss you a whole lot if we don't see each other."

Laurel said, "We've managed to see each other every night this week."

"Yeah, but…" Dana hesitated. "I miss you whenever you're not with me. During the day, you know. And night. All the time, actually."

She couldn't be any sweeter if she tried. Laurel kissed her cheek. The pale skin felt warm beneath her lips, betraying Dana's bashfulness. "What do you want to do tonight?"

"We could rent a movie." Dana touched her inner thigh, setting off a ripple of arousal in Laurel's body. "Is there anything you want to see?"

Laurel experienced a moment of pure inspiration. "Actually, I was thinking we could do something else tonight." She moved her hand to Dana's thigh, then slid over warm denim to trace her fingertips along the seam that ran between her legs. "What do you think?"

She could hear the catch in Dana's breathing. "I think we'll do whatever you want. Anything you want."

Exactly what I was thinking. Laurel palmed Dana's steamy center, pressing into her as she whispered hotly into a delicate ear. "I have three fantasies. Want me to tell you about one of them?"

"Three fantasies?" Dana shivered and exhaled, tightening her grip on the steering wheel. She shifted a little, easing her thighs apart to make room for Laurel's busy hand.

"Yes."

"Have you been thinking about it or are these spontaneous fantasies?"

"I've been thinking about it a little," Laurel lied. *Only all the time.* She tried to decide which of her many ideas to broach first. And how exactly to do it.

Dana turned to look at Laurel, all at once serious. "Do you know how much I love that we can talk about sex like this?"

Laurel grinned. "Me, too." She hesitated a moment, making a decision, then said, "This one is really dirty."

"Ooh." Dana shifted, and Laurel continued to rub her gently. "A dirty fantasy, even?"

Laurel took in the delighted look on Dana's face. "You sound excited about the seedy side of my imagination." She squeezed Dana through her jeans.

"There's nothing wrong with that."

"No, there's not," Laurel agreed. She bit her lip, turned on beyond measure at the thought of sharing this particular fantasy with her lover. *Especially knowing that she'll try to fulfill it.* "You have no idea how much I enjoy knowing that you want to do this with me."

"Laurel, there's nothing particularly sweet or noble about my wanting to have hot sex with a beautiful woman. Especially when I happen to find her completely adorable."

Over a month in, and Laurel wasn't close to tired of hearing the increasingly mushy declarations from Dana. She suspected that she never would be. "I want you to...be rough with me."

For a long while, Dana said nothing. She flipped on her turn signal and exited the highway near Laurel's apartment, sticking to the speed limit as she navigated them through the neighborhood. When she spoke, her voice was husky. "Be rough with you how, baby?"

A LITTLE ROUGH

L aurel unlocked the door to her apartment and gestured Dana inside. She took deep, steadying breaths as she entered, trying to calm her nerves.

"Do you remember the night we met?" She followed Dana into the tiny kitchen, cradling a purring Isis in her arms.

Dana smiled at the silly question. "Of course."

"I told you then about...some things I like." Laurel shifted Isis to one side and opened the refrigerator. "Rough things."

"Spanking?" Dana's voice came out in a breathless murmur that sent a jolt of longing to Laurel's core.

Laurel nodded. "That's part of it." Handing Dana a bottle of beer, she said, "I want you to spank me, talk dirty to me. I want you to take control. Hold me down on the bed."

"Baby..." Dana released a shaky breath and fumbled as she twisted the cap off her beer. She wasn't averse to delivering a sharp smack to Laurel's bottom when she took her from behind, but that had been the extent of their play over the past month.

Laurel studied her closely. "I know we've...flirted with that, in bed, a few times. Sometimes I get the feeling that you'd really enjoy dominating me. Is there any particular reason you've never gone further with it than you have?"

Dana shook her head. "No," she whispered. "I mean, the thought turns me on. Very much. But I guess—"

"What?" Laurel pressed a kiss into the black fur between Isis's shoulder blades and set her down.

"I can hear her motor from over here," Dana said, knowing she was creating a distraction. She wasn't quite ready to explain herself.

"What can I say?" Laurel said softly. "She's happy to see me."

Dana took a much-needed swallow of beer. "I think I make the same noise when I see you, sometimes."

"I think you do, too." Laurel took a step toward her and scratched one fingernail over the crotch of Dana's jeans. "You didn't answer my question."

Dana's throat rasped when she spoke. "I was sort of waiting for you to ask for it. I didn't know how to initiate that. And—"

"And what, honey?"

"I guess I'm afraid of hurting you." Dana's voice was quiet, almost worried. "I fantasize things, but—"

"You won't hurt me," Laurel said. It was a statement of fact, something she knew deep in her heart.

"You want me to slap you," Dana murmured. "You want me to hold you down, be rough with you. How can you be sure I won't hurt you?"

Laurel pulled her hand from between Dana's thighs, resting it on her knee. "You're so gentle, instinctively, I just don't think you would ever hurt me past the point of it being pleasurable."

Dana blinked and darted her eyes in a sidelong glance. "What do you mean?"

"I mean that the point of the whole thing is to experience a little pain. Not *real* pain, but…the kind that hovers right on the edge of pleasure. A good pain. When I say I want you to spank me, I mean I want you to really *spank* me." Even though she was more confident talking about these things than her lover, Laurel felt her cheeks flush a little with the admission. "And I want you to fuck me hard. I want you to…say nasty things to me."

"I've never actually touched anyone roughly before. What if I do it wrong?"

"That's why we'll have a safe word, darling." Between Dana's inexperience and their newness as a couple, Laurel knew a safe word was essential. They were still learning each other's limits.

"A safe word? Like 'stop, you dumb bitch'?"

Laurel let out a burst of laughter. She stroked Dana's face. "No, our safe word will be something we would absolutely never say during sex. It shouldn't have anything to do with 'stop' or 'no.'" She moved her head so that Dana could see her playful smile. "When we play like that, we may get confused by those words."

Dana's pale throat worked as she swallowed. "How about 'quicksilver'?"

"'Quicksilver'? Where the hell did that come from?"

Dana struggled to answer the question. It was, quite simply, the first thing that popped into her head. She didn't know what that said about her. "I'd never say it during sex. Would you?"

"'Quicksilver' it is."

Dana's body relaxed slightly, as if she were relieved that at least one detail had been ironed out. Laurel could practically feel Dana's mind churning, however, and so she waited for her to speak again.

"So could you give me an idea?" Dana asked after a brief hesitation. "I mean, of what sort of thing you fantasize about?"

Laurel cocked her head, curious. "Have you ever fantasized like that? I mean, about taking control with me?"

"Yes," Dana whispered. "Ever since the elevator, actually. And, you know, I always loved stories and movies…like that. I've always imagined…"

I knew it. Laurel grinned. *My baby is a freak just like me.* She took Dana's hand between her own. "So you want to know my fantasy?"

With an anticipatory grin, Dana replied, "Please."

"Okay, I guess it starts with…well, you're upset with me about something."

Immediately, Dana looked perplexed. "Why would I be upset with you?"

Struggling with the details, Laurel shrugged. "I'm not sure, honey. That's not really the important part of this fantasy."

"But I can't even imagine being mad at you about something."

"Pretend I interrupted you when you were trying to write a proposal by giving you a lap dance," Laurel suggested. "It worked once."

"I don't really think it's sexy for me to be a jerk. And I don't know if I can be mean to you like that anymore."

Laurel stifled a sigh, giving her hand a soothing squeeze. "Dana, baby…it's not so much that you're *mad* at me in the fantasy. More like…you're disappointed. Or disapproving. I don't know why, exactly. The important part is that you want to punish me for something."

"Oh." Dana managed a resolute nod. Fantasy was just that, she reminded herself. When she imagined fucking Laurel in a prison cell, she didn't try to figure out why they had been incarcerated. "Okay, so you need to be punished."

The words sent a riot of goose bumps erupting across Laurel's flesh. *Oh, yeah, baby. Punish me.* She regained her composure, trying to sound matter-of-fact so Dana could process the information without feeling cornered. Laurel only wanted this if Dana was completely on board. "So you take me over your knee—"

Dana let out a high-pitched whimper. "Oh my God."

"Too kinky?" *Please don't say that's too kinky.*

"Too perfect," Dana said in a throaty voice. "I think you're just too perfect for me." She stared into Laurel's eyes. "And I think I can definitely get into kinky."

Laurel touched Dana's breast through her T-shirt. Her nipples were already hard, pebbled beneath the soft fabric. "So you want to take me over your knee?"

"If the fact that I'm soaking wet is any indication, yes."

Gaining confidence, Laurel said, "You spank me, really hard, until I'm squirming in your lap."

"With my hand or something else?" Dana leaned into Laurel's fingers, which toyed with her nipple. She couldn't believe she was talking about dominating someone out loud. The Internet had prepared her for the idea that she would love to take command of a woman, but her visits to those light BDSM Web sites were her dirty little secret. That she was exploring the idea of doing this for real was almost too much.

Laurel lifted her other hand to Dana's hair, running her fingers through auburn strands as she stared into slightly dilated pupils. She could see Dana's naked desire. "With your hand would be hot. Or with a paddle, if I decided to buy one at some point—"

"I've got the URL of a great online sex toy store," Dana breathed. She'd been exploring these over the past few weeks, imagining all the things she and Laurel could try together.

"Computer geek." Laurel gave her an impulsive kiss on the nose. "For tonight, your hand will be fantastic."

Dana shivered. "What happens after I spank you? When do I stop?"

"You spank me until my ass is red, until I'm a little sore." Laurel spoke quietly, aware of the power her words were having over Dana. "And then you slip your hand between my legs and realize how wet I am."

"How wet being spanked makes you?"

From Dana's tone, Laurel knew she'd caught on to the fantasy. "Yes. And you decide that this makes me a very *bad* girl." She lowered her hand once more, to cradle Dana's breast. She could feel Dana's heart, and the nipple beneath her palm was rock hard. "So you proceed to tell me, then *show* me, just how bad I am."

For a moment Dana sat in total silence, mouth agape. She cleared her throat, licked her lips, and shook her head a little as if to clear it.

"You look nervous, honey."

Dana shook her head. "No, just so horny it hurts."

"Yeah?"

"Oh, yeah." Dana placed her hand over Laurel's, squeezing until she felt added pressure to her breast. "I don't want you to think that I'm going to be fulfilling a one-sided fantasy here."

"Still worried you're going to hurt me?" Laurel asked.

"I've got more than one worry going on, as usual."

"What else?"

"I hope I can play the part," Dana said. "I hope I can keep a straight face. I'm afraid I'll feel goofy."

"If we giggle once or twice, it's not gonna be the end of the world." Laurel looped her arms around Dana's waist. "Sex is supposed to be fun. This isn't summer stock theater, it's making love."

Dana's shoulders relaxed, and she set her bottle of beer down on the counter. "Okay. Cool."

"Let's just see what happens, all right?" Laurel asked. "No pressure."

"No pressure," Dana repeated. "All right."

Laurel sensed that her lover needed the reassurance of receiving direction. That should make it easier. Pressing her body close to Dana's, she leaned up and put her lips next to her ear. "I'm feeling so slutty tonight. I'm not going to think anything you do to me is goofy."

"Slutty, huh?" Dana moved her hands to Laurel's bottom, gripping her hard.

Laurel's blood surged at the rough handling. She pressed her face into Dana's neck. "And I trust you enough to show you what a slut I can be with you."

Warm hands slipped inside Laurel's T-shirt, up over her back, under her bra straps. "I'm so lucky to have a girlfriend who loves sex as much as you do," Dana mumbled.

"And who's so good at it, too," Laurel reminded her.

"Of course." Dana gave her a deep, wet kiss and released her with a gentle pat on the behind. "Why don't you go get ready for bed? I'll turn off the lights and lock the door. You know, and make sure Isis is all settled for the night."

Translation: *she needs a minute alone to prepare.* Laurel left her with a teasing smile. "Don't be long."

"I promise."

Laurel maintained her cool until she was three steps inside of her room. Then, door safely closed behind her, she took a running leap and flounced onto her bed. *Holy shit.*

She breathed in and out and put the palm of her hand over her thumping heart. This was a fantasy she'd had for years but had never fully acted out with her past lovers. She'd come closest with Lindsey, but the trust hadn't been there between them and so she was never really able to let go. Dana made her feel utterly safe and loved, and therefore capable of letting her dark side out to play. She hoped Dana had the same trust in her.

Laurel stood and crossed to her dresser, wondering what she should wear. She opened her underwear drawer, scrutinizing her choices. She had that little lacy black thing that Dana loved so much. Or maybe something a little more innocent...the white babydoll? She wasn't quite sure what she wanted to project: naughty girl or dirty slut. Each had its appeal.

Laurel unbuttoned her jeans and let them drop around her ankles. She stepped out of them as she rooted through the drawer. Her T-shirt and bra followed. She stood in her pale blue cotton boyshorts, shivering when her nipples grew even harder in the cool apartment.

Fuck, I'm turned on. She spared a moment to slide her hand in the front of her panties, planting her feet apart so she could glide a fingertip along damp, swollen folds. Exhaling through her nose, she braced one hand on the dresser and explored her aroused pussy with her fingers.

The bedroom door opened behind her. "What are you doing?"

Laurel jumped, startled at the sound of Dana's voice. She turned and gave her lover a sheepish grin, her hand still deep in her panties. "I…"

Dana crossed the room in four long strides. She reached out to take Laurel's wrist in an almost painful grip, pulling her hand from her underwear with a vicious tug. "Did I say you could start without me?"

Her voice was deadly serious, though deep affection still glimmered in her eyes. She moved her hand from Laurel's wrist to her upper arm. Though she loosened her grasp slightly, it remained the harshest touch she had ever used with her lover.

Their game had begun.

Laurel sensed that Dana was waiting for some cue from her, and so she gave a tentative shake of the head. "I'm sorry."

"You can't keep your hand out of your panties for a minute, can you?"

Laurel shivered as Dana instinctively tapped deep into her desire to be made to feel naughty. "I just wanted to see—"

"What?" Dana interrupted. "You wanted to see if your pussy was wet enough for me?"

Sensing she wouldn't be allowed to offer a real response anyway, Laurel merely nodded. She flexed her arm in Dana's hold, testing her limits.

Dana leaned close and hissed into her ear. "That's *my* pussy. And I didn't give you permission to touch it."

Wow. She was good. Eager to take one last opportunity to encourage Dana, Laurel whispered, "This is perfect."

Dana's eyes flashed with pleasure, then became shuttered and closed. She reverted fully into the fantasy, at once becoming the strict dominant that Laurel had always known lurked beneath the surface. "I want you to apologize, Laurel."

Laurel bit her lip, acutely aware of how very naked she felt. Dana's tense arm brushed the side of her bare breast. "I'm sorry," she said. Wholly obedient.

Dana shook her head. "Not good enough. I don't believe it."

"You don't?" Laurel released an incredulous giggle. "What do I have to do to convince you?"

The iron grip on her upper arm tightened just a little, and Dana dragged her over to the bed. "You'll have to take your punishment." She sat down, pulling Laurel across her lap. "And *then* tell me you're sorry."

Despite the fact that she had often fantasized about being in this position, Laurel's face grew hot with mild embarrassment at being laid over Dana's knee like a disobedient child. She felt herself getting wetter.

"You know you did something wrong, don't you?" Dana murmured.

Laurel swallowed hard. "Yes."

Smack. The first blow came down hard on her right cheek, painful enough to make her gasp in shock.

Dana paused. She was really doing this. And from the way Laurel was nearly gasping for air, she was doing it well. Her entire body was tense and still, but she trembled inside. She had never been so aroused in her life, but the fear that she was going too far lingered. "Quicksilver?" she ventured.

Laurel released a shaky chuckle. *Are you kidding me?* She shook her head, resting the side of her face on the comforter. "No."

Smack.

Laurel moaned at the second firm slap, wiggling on Dana's thighs. "I really wasn't trying to start without you—"

"Did I ask you what you were really trying to do?" *Smack.*

Laurel gave her a vigorous shake of the head. "I'm sorry."

"Oh, I know you're sorry." Dana rested her hand on Laurel's right cheek. "I love these panties, baby, but they need to go. I want to see your ass getting nice and red for me." With that, she hooked her fingertips in the waistband and yanked the cotton briefs down, exposing Laurel's bare bottom.

Laurel felt wetness coating her inner thighs and wondered when Dana would discover just how hot she was making her. She was a natural at this.

Dana groaned as she tugged Laurel's underwear down to her knees. "God, I love your ass."

Laurel didn't say anything to that, though her chest burned with pleasure.

Smack.

Laurel squirmed, trying to contend with the sensations and feelings building with each slap. They were painful enough to make her flesh tingle, and so exquisite they made her want to weep. This was exactly what she wanted.

"I told you to get ready for bed," Dana said. Her tone was almost as hard as the spanking she continued to deliver, punctuating her words with measured smacks. "I did *not* tell you to come in here and touch yourself."

Sweat beaded on Laurel's forehead. She closed her eyes tight, riding out the pain. "I'm sorry, Dana," she gasped.

"What?"

"I'm sorry!" Laurel repeated. "I'm sorry I was touching myself."

Smack. "Why?"

The question threw Laurel for a moment. She tried to remember what Dana had said when she caught her, hand in panties. "Because you didn't tell me I could," she whimpered.

"That's right," Dana said. "And whose pussy is it that you were fingering?"

"Yours," Laurel said without hesitation.

"Tell me."

Her buttocks throbbed, hot and sore. She could feel her pussy literally dripping, and again she wondered when Dana would discover her arousal.

"*Tell* me," Dana repeated, applying her hand once more.

"My pussy belongs to you."

Smack.

"It belongs to you!"

Dana stared down at the flesh quivering beneath her palm. As she drew her hand back, she saw its imprint, faintly white before hot color washed through. Both ass cheeks were hot. They had to be stinging. She stopped slapping, and let her hand come to rest, rubbing soothing circles on the warm flesh. "Now tell me you're sorry," she drawled. "And mean it."

"I'm sorry," Laurel mumbled. "I'm really sorry, Dana. I...wasn't thinking."

"Does your ass hurt?"

Laurel was honest. "Yes."

"It looks like it hurts." Dana's fingers traced gentle patterns. "I really marked you."

Laurel shivered at the quiet comment. She concentrated on the now gentle touch of Dana's hand. "I've never been spanked so hard."

"Maybe I was a little harsh with you," Dana murmured. She continued to run her fingers back and forth over the punished flesh. "My hand actually hurts."

Laurel remained still. Her panties, caught around her thighs, prevented her from spreading her legs like she wanted. "I'm sorry," she said again.

"Are you?"

Panting with rising excitement, Laurel shifted beneath Dana's hand. Her lover was stroking a path from the cleft of her buttocks now, venturing closer to the juncture of her thighs on every up and down pass.

"I'm very sorry," Laurel repeated. "And I mean it."

"Do you really mean it?" Dana sounded calm and casual, a stark contrast from the cold disciplinarian she'd been channeling just minutes ago. "Or do you just want me to stop spanking you?"

Laurel stayed silent, for a moment uncertain how to answer. She couldn't honestly say she wanted the spanking to end.

"Would you rather I be nice to you instead?" Dana slid her fingertips down along Laurel's ass, pressing between her thighs.

Laurel froze when she felt Dana encounter the slick, abundant wetness coating her labia and spilling onto her inner thighs. Dana stopped speaking, though her fingers continued to explore her swollen pussy.

"What's this?" Dana asked in a soft voice.

Laurel felt her face flood with inexplicable shame. She closed her eyes, overcome by just how amazing Dana was making this entire scenario. "I'm—"

"You like this," Dana said. She rubbed the pads of her index and middle fingers along Laurel's sensitive folds, then delved into her entrance with just the tip of one. "You're all wet."

When Laurel didn't respond, Dana drew back and delivered a

sharp smack to a particularly sore spot on her bottom. Laurel grunted in pain.

"Does it hurt?" Dana asked. "Or do you like it?"

Laurel bit her lip to keep herself from gasping when another hard slap landed on her bottom. "Both."

"Is that the problem?" Dana murmured. "You like being bad?"

Laurel was certain of two things: her ass had never felt so incredibly tender, and she had never been as painfully desperate to be fucked as she was at that moment. She spread her thighs as far as her panties would allow.

"It makes you *wet* to get spanked like a naughty little girl?"

Laurel released a load moan, startling herself. The sound must have inflamed Dana, because it brought on a flurry of softer slaps that landed in one tender area on the fleshy part of her left cheek. They were almost too soft, teasing her with the promise of more.

"Answer me," Dana demanded. "Is that why you're wet?"

"Yes," Laurel whimpered. Her voice sounded pleading and strange to her own ears. "I like it when you spank me."

"I thought you told me it hurt."

"It does."

Dana delivered another slap, without a word. She was so turned on in that moment, she didn't trust herself to speak.

Laurel flinched. Dana wasn't relenting, and Laurel wasn't anywhere near saying their safe word. "It hurts," she whimpered.

"You like being hurt?"

Laurel exhaled slowly. "Yeah."

"Such a dirty little slut," Dana drawled.

Laurel opened her eyes wide, shocked at her body's reaction to the throaty words. Her pussy felt swollen and heavy, and achingly empty. She was sure that she was smearing her juices onto Dana's blue jeans. *I love her for doing this with me.*

Dana worked a finger between her buttocks, probing at her anus with the tip. "You've thought about this, haven't you? Being my slut. Letting me hurt you."

Laurel's heart was thumping so hard, she wondered if Dana could feel the vibrations where the palm of her hand still rested on her throbbing backside. "Yes."

Dana released a shaky sigh. She patted Laurel on the bottom, three times. Her hand was gentle on tingling flesh. "Stand up."

Laurel stood, and immediately Dana grabbed her arm and pulled her down onto the bed, face first. She let out a tiny noise of surprise, then a groan when Dana forced her to turn over onto her back. The comforter felt rough and uncomfortable against her aching bottom. She watched Dana tug the boyshorts from her ankles.

"I'm not sure how to punish you." Dana ran her palms along Laurel's inner thighs, pushing them apart. She didn't touch Laurel's pussy, content simply to expose her. "Fuck," she murmured, staring down at Laurel's blatant arousal. "This doesn't look like a punishment to me."

Face hot, Laurel was eager to play along. "I'm sorry, I didn't mean to get so wet."

Dana reached down and covered Laurel's sex with her hand, squeezing hard. Laurel gasped. Dana slapped at Laurel's left foot, encouraging her to tilt her leg outward and plant it on the bed.

Now Laurel was truly exposed.

"So you like having your ass slapped?" Dana's lips twitched, and for an instant she thought she was going to break into an amused grin. Instead, she sobered herself. As much fun as she was having, and as excited as she was about being able to play this role, she knew she had to stay in character for Laurel.

"Yes," Laurel said. She looked at Dana's hand, wanting nothing more than to feel her fingers deep inside.

"What else makes you wet?" Dana sat between Laurel's thighs, staring down at her open pussy. She swirled her finger through copious wetness. Lightening quick, she moved her hand to Laurel's breast, plucking hard at her nipple. "Does that make you wet?"

Laurel closed her eyes and shook with pleasure.

Dana clamped the nipple harder, skirting on the edge of real pain. Opening her eyes, Laurel groaned at the sight of her rock-hard nipple and the reddening flesh around the areola. Dana switched to the other breast, squeezing hard before taking the nipple in the punishing vise of her fingers.

"Dana," Laurel gasped.

At once Dana stopped. She stared into Laurel's eyes, afraid she'd gone too far. She was ready in that instant to back off and revert to the familiar sweet, hot caresses of the past few weeks. Laurel must have seen the question in her eyes. She shook her head and moved her hands up to grip the headboard, and Dana gave her what she wanted.

"Look at your pussy." She leaned over Laurel. "You look like a slut who needs a good, hard fuck."

Laurel shuddered beneath Dana's weight. Warm breasts pressed against her own, trapping her against the bed. She let go of the headboard and placed the palms of her hands against Dana's shoulders, between their bodies, and gave her an experimental push, hoping her "resistance" wouldn't be misinterpreted.

So fast it left her breathless, Dana reached up and gripped her wrists, slamming them onto the mattress above her head. Dana shifted her whole body on top of Laurel's and held her down on the bed.

"Are you refusing me?" she whispered into her ear.

"No." Laurel struggled out of the hold. Her clit throbbed.

"No, I'm not refusing?" Dana asked. "Or no, I'm not a slut who needs a good, hard fuck?" She forced a denim-clad leg between Laurel's thighs.

Laurel bucked against her, marveling at her own wetness. "I'm not refusing."

"Then why are you struggling?"

"I'm…just…" Laurel whimpered, moving against Dana's thigh. "Please, Dana."

"Please what?" Dana tightened her grip on Laurel's wrists. "Don't tell me you don't want me to fuck you."

Laurel shook her head. "I want it," she said.

Dana grinned and transferred both wrists to one hand. Her grip was less severe, but Laurel wasn't going anywhere. She shifted to the side, lying next to Laurel's prone body. Bringing one hand down to hover above Laurel's abdomen, she said, "Spread your legs wider."

Laurel obeyed. She felt like a whore, spread so wide, and she experienced a renewed flood of arousal at the thought.

"I wonder what I could do to get you wetter." Dana brought her hand down to give Laurel's pussy a gentle, teasing slap.

The contact sent an electric shock wave of sensation throughout Laurel's body, originating from her erect clit. Hot juices dribbled down the crack of her ass, a shameful testament to her pleasure.

"You feel awfully wet," Dana said. "Do you like having your pussy smacked, too?"

Laurel writhed. Tears stung at her eyes, an instinctive reaction to the taunt. She struggled with her instinct to close her trembling thighs, but faltered and trapped Dana's hand between them.

Dana released Laurel's wrists and slapped at her left thigh, hard. "Open. Your. Legs," she ground out.

Undone by her stern tone and the intractable set of her jaw, Laurel obeyed, easing her thighs apart.

"Spread them wide like the little slut you are," Dana said. She chuckled a little, breaking character for a split second. Laurel brought her hands down and tried to cover her tender labia. She looked deep into Dana's sparkling eyes, searching for the love she knew she would find there.

"You look beautiful right now," Dana murmured. "Put your hands above your head and keep them there." Her gaze was tender, urging Laurel to do as she said.

Laurel raised her arms and grasped the headboard with both hands. She could feel her entire body shaking. She had never felt so out of control—and so in love—in her life.

Dana combed the backs of her fingertips through the trimmed thatch of hair between Laurel's thighs, and slipped down to rub her clit. "I love the look on your face when you're not sure if something hurts or feels good."

Laurel bit her lip when Dana began playing with her pussy. She stroked up and down her lips, tugging on the short hairs there, then slipped inside and traced the edges of her swollen pink folds. Laurel's hips pumped against the deliberate touch.

After a moment, Dana drew back and gave her a gentle pat between the legs. Her fingers ground wetly against Laurel's clit, and Laurel cried out.

Dana reached up and covered Laurel's mouth with the palm of her hand. "Quiet, little girl. Do you want the neighbors to know how bad you are?"

Laurel groaned, closing her eyes in pleasure. She didn't know how Dana had guessed what being forced to keep quiet would do to her, but she was enjoying every second of this game. She could feel the pads of

Dana's fingers slip-sliding over her clit. Laurel moaned and got louder when Dana pressed her hand even more firmly over her mouth.

"Everyone is going to hear what a slut you are for me." Dana seized Laurel's distended clit between her fingertips. "Do you want people to know what you let me do to you?"

Laurel bucked her hips. *God, Dana, stick something inside me.* She ground her pelvis against her lover's hand, keening in desperation. *Rub something! Anything!*

All at once Dana retreated. She took her hands off Laurel's body and sat back. Laurel continued to grip the headboard. Her fingers felt locked.

"You can let go of that, baby," Dana said. "I want you to show me how wet you are."

Biting her lip, Laurel slid her hands over her belly, between her legs. She hesitated, fingertips resting on her slippery inner thighs.

"It's mine. Show it to me."

Laurel spread herself with her fingers, feeling a flush rise on her face and chest. She watched Dana appraise her with interested eyes. She knew she was as wet as Dana had ever seen her.

"Do you like showing me your pussy?"

I thought she was shy about talking dirty! Laurel's mouth fell open a little. "Yes," she breathed.

"You want me inside?"

"Yes," Laurel said, more loudly this time. Her face burned at how wanton she felt.

Without warning or preamble, Dana entered her with a single finger, in one smooth thrust. Laurel moaned and arched her back in appreciation. She kept her hands still, holding herself open.

"You want me to fuck you until you come, don't you?" Dana pulled out, then pushed back inside. "You've been waiting for this since the moment I put you over my knee."

"Yes," Laurel repeated. She was prepared to say anything to keep Dana's finger moving.

But instead, Dana pulled out. And climbed off the bed.

Laurel planted her elbows on the bed and propped herself up. She stared at Dana, unable to believe she would leave her like this. "Where are you going?"

Dana stood at the side of the bed, smiling in amusement. She took Laurel's upper arm in her hand, pulling her into a sitting position. "You're being punished. So you get to make me come first."

Like that's punishment. Laurel nodded as Dana guided her shaking hands to the button on her blue jeans. "What do you want me to do?"

Dana pulled off her T-shirt. "Take off my jeans," she said. "And then I want you on your knees beside the bed. You're going to suck me off."

Laurel fumbled with Dana's zipper, not only because she was too excited to be smooth, but also to excite that part of Dana that she could see getting off on their dynamic of dominance and submission. She eased the tab down, then tugged her lover's jeans over her hips and thighs.

Dana stepped out of her jeans and wound her fingers in Laurel's hair. Pulling Laurel's face to the crotch of her lavender panties, she growled, "You want this pussy, don't you?"

Laurel nodded. The cotton was damp against her nose and lips, and Dana's scent hung heavily in the air. Her mouth watered for a taste. "Please."

"Kiss it."

Laurel pursed her lips and kissed the spot over Dana's clit. She pressed forward slightly, nudging Dana with her nose.

Exhaling shakily, Dana tugged on her hair. "Take a little taste."

Laurel poked her tongue out and licked over Dana's panties, sampling her through the thin material. Taking a chance, she hooked her fingertip in the crotch of the panties, pulling it to the side. This time, she was able to slide her tongue along bare flesh.

Dana pulled on her hair, forcing Laurel's face away from the space between her thighs. With her free hand, she gripped Laurel's arm and guided her onto the floor. "On your knees, little girl."

Laurel settled on the carpet, turning to face the bed. Dana tugged her underwear down and kicked them away carelessly. She sat on the bed and spread her legs, threading her fingers through Laurel's hair.

"Come on," Dana urged. She pulled Laurel closer until her face was only inches from Dana's patch of dark, curly hairs. "I want you to show me how a good slut licks pussy."

Laurel rocked forward on her knees and lowered her head so she could take Dana's labia in her mouth. She moaned at the salty-sweet musk of her lover's juices.

"Oh, you like that," Dana murmured. She stroked Laurel's hair, spreading her thighs wider to allow her better access. "Don't you?"

Laurel mumbled her agreement, running her tongue up and down over Dana's pussy. She could feel the wetness spilling from her, and it stoked her arousal. Reaching between her own legs with a discreet hand, she stroked at her labia and clit with her fingertips.

"Suck it." Dana brought her free hand to cradle Laurel's jaw. "Suck me, baby."

Laurel changed tactics and obediently sucked Dana's clit into her mouth. She lapped up and down the distended shaft with the very tip of her tongue. She pulled out every move she knew Dana liked, desperate to make her happy.

"Oh," Dana gasped. She lay back on the bed, releasing Laurel's jaw and bringing her hand up to pinch her own nipple. Her other hand stayed tangled in Laurel's hair. "So nice, baby."

Laurel rested her hands on Dana's thighs as she worked her mouth. She murmured in pleasure as she moved her tongue, letting Dana know how much she enjoyed what she was doing.

Dana's thighs started to tremble. She moaned and arched her back, tightening her hand in Laurel's hair. "That's right," Dana growled. She forced Laurel's face harder between her legs and pumped her hips against her tongue. "Make me come with your mouth."

Dana's clit was as swollen as Laurel had ever felt it. She took it between her lips with no problem, batting at it with the tip of her tongue. Dana groaned, thighs shaking, and her whole body tensed as a flood of hot wetness coated Laurel's chin. Laurel felt a rush of pride at her accomplishment.

As soon as Dana's convulsions subsided, she pushed Laurel away and rose to her feet, towering over a still-kneeling Laurel. "Get on the bed. It's your turn."

With shaking legs, Laurel crawled onto the mattress. "How do you want me?"

Dana crossed the room to Laurel's oak dresser. "On top."

Laurel settled back and watched as Dana pulled the harness from the sex toy drawer, along with Laurel's favorite dildo. Her clit pulsed in anticipation.

"You approve?" Dana smiled over her shoulder as she fastened the harness around her waist.

"Wholeheartedly."

"Good." Properly equipped, Dana strode back to the bed.

Without being told, Laurel scooted over to make room, and Dana lay down on her back. Her orgasm had taken the edge off slightly, and now she could focus solely on Laurel's pleasure. She slipped right back into her dominant role.

"I want to watch my naughty slut fuck herself." She grasped Laurel's arm. "Climb on."

Laurel straddled Dana's hips, planting one knee on either side of her body. She reached between their bodies and grasped the base of the dildo Dana wore.

Dana covered her hand with strong fingers. "But first ask me if you can have my cock."

Laurel blushed at her eagerness. She forced herself to slow down and meet Dana's eyes. "May I have it?" she murmured. She rubbed the head over her clit, shuddering at the fierceness of her desire. "Please, Dana."

"Take it." Dana rested her hand on Laurel's hip, encouraging her to lower herself onto the dildo. "Take it inside, baby, and fuck yourself on it."

Laurel brought the tip of the dildo to her entrance, pressing it inside with careful patience. This particular dildo was one of her larger ones, and it always took her a few moments to adjust to its size. Dana gripped her hips with both hands and held on as Laurel took in its length.

"That's what you've been wanting," Dana murmured. She reached between them and rubbed gentle circles on Laurel's swollen clit, relaxing her pussy and easing the passage of the dildo as it slid inside. "Isn't it?"

Laurel dropped her head, exhaling through her nostrils. This was the fullness she had craved. "It feels so good."

With both hands on Laurel's hips, Dana encouraged her to rock up and down on the dildo. "That's right. Fuck me, baby."

Given permission, Laurel moved in earnest. She put her hands on the headboard and ground her hips into Dana's, riding her hard. "Dana," she said through gritted teeth.

Dana delivered a hard smack to Laurel's bottom. Still tender from her spanking, Laurel winced and fucked Dana faster.

"That's right," Dana said. "Fuck yourself. Show me what a hungry little slut you are."

Laurel's pussy tightened around the dildo, and she moved faster. When Dana smacked her ass again, she groaned and jerked her hips back and forth. She set a fast pace, desperate to come after being teased for so long.

Dana lay still on her back, staring up as Laurel did all the work to get herself off. "Do you want to come?"

Laurel nodded. Sweat gathered on her brow, and a single droplet snaked a lazy trail down her temple, over her jawline. She leaned forward, still gripping the headboard, and moved her hips at a furious pace. She was close, but release proved elusive.

"You want me to hold you down on the bed and fuck you hard until you come all over this cock?"

"Yes." Laurel released a keening moan when Dana's hips began moving, thrusting the dildo up into her pussy. "Fuck, Dana, please—"

Dana wrapped her arms around Laurel's body and rolled them over until she was on top. Laurel's thighs were spread wide, legs wrapped around Dana's waist. The move took Laurel by surprise, and she felt weak for a moment as she registered her loss of control.

Dana grabbed her wrists in a tight grip, then slammed them onto the bed above Laurel's head. She brought her lips to Laurel's ear as she began a series of forceful thrusts. "Let me fuck you, baby."

Laurel gasped and squirmed beneath Dana. "Oh, God—"

"You're getting tight, aren't you, honey?" Dana loosened her fingers on Laurel's wrists, but didn't release her grip. "You want to come all over me."

"Yes," Laurel begged.

Dana increased the speed of her driving thrusts. She brought a hand down between their bodies, pinching Laurel's nipple between her fingertips. She tugged and twisted on the erect nub until she wrenched free a mild cry of pain. "I can't believe it makes you wet when I get rough with you like this," Dana whispered. Her thrusts grew harder, more demanding. "I love fucking you like the naughty little slut you are."

Laurel's pussy clenched and throbbed at the words, and a dense ball of pleasure formed deep in her belly. Dana pounded against her hard enough that her clit was bumped by the harness on every forceful stroke. Laurel kept her hands above her head as Dana tortured her nipples, closing her eyes and concentrating on the orgasm that promised to rip through her body.

"Ask me to fuck you harder," Dana panted. Her body was damp with sweat, heavy on top of Laurel's. She still held one of Laurel's wrists in her hand. "Beg me, Laurel."

Laurel felt the orgasm tingling in her toes. "Please," she begged, "fuck me harder." She squirmed beneath Dana, trying to bring her hips up to meet the vigorous strokes.

Dana released her nipple and brought her hand up to pin Laurel's free wrist to the bed once again. When she had her fully restrained, she increased the strength of her pounding.

"Come for me," Dana commanded. "Let me hear you come all over that big cock." She pressed her face into Laurel's neck, biting the tender skin there.

It was more than enough to send Laurel over the edge. She opened her mouth and called out as her pussy contracted in pleasure. The orgasm hit her hard, making her voice crack and her legs shake, leaving her limp and boneless beneath Dana's weight. She closed her eyes and rode it out for as long as possible, biting her lip as Dana continued to pump into her. Tears leaked from the corners of her eyes, the strength of her release leaving her overwhelmed and unable to speak.

"Stop," Laurel finally gasped. An instant of thought, then, "Quicksilver."

Immediately Dana stopped moving. She released Laurel's wrists and planted her hands on the mattress so she could push away from their sweaty embrace. "Are you all right?"

Laurel released a helpless sob of ecstasy. She threw her arms around Dana's neck, pulling her into a strong hug. "Oh my God," she gasped. Aftershocks rumbled through her body, causing her pussy to tighten around the dildo that still rested inside. "Dana, that was amazing. That was…exactly what I wanted."

Dana felt her body vibrate with quiet joy. That had perfectly satisfied her own dominance fantasies. Was it possible that they were truly so compatible? "It was fun. I really did okay?"

Laurel loosened her grip, drawing back to meet Dana's tender gaze. At once, her sweet, sensitive lover was back. "You're a fucking natural at that."

Dana beamed, feeling a swell of cocky pride. "I thought I did okay."

"Okay?" Laurel repeated incredulously. "That couldn't have been more perfect. I came so hard—"

"Really?"

Laurel gave her a sincere nod. "But, honey?"

"Yeah?"

"You need to pull out of me now." Laurel wrinkled her nose, shifting under Dana. "I'm thoroughly ravished."

"Oh. Sorry." Dana shifted, unsure of how best to extricate herself from their embrace. "Why don't you help me?"

With a nod, Laurel tensed her muscles and helped push the dildo out of her body, groaning at the sensation. Dana backed off to sit on her knees, and began the involved task of releasing herself from the harness.

"I wasn't planning on using this, actually," Dana murmured. She moved with languid grace, a peaceful smile on her face. "I just felt you under me and inspiration struck."

Laurel marveled at the sexy confidence of her lover. Sometimes she couldn't believe this was the uptight project manager she'd met in the elevator that night. "I love feeling your body against mine when you're inside me."

Dana grinned and kept unbuckling.

Stretching, Laurel pulled the quilt that was bunched at the end of the bed over her body. A loud yawn forced its way out of her mouth. "Honey, you wore me out."

Dana discarded the dildo and harness on the floor. "Getting old, huh? Twenty-five and one little orgasm lays you out?"

"There was nothing little about that orgasm."

A familiar look of self-satisfaction stole over Dana's face. "Of course there wasn't."

Laurel chuckled and reached out with a lazy hand to tug Dana under the quilt with her. "Come cuddle me."

"Actually, I wanted to do something else first." Dana climbed off the bed and walked to the bathroom. "Don't pass out just yet," she called over her shoulder.

After a moment, Laurel heard the bathtub faucet begin to run. Eyes closed, she couldn't suppress a blissful smile. *A hot bath. Lovely.* She covered her damp sex with one hand, exhaling at the feeling of her fingertips brushing against sensitive skin.

"Baby?"

Laurel attempted to pick her head up off the pillow when Dana came back into the room, but failed miserably. Her muscles felt like jelly. "Yeah?"

"Aww," Dana cooed. She crossed over to the bed, dropping onto her knees next to Laurel. "Are you too tired for a bath?"

"Just too boneless to actually stand up." She turned her grin on her lover. "You fucked me hard."

Dana wrapped her arms around Laurel's shoulders and gathered her into a reverent hug. "Yes, I did." She tugged Laurel into a sitting position, supporting her weight with the embrace. "And now I want to wash you."

Laurel allowed Dana to lead her by the hand to the bathroom. The tub was full of steamy, fragrant water, and two of her favorite candles were lit on the edge. Dana gave her a shy smile when Laurel whimpered at the sight.

"Get in," Dana said. "I want to wash your hair."

Laurel was already testing the temperature with her toe. "You aren't going to get in with me?"

"I will in a couple of minutes." Dana settled next to the tub and picked up a sponge. "Let me just pamper you first."

"I'm not about to argue." Laurel sat down in the hot water, groaning as her aching muscles began to relax. "Oh, that feels wonderful."

Dana poured some body wash on the sponge and rubbed it over Laurel's upper back. "You worked up a little sweat, honey."

"So did you."

"I think that's the most exercise I've gotten in months."

Laurel leaned forward to give Dana better access to her back. "That was some of the hottest sex I've ever had. I felt so safe with you."

In the candlelight, she could see color rise on Dana's cheeks.

"I didn't...go too far?"

"Oh, no. You gave me exactly what I wanted."

"Lean back, darling," Dana said. When Laurel complied, she rubbed the sponge over Laurel's tender breasts. She was silent for some time, then murmured, "I felt safe with you, too."

"Yeah?" Laurel moaned quietly when Dana's hand ventured down over her belly.

"Yeah," Dana said. "I don't think I could have done something like that if I didn't trust you so completely."

In a way, it was funny that Dana, having played the dominant role, would feel like that. But Laurel understood what she was saying.

"Trust is what makes something like that so good." Laurel shivered as she reflected on their lovemaking. She cupped Dana's pale breast in her hand and pinched her nipple lightly. "This is an amazing gift. Knowing that I can share my fantasies with you, and that you'll play them out with me—"

"I'll have to remember that for your birthday. It's a cheap gift."

Laurel swatted Dana's arm. "Shut up."

"No, I mean it. It really fits within my budget."

Laurel smacked Dana's arm again, harder this time. "Stop before I decide you're not the best thing that's ever happened to me."

Dana dropped the sponge and wrapped her arms around Laurel's middle. "I am?"

"Without a doubt."

Teasing fingers traced patterns down over her belly, then between her thighs. With a low groan, Laurel parted her legs to allow Dana to stroke the swollen lips of her pussy.

"I am so crazy about you, Laurel." Dana buried her face in Laurel's neck, breathing hard. Her fingertips sought out Laurel's clit, still impossibly swollen, and she began rubbing gentle circles around the ridge of flesh. "I feel so much that sometimes I don't know how to tell you."

"Kiss me." Despite her exhaustion, Laurel felt her ardor rising once again. "I always know how you feel when you kiss me."

Wordlessly, Dana did as she asked. She pulled her face from Laurel's neck and found her lips, slipping her tongue inside her mouth with a quiet moan. Laurel looped her arms around her neck and kissed her back.

Despite their rather inauspicious beginning—that messy, fumbling first kiss in the elevator—Laurel thought that kissing Dana was the most delicious thing she had ever done. If she could, she would spend every evening on the couch, just making out. Dana had honed an uncanny ability to communicate the depth of her emotions with her lips, and it was when Dana's tongue played inside her mouth that Laurel felt the safest and most secure in their relationship.

As they kissed, Dana brought her to a slow, sweet orgasm with the pads of her fingers. She never left Laurel's mouth for a moment, alternating between long, wet explorations with her tongue and gentle nibbles on her lips. She kept one arm wrapped around Laurel's back while the other worked between her thighs, and when Laurel came, she held her trembling body tight.

Dana drew back when Laurel had recovered from her orgasm. "I wanted to make soft love to you, too, baby. I hope you don't mind—"

Laurel shook her head, closing her thighs and trapping Dana's hand between them. "I was wrong earlier, when I said that tonight couldn't have been more perfect."

"Yeah?" Dana slipped her hand from between Laurel's thighs, opened the drain, and reached up to turn the faucet on again. Hot water poured into the bathtub, warming Laurel's body.

Laurel moved forward so that Dana could climb into the bathtub behind her. "I have a gift for you."

"I'm not sure what more you could possibly give me right now."

"I quit my job at the club last night."

Dana's heart sang at the words she had been hoping to hear for almost a month now. She was thrilled, but with that came a sharp stab of guilt. Did Laurel do this for her? "I hope this isn't because I—"

"This is because I wanted to do this. For you. Because you've made my life more perfect."

Tears filled Dana's eyes, and she was almost glad Laurel was facing away from her. She wasn't sure she had ever felt so much, about anything. Her heart ached in the most pleasant way imaginable. Dana eased her legs around Laurel's waist and pulled her back into a strong hug with both arms. Inhaling the scent of Laurel's hair, she whispered, "You deserve perfect."

Laurel leaned back into Dana's embrace with a contented smile. *And I've got you.*

AFTER THREE MORE MONTHS

L aurel woke up on the morning of her twenty-sixth birthday to a soft hand sliding up the inside of her thigh. She whimpered, half asleep, when warm fingers slipped through the wetness she was surprised to feel between her legs so early. Either she'd been having one hell of a dream, or Dana had been teasing her for a while now.

Laurel decided to play possum and see what developed.

Dana's fingertips creep-crawled over her abdomen, sweeping across her belly before moving down to play with the damp curls covering her sex. She tugged on the short hairs, pulling a low groan from Laurel's throat.

"You awake, honey?"

Laurel kept her eyes closed, eager to see where this was going. She arched her back a little and let her thighs fall open for Dana's hand. Murmuring sleepily, she turned her face to the side.

"Not yet, huh?" Dana whispered. She rasped blunt fingernails over Laurel's sensitive outer lips and traced gentle patterns across her slick labia with the pad of her thumb. "Maybe I need to try harder."

Yes. Laurel eased her legs apart another inch. *Try harder.*

Groaning when her mother's old quilt was pulled from her naked body, Laurel felt her nipples harden in the cool air and under Dana's hot gaze. She didn't need to open her eyes to know that her lover was studying her body with that intense stare. Laurel's nostrils flared with arousal when a fingertip pressed against her opening, but didn't go inside.

"I wonder what would wake my girl up," Dana murmured.

Laurel suspected that the words were as much for her as they were an out-loud musing, and she fought not to smile at the quiet question. *I wonder what you'll do to find out.*

The bed shifted under Dana's weight, and Laurel could feel her changing position beside where she lay sprawled on her back. Her body tensed in anticipation of Dana's next move.

A soft, wet tongue snaked a lazy trail from just below Laurel's belly button to the hair between her thighs. Laurel whimpered and spread her legs even farther apart, now wanton in her pose.

"I bet this wakes her up," Dana mumbled. And then she stopped talking.

Laurel opened her eyes when Dana's tongue eased between the folds of her sex, lapping up some of the wetness her sleeping body had produced. She couldn't stop a shaky sigh, and she tangled her fingers in Dana's tousled hair.

Dana paused in her gentle licking, looking up into Laurel's eyes with a pleased smile. She was naked and stretched out on her belly between Laurel's thighs. "Good morning, birthday girl."

"Good morning."

Pulling her open carefully, Dana lowered her face and dragged her tongue up the length of Laurel's pussy. She flicked at her clit with the tip of her tongue, then drew back with a wide grin. "I made you breakfast in bed."

Laurel looked at the tray of food sitting on the table near her oak dresser. The thought of Dana—boardroom, sales-pitch Dana—slaving in the kitchen was enough to make the day special. "Breakfast? For me?"

Dana gave her a loving lick, from bottom to top. "All for you, honey." She inhaled, nuzzling into Laurel's slick folds. "But I want to eat first."

Laurel cradled the back of Dana's head in her hand, holding her close. "Will mine get cold?"

Sucking Laurel's swollen clit in a hot, wet kiss, Dana took a while to answer. Finally she retreated, licking her lips. "Fresh fruit and dry cereal. And orange juice."

Perhaps she didn't slave, but she certainly thought ahead. Laurel urged Dana back to task with a lazy grin. "Perfect."

Dana kissed and sucked until Laurel's hips were pumping into her face. She pulled away with a soft chuckle. "You aren't going to come so soon, are you?"

Laurel glanced at the alarm clock on the bedside table. "You have to be to work in a half hour."

Dana shook her head. She crawled up the length of Laurel's body, reaching out to turn the glowing digital display toward the wall. "Not today," she murmured. Her lips captured Laurel's in a lingering kiss. "Today is your day."

Wow. Laurel held on to Dana's shoulders and grinned up at her lover. Her stomach turned over in pleasure as she licked the taste of her own arousal from Dana's mouth. "You took the day off?"

Dana pressed her thigh into Laurel's wetness. "I did. I wanted to be with you."

Laurel couldn't have wiped the goofy smile off her face if she'd tried. "Really?"

"I told you that you're more important than project management."

Laurel hugged her tight. "And you're the sweetest, most lovable, cuddly—"

"Teddy bear?" Dana finished. She drew back and gave Laurel a look of distaste. "Puppy?"

"*Sexiest*, gorgeous, wonderful woman. In the world."

"Nice save." Dana lowered her face and whispered into Laurel's ear. "Now tell me what you want."

"For my birthday?"

"Right now." Dana rotated her hips, grinding into Laurel. "From me." She ran her fingers down the side of Laurel's face, onto her throat. "What do you want, baby?"

It didn't take Laurel long to decide. "I want you to fuck me."

Dana looked like she was the one being given a present. Her whole face lit up with her smile. "Yes."

Laurel spread her legs wide. "I want to feel you fucking me, honey. I love how you feel inside me." She watched as Dana trembled slightly with the words, as she always did. And like always, Laurel felt a rush of power at the sight.

Dana slid her hand between their bodies, capturing Laurel's lips in yet another kiss. She pushed her tongue into Laurel's mouth at the same time she thrust a finger into her pussy, wrenching a moan from Laurel's throat.

Tearing her mouth away from Laurel's, Dana whispered, "More?"

Laurel nodded and closed her eyes. "More." She was soaking wet, eager for more of Dana. "I need to feel full."

Dana eased her finger out of Laurel, then pressed back into her with three. She lowered her face to Laurel's shoulder and talked low into her ear. "I woke up thinking about filling your pussy like this."

Laurel tightened her arms around Dana's shoulders, hugging her close. "You're so good, Dana."

Dana smiled against her throat. "Harder?"

Laurel nodded, bucking her hips up to meet Dana's strokes. "Harder." She exhaled through her mouth. "Fuck me harder."

Pounding into her so hard that the back of her hand slapped firmly against Laurel's ass, Dana surged up and caught Laurel in a hard kiss. Breaking away with a soft cry, Dana whispered, "You're so beautiful, Laurel." Deep emotion rang clear in her voice. Her fingers rubbed at a spot that made Laurel's lower belly burn with pleasure. "I…love you."

Laurel's hips froze beneath Dana's hand. She held her breath, searching Dana's eyes. "You…?"

Dana's hand stilled. She stayed deep inside Laurel, looking down at her tenderly. Her breasts pressed against Laurel's, both of them breathing heavily as they stared at one another.

"I love you. A lot."

Laurel blinked rapidly, eyes stinging. When Dana's face began to give way to a look of panic, Laurel squeezed her hard around the shoulders. She buried her nose in Dana's hair, breathing in her scent as she focused on the sensation of strong fingers stretching her wide open.

"I love you, too." Hot tears spilled onto her cheeks. She felt like she had been waiting forever to say the words out loud. "I love you, Dana."

Dana released a quiet little cry, easing her free hand beneath Laurel's neck. She gripped the nape and gave her a watery grin. "And it's not even my birthday."

Shaking her head dazedly, Laurel laughed and shifted her hips on the mattress. "Make me come, honey. I want to come on your fingers."

Staring deep into Laurel's eyes, Dana began moving her hand again. She made circles over Laurel's hard clit with her thumb. Somehow, she kept Laurel on the edge for what felt like hours before releasing her in an explosion of sound and juices that ended when Laurel collapsed limp onto the bed.

Laurel pulled Dana's full weight onto her body after she came, delighting in the feeling of her lover's heartbeat thrumming hard against her chest. "You love me?"

"You have to ask?" Dana mumbled. She lifted her head and gazed down into Laurel's eyes. "It's only taken me a few months to work up the courage to say it."

"Well, it's the best birthday present I've ever been given." *And you have no idea how much I've been hoping you felt the same way.*

She knew it was a big deal for Dana to be so open with her feelings. Laurel had acknowledged that she was in love since their night of rough sex, but she was careful not to push Dana for any declarations. Laurel was her first girlfriend, after all, and so everything between them had been a new experience for Dana. Laurel was content to move at Dana's pace, despite the fact that she had been falling in love almost since the night they met in that elevator.

"The best, huh? So does that mean you don't need the present I was going to give you?"

"I didn't say that." Laurel lifted her head, giving Dana a slow kiss. "But maybe first I could—" She slid her hands down the length of Dana's back, tracing her fingernails over silky smooth skin.

Dana shook her head and rolled off. "No. I'm feeding you breakfast now."

Petulantly, Laurel watched Dana go to the tray of food. The sight of her lover's pale, round bottom made her fingers itch to reciprocate the pleasure she'd been given. "But—"

"No way, Doc. I've been planning this morning for weeks. We're playing by my script now."

Laurel felt warm delight at the nickname. *Doc.* It still didn't feel quite real. In a week, she would be starting her new job at the veterinary clinic only two miles from her apartment.

"My script," Dana continued, "has you eating breakfast after experiencing a fabulous orgasm." She sat on the edge of the bed, gesturing for Laurel to sit up.

Laurel regarded her fondly as she propped herself against the headboard with her legs crossed, totally at ease with her nudity. "Well, I *did* just have a fabulous orgasm," she acknowledged.

Dana handed her a bowl of fresh fruit: strawberries, raspberries, cantaloupe, and grapes. Looking inexplicably sheepish, Dana said, "I know they're your favorites."

"They are," Laurel said. She took a bite from one large strawberry, holding out the other half for Dana. She watched straight white teeth take a neat chunk from the fruit, and groaned as her still-sensitive pussy throbbed at the sight. "You're my favorite, too."

Dana blushed, picking at the quilt and looking quite pleased with herself.

"So what are we going to do today?"

"Anything you want. We could go to a movie, go shopping... I'll even go to that silly ceramic-painting place with you, if you want." Dana paused. "Or we could stay in bed for a while."

That was the best idea she'd heard so far. "Let's start by staying in bed."

"Fair enough," Dana said. Stroking Laurel's bare back with her fingers, she asked, "Want your birthday present now?"

"I thought you caved and gave me my present last night." Laurel held up her arm, turning her wrist so she could admire the gold bracelet once again. "And I love it."

Dana looked thrilled all over again. "Well, I have something else for you."

"You spoil me."

"I shouldn't?"

"I wasn't telling you to stop." Laurel munched on her cereal, more interested in making it through the meal so she could touch Dana's body rather than actually tasting the food. "I was just making an observation."

"Very astute."

"So..."

Dana gave her a wide smile of satisfaction. "So?"

Laurel huffed a little, but played along. "So what did you want to give me?"

Dana's eyes sparkled. "Your three fantasies. The ones you mentioned that night...when I spanked you."

Blinking, Laurel said, "Yes, I remember."

Dana gave her an eager nod. "The other two. Anywhere, anytime."

"You mean—"

"I want you to have them. All three." Raising an eyebrow at the tray that sat between them, Dana asked, "Are you done with your food?"

Laurel gave her a distracted nod and Dana moved the tray of mostly eaten breakfast from the bed to the floor.

"I want to…allow you to experience your fantasies. You tell me something you've imagined doing, or that you like, something that turns you on, and I'll do it with you. No hesitation, no questions asked. You can redeem two more fantasies whenever you want."

Laurel slid down under the covers and invited Dana in beside her. Planting her elbow on the bed, she leaned over Dana. Her breasts pressed into Dana's side as a gentle hand stroked her bare back. She looked deep into Dana's eyes, aware of the enormity of this gift.

"Any fantasy?"

Dana nodded and swallowed. Her eyes were alight with a nervous sincerity that made Laurel's pussy clench in deep lust. "Anything. I would try anything with you at least once, if it would make you happy."

If Dana could have gift-wrapped her trust and love, Laurel imagined that this was precisely how she would have felt when opening it. "Three fantasies?"

"And today doesn't count." Dana's lips twitched into a shy smile. "So, uh…happy birthday, Laurel."

Laurel wrapped Dana in a warm, heartfelt hug. "You're right," she said. "It is."

Her mind was already racing with the possibilities.

That Friday

Laurel greeted Dana at the door of her apartment wearing only a fluffy pale blue bathrobe and a wide smile. Dana held a dozen red roses in her hand and leered appropriately at her as she stepped inside.

"You're glowing," Dana said as she handed over the flowers. When Laurel took them, Dana eased an arm around her waist and drew her in for a brief kiss. "Absolutely glowing. And you smell good, too."

"Thank you. I'm nice and clean."

Dana tugged on the belt to her robe, then discarded it on the floor. She parted the terrycloth material and eased her hands inside to stroke Laurel's breasts. "I can see that. And I'm finding you very hard to resist."

"Then my evil plan is working."

"That it is." Dana moved her hands from Laurel's breasts to her bottom, giving her a firm squeeze. "Is this part of the second fantasy?"

"Actually, yes." Laurel gave Dana a coy grin. "I tried something new today."

"What's that?" Dana lowered her mouth to Laurel's neck and trailed tiny, sucking kisses across her throat.

"An enema."

Dana drew back and gave Laurel a look of shocked uncertainty. "Excuse me?"

"I wanted to be clean," Laurel explained. "For tonight. For the second fantasy."

"And what, pray tell, is the second fantasy?" Dana kept her hands on Laurel's buttocks, gripping and releasing each cheek in turn. "I hope like hell it doesn't have anything to do with giving *me* an enema, too."

Laurel chuckled. "Oh, it wasn't that bad. I feel immaculate."

Relaxing into a wicked smile, Dana backed them farther inside, steering Laurel toward the couch. "What do you want me to do with that pristine ass, darling?"

"I want you to fuck it," Laurel said. Her lips twitched when she saw a flash of heat in Dana's eyes at her quiet words.

"With my fingers?" Dana's throat worked, and she exhaled shakily.

Laurel shook her head as she sank onto the couch. *Been there, done that.* Now was the time to try new things. She pulled Dana down onto the cushion next to her. "With a dildo. I actually bought one for the occasion."

Dana looked at her with a mixture of lust and awe. "Really?"

"Really." Laurel trailed her fingertip along Dana's jaw, then her collarbone. "I've always fantasized about having anal sex involving more than a finger, but I've never tried it before. I've never had someone I wanted to try it with."

"Am I supposed to—"

"Wear it," Laurel said, guessing what Dana's question would be. "I want to feel you against my body while you're inside me."

Dana shivered in her arms. "Are you nervous?" she asked.

"Somewhat. I'll be honest, it's a little intimidating." She gave Dana a meaningful look. "But I trust you."

"Even though I've never done this before?"

Laurel held back her giggle at the tentative question, sensing the emotion behind the words. "That just makes us even," she said. "Have I managed to come up with another fantasy that makes you nervous?"

Dana dropped her eyes. "I—"

Laurel put her hand on Dana's cheek, and slid it down to cup her chin. "Don't be embarrassed to tell me when you're uncertain about something."

Dana lifted her gaze so she could look into Laurel's eyes. "Again, I just don't want to hurt you."

"You won't," Laurel said. She'd anticipated this and was prepared to respond. "I won't let you hurt me. We're going to go slow, use lots of lube, and talk to each other." Slipping her hand into Dana's, she added, "If it hurts or I don't like it, I'll stop it. I promise."

"Quicksilver?" Dana's half-smile didn't entirely disguise her apprehension.

"I promise," Laurel repeated. "Please trust me on that."

Dana gave her a sage nod. "Okay. Will you give me five minutes to get ready?"

Get ready? Laurel tried to decide what Dana needed to prepare and wondered if she simply needed some space to gather herself. Pulling the two halves of her robe together and retying her belt, she left her lover with a throaty murmur. "Don't take too long. I've been thinking about this *all* day."

"Why don't you go lie down and think about it some more?" Dana raked her eyes over Laurel's body like she was on display. "Get yourself wet for me."

Laurel was well aware of the slickness already coating her upper thighs as she walked toward the door. "That won't be a problem."

"Just don't make yourself come," Dana called after her.

Laurel escorted Isis from the bedroom and closed the door. She threw open the lid of the wooden trunk next to her bed and took out the still-boxed double dildo that had arrived in the mail just the day before. *That was cutting it close*, she mused, and opened her new toy.

She tossed the box in the trash can and stooped to remove two condoms from one corner of the trunk, and a large bottle of lube from the other. Supplies in hand, she went to the bed.

She lay on the bed with the toy next to her on the nightstand, her robe spread open beneath her, and her hand moving between her thighs, Laurel started worrying about what Dana was doing. It had definitely been five minutes since she'd come in here. Maybe even seven.

Was Dana really that scared? Was she trying to avoid this? Laurel didn't want to force her into anything she found distasteful. Or frightening.

Sitting up on the bed, she tried to decide whether to break down and go find Dana or give her another minute or two to get ready. Thirty seconds later, Laurel went back into the front room, decision made. If Dana had reservations about this, she wanted a chance to change her fantasy before the evening was spoiled and the mood destroyed.

Cross-legged on the couch, Dana was hunched over Laurel's laptop computer with a look of intense concentration on her face. She'd turned off the lamps in the room, and the glow from the screen lit her up in a way that made Laurel sigh in appreciation. She stood and watched Dana read for almost twenty more seconds before Dana looked up and blinked in surprise.

"Hey," Dana said. She dragged her gaze up and down the length of Laurel's nude body. "I'm taking too long, aren't I?"

Laurel nodded and crossed the room to stand in front of Dana. Those languid green eyes were just about level with the dark patch of curls Laurel had trimmed for the occasion. Dana immediately set aside the laptop and reached up to grip Laurel's buttocks in both hands. She brought her mouth between Laurel's legs and gave her a wet kiss.

"I'm sorry," Dana mumbled. She nuzzled into Laurel, pushing her nose between slick folds, grazing her swollen clit. "I was just about to join you, I swear."

"What are you doing out here?" Laurel asked. She ran her fingers through Dana's thick auburn hair, holding her face close. She was rather enjoying the intimate apology.

"Research." A silky, repentant tongue lapped down and up her labia; lips sucked at her clit. "About anal sex."

Laurel groaned. "Online?"

Dana nodded and spread her with gentle fingers. "Frequently asked questions." She played the tip of her tongue over intricate folds, sending a shuddering thrill to the tips of Laurel's toes. Pulling back, she said, "I learned a lot."

"Oh, yeah?" Laurel lifted one foot and planted it on the couch beside Dana's hip, opening herself up to the mouth that was still engaged in slow exploration. Her hand continued to stroke Dana's hair. "Feeling more confident now?"

Dana gripped her calf with one hand and spent some time moving her mouth up and down in worship; she laved her tongue over a swollen clit, pressed inside her opening, then farther down, teased the tight ring of puckered flesh. The foot that remained on the carpet began to tremble, and Laurel's legs shook at what Dana was doing with her tongue. She tugged on Dana's hair, pulling her away.

"I need to sit down."

"I need to lick you until you come," Dana countered. She growled and nuzzled her patch of dark hairs with her face.

"Can we compromise?" Laurel giggled. When Dana brought her mouth back against her pussy and shook her head, emitting a pleased hum, Laurel pitched to the side with a little squeal.

Dana caught her around the waist and helped ease her onto a warm lap. "Okay, okay. Compromise. Let's go to the bedroom and I'll lick you."

"Aren't you going to tell me what you've learned?" Laurel asked. She watched Dana's hands stroking her bare breasts. She leaned into the caress, feeling her nipples harden against Dana's palms.

"I'll tell you on the way to the bedroom," Dana said distractedly. She stared at Laurel's breasts with a look of intense hunger, as she often did.

I'm not sure I've ever seen a woman so in love with the female breast before, Laurel mused. She wasn't even sure she'd had that many male customers at the strip club who had so thoroughly devoured her chest with their eyes. She ran a hand through Dana's hair and smiled when both of her lover's hands squeezed her firmly, thumbs making circles around her tight nipples.

"You know, your breasts were the first thing I noticed about you," Dana said.

Laurel erupted into giggles. "How romantic, honey."

Dana gave her a helpless shrug and a sheepish smile. "What can I say? You shoved them right in my face as soon as we met. I couldn't help but notice." Bending forward, she caught a nipple between her lips and sucked.

Laurel kept her hand on the back of Dana's neck. "I could tell you liked them," she murmured. "I was turned on, dancing for you. My nipples were so hard."

Dana nodded and kissed over to her other nipple. "Loved them. Most perfect breasts in the world."

As much as she didn't want to lose the wet heat of her mouth, Laurel had to forcefully disengage Dana from her task. At this rate, they would never make it into the bedroom. "Darling, the bed?" she gasped as Dana leaned in for another nibble to her areola.

"Right," Dana mumbled. She helped Laurel to stand, and rose

behind her so she could wrap strong arms around her stomach. Kissing the back of Laurel's neck, she whispered, "The first thing I learned is that I'm going to have to get you very wet and excited. Very ready."

Laurel walked them to the bedroom with Dana still wrapped around her middle. "That sounds like fun."

"I think it'll be a lot of fun," Dana said. She closed the door behind them, giving Laurel a smoldering grin.

Laurel turned to face Dana when they reached the bed, raising her hands to unbutton Dana's white dress shirt. Dana was wearing the power suit minus the jacket, and she looked deliciously sexy. "You already had dinner, right?"

"I grabbed something on the way over," Dana said. She allowed Laurel to undress her with a lazy smile on her face. "I thought that hopping right into bed sounded like an excellent way to end the workweek."

"An excellent way," Laurel echoed. After pushing Dana's shirt over her shoulders, she reached around and took off her bra with both hands. She nodded over to the nightstand as she moved to unbutton Dana's pants. "Did you see what I bought?"

She watched Dana discover the toy with a widening of her eyes. "Wow."

"What do you think?" Laurel asked. She knelt on the carpet as she pulled Dana's pants down her legs and helped her step out of them. Kissing her soft belly on the way back up, Laurel slipped her hands into the back of Dana's black panties and held her in a loving embrace. "Look interesting?"

"This does seem to be the night for trying new things," Dana said. She pulled away from Laurel so she could retrieve the double dildo from the nightstand. Pointing at the more bulbous end, she asked, "This part goes inside me?"

Laurel cleared her throat and nodded. She knew the end that went in the wearer was a little larger than Dana was used to accommodating, and she watched her carefully for an honest reaction. "According to the reviews I read online, you don't even have to use a harness with it."

Dana weighed the purple silicone object in her hand. "Nice," she said, and raised her eyes to Laurel's. "Lie on the bed."

Laurel obeyed without question. There was excitement shining in Dana's eyes, pure and simple, and she saw it instantly. She knew she wasn't going to have to change her fantasy. That little bit of online research Dana had sneaked in seemed to have injected her with new confidence, and so Laurel was grateful she'd taken the seven minutes to do it.

Dana laid the toy back on the nightstand and climbed into bed. Pulling Laurel into a heated embrace, Dana managed to get her flat on her back before she knew what was happening. A hand rubbed down her side and over her hip before slipping between her legs.

"I love having sex with you," Dana growled. She rubbed her fingertips over Laurel's clit, then moved down to slip one finger inside. "I've been daydreaming about this all day."

"That must have made work fun," Laurel said. She gave Dana a playful smile, then a low moan when the thrusting started in earnest.

Dana chuckled. "If my developers had any idea what I think about during project meetings—"

"They'd be impressed," Laurel said. "I happen to know that you've got quite an imagination."

"Nah." Dana's thumb found Laurel's clit as her finger continued to work in and out of her slick opening. Pressing a second finger inside during one smooth thrust, she said, "I've just got a really kinky girlfriend."

"I can't help it if you inspire me," Laurel said. Then she closed her eyes and enjoyed how Dana fucked her so perfectly it curled her toes.

"Just like you inspire me." The hand left, fingers removed and thumb taken away, and Laurel groaned in disappointment. It turned into a loud moan a moment later, when Dana's mouth replaced her hand.

Dana was masterful at oral sex. Those times when Laurel lay with her legs spread and Dana's tongue on her pussy were like pure Zen, a state of perfection she had never attained with another lover. Tonight, she nearly died when the tongue that lapped at her clit suddenly moved down and hands spread her buttocks, and all of a sudden Dana was licking her anus.

Laurel arched her back, allowing Dana to pull her closer to her face. Her clit throbbed at the new sensation of being licked in such a sensitive place, and when Dana pressed just the tip of her tongue inside the tight pucker, Laurel cried out in pleasure.

"Dana, please—" she whimpered. She was so close her whole body was shaking. *How did that happen so fast?*

A gentle thumb found her swollen clit and rubbed in large circles, applying just the amount of pressure she liked as Dana continued to lick at her anus. After a moment, all movement stopped and Dana pulled away right as she hovered at the brink, causing Laurel to gasp her alarm.

"It's okay, honey," Dana panted. "I just want you to turn over. Butt in the air."

Laurel moved quickly, eager for Dana to touch her again and send her crashing into orgasm. She was ready, body slick with sweat, pussy wet and open. She thrust her ass into the air and laid her face on the pillow, moaning into it when Dana pulled her open with one hand and moved the other to her clit. Exposed, she whimpered when Dana began licking her anus once more.

It didn't take her long to come. Only thirty uninterrupted seconds of her lover's fingers on her clit and tongue in her ass, and she was moaning and trembling and falling onto the mattress to recover. Dana moved up on the bed and gathered her into a loving embrace as she collapsed, hugging her close.

"That was another thing I learned online," Dana said, and kissed her face. "To relax and stimulate you, get you nice and open. I was going to do it before I fucked you, but I got impatient and wanted to try it now."

Laurel managed a dazed chuckle. "I'm glad. I enjoyed that a lot."

"I could tell," Dana said, and shot her a confident grin. "Should I try to put that toy in me now?"

Sitting up, Laurel leaned over Dana's chest to grab the double dildo from the nightstand. "Let me."

Dana propped herself up on her elbows, looking down at her own body. "God, I'm already so wet—"

Laurel's mouth watered at the thought. "No good," she said, and snagged a condom. "This thing is supposed to stay inside you. We don't want you *too* wet."

"Oh." Dana shifted on the bed, squirming beneath Laurel. "Um, should I—"

Laurel crawled down Dana's body and set the toy aside, then pulled Dana's leg over her shoulder. She felt Dana fall backward against the pillows. "I'll take care of it," Laurel murmured. She dragged the length of her tongue up along puffy labia, pulling sweet wetness into her mouth. "Lick you clean."

Dana groaned and tangled a hand in her hair. She tilted her hips, brushing dark curls against Laurel's nose. "I think this is my favorite thing in the world."

Laurel made a happy noise as she slid her tongue over slick, fragrant flesh. It was her favorite thing, too. Especially with Dana, who made the best noises she had ever heard.

By the time Dana's pale thighs trembled and her hips began to thrust against Laurel's mouth, the air was filled with breathy, wanton moans and whimpers, and Laurel was nearly ready to come again just listening to her. Laurel teased her opening, then moved back up to suck at her clit. She stroked the swollen shaft with her lips, flicked at the tip with her tongue.

Dana came with a loud cry. Her back arched and her heels dug into the mattress, nearly dislodging Laurel from her spot between her thighs. Laurel hung on and lapped at her until she calmed, relaxing boneless on top of twisted sheets.

"Holy shit," Dana said, when she finally spoke. She pushed Laurel's face away with a gentle hand. "Honey, you're going to wear me out before I can fulfill your fantasy."

"I wouldn't want that," Laurel said. She grabbed the dildo and covered the more bulbous end with the condom, then pressed it against Dana, who was as wet and relaxed as she had ever seen her. "Are you ready for this?"

"Definitely," Dana murmured. "Go ahead."

She took the toy easily. Laurel was a little surprised by how smoothly it slid in, and by the way Dana spread her legs wide and accepted it with a loud groan of pleasure. She settled it into position, so that the longer, slimmer shaft jutted out from between Dana's legs.

"Nice." Laurel slid her hand down the length of the toy. "How does it feel?"

Dana gave her a lazy grin. "Very good. May I fuck you for a minute?"

Laurel scooted up on the bed so she could lie at Dana's side, then spread her legs. Playing with new toys always made her a little giddy. "I love a girl with initiative."

Dana set a time record for rolling a condom onto a dildo and settling into position between Laurel's thighs. The hard length of the toy pressed against Laurel's labia, and she planted her feet and rubbed her pussy up and down over it. Knowing that the other end rested inside Dana's body, that they would soon be joined so intimately, was making her so hot she could hardly stand it.

"Go inside me," Laurel said. "I want to feel you inside me."

Dana reached between their bodies and guided the head of the dildo to Laurel's entrance. "You're so sexy, baby. I want you so much."

"Then take me," Laurel said. She wrapped one leg around Dana's hip and curled an arm across her shoulders. Pushing her hips up, she coaxed her lover inside. "Please."

Silently, Dana entered her, then planted both hands on the pillow next to Laurel's head. Her hips moved slow and steady, inch after inch sinking into her, the progress unhurried and torturous. Dana moved one hand to Laurel's hip, pulling her tightly against her groin.

"Oh, I like this," Dana breathed. She kissed Laurel's neck, exhaling with a moan.

Laurel moved beneath Dana, hissing in pleasure at the way their breasts pressed together. Dana's hips pressed against her slowly at first, then faster, harder, filling her with ardent strokes. Laurel wrapped her arms around Dana's shoulders, holding her tight. She met the thrusts with enthusiasm, her sweat-slicked skin sliding against Dana's as they moved in desperate rhythm.

"I love fucking you like this," Dana murmured into her ear. She ground her pelvis into Laurel, buried to the hilt. "I love *feeling* it when I fuck you. Feeling it deep inside me—" She stopped talking, groaned, shuddered in pleasure.

Laurel held Dana tight, running her hands down her back until she could grip her ass, which clenched and relaxed as she pumped into Laurel's body. "Do you think you can come again?"

"Yes," Dana said, teeth gritted.

Laurel was sure she could also come again, but she wanted to hold out and let Dana penetrate her anally while she was as excited as possible. Still, she wanted to feel Dana come inside her. She tightened her legs around Dana's hips and scratched her fingernails up over the small of her back.

"Do it, honey," Laurel whispered. She latched onto Dana's neck with her mouth, sucking hard, teeth scraping over porcelain skin. "I want to feel you come."

Propping herself up on her hands, Dana jerked her hips more rapidly, fucking both of them and grinding wantonly against the juncture of their toy. Laurel closed her eyes as the pleasure rose in her abdomen and between her legs, trying not to give in to the climax that lurked just beyond her reach. She moaned and grunted and gasped along with Dana, letting her hear how good this felt, but she kept a tight lid on her control. She wasn't ready to let go.

Her control was nearly shattered when Dana stiffened, lifted her head, and trembled as she came with a burst of sound. Sweat dripped from Dana's face onto Laurel's neck, snaking lazy trails across her skin. Her face was contorted with ecstatic release. After a moment she relaxed and rested on Laurel's body, heavy and sated, covering her upper chest with passionate kisses.

"Oh, Laurel. God, Laurel—"

Laurel was almost beside herself with wanting. "I want to try it now, honey. In my ass—"

Dana nodded and pulled out, panting for air. "I know."

"You've got me so turned on I don't know what to do with myself."

Rather than offer suggestions, Dana merely kissed her way down Laurel's body until her mouth covered her hot pussy once again. Laurel groaned in appreciation and spread her legs wide, feeling ready for just about anything Dana could give. She went wild when Dana's tongue began lapping at her anus again.

"Oh, fuck, Dana." Laurel squirmed on her tongue, keening in pleasure. "Oh, please. Please, please, please."

Dana drew back and sank a heavily lubricated finger into her ass. Laurel blinked in surprise; she hadn't even seen her go for the bottle of lube. She took the single finger easily, and the tender penetration felt absolutely delicious.

"Yes," Laurel hissed. She gritted her teeth and writhed around on Dana's hand, face twisted in pleasure. "Yes. Yes."

"Feels good," Dana said, not so much a question as a statement of fact. She twisted her finger, thrusting in and out of the tight opening.

Laurel nodded in agreement. "Try another one," she gasped.

She expected it to be harder to take two of Dana's fingers, but they slipped right in and pressed deep inside her ass with no resistance. Grunting in pleasure at the sensation, Laurel willed herself to relax so she could experience the incredible satisfaction of being filled so thoroughly. It was the first time she'd taken more than a single finger there. She looked into Dana's loving green eyes and shared an excited smile at their accomplishment.

"You still feel good?" Dana asked, wearing a goofy grin.

"Excellent," Laurel said. "Like I can take more."

Dana pushed and pulled her fingers in gentle, driving rhythm. Laurel could feel her twirling and rubbing, spreading them slightly apart, in an effort to open her up for the dildo. She closed her eyes and smiled in contentment.

"Oh, God, Dana," Laurel whispered.

"We're going to do this with you on your back," Dana said. She continued to fuck her using her fingers, slow thrusts, and deep. "That Web site said that it's the most comfortable position."

Laurel gazed up at Dana with a grateful moan. "Perfect. I want to look at your eyes."

Dana withdrew her fingers and placed the head of the silicone shaft against Laurel's relaxed anus. She could feel Dana pour more lube onto the dildo, and it dribbled down her buttocks as Dana's hand worked it up and down the length of the toy. "We go at your speed, okay? I'm going to provide pressure, but I want you to guide me."

Laurel bit her lip and nodded, trying desperately not to tense up now that the moment was here. "I'm ready."

Dana pressed forward slightly, pushing against her anus with the tip of the dildo. "Rub your clit, honey, and push against me when you try to take me in."

"Push against you?" Laurel repeated.

"As if you're trying to…expel," Dana explained. "I, uh, read it."

"Well, if you read it online, it must be true." Laurel reached down and started rubbing circles over her engorged clit. Groaning, she tacked on an affectionate, "Geek."

Dana held the base of the toy with one hand and used the other to pinch Laurel's left nipple, then the right. "You love this geek."

"Yes, I do," Laurel said. She took a deep breath, relaxed, then bore down on the dildo while pushing her muscles against the pressure. She sucked in a shocked breath when she opened up and accepted the first half inch inside with a slight, burning sting. "Oh."

Dana continued to pinch and twist at her nipples. "Keep rubbing your clit, honey. Relax and open up to me."

Laurel gave her a determined nod. "Go inside me a little more."

Using her hand to steady her, Dana pressed deeper. Laurel felt her anus relax and accept the whole head of the dildo. Her muscle tightened down around the slimmer shaft, and Laurel held up a shaky hand to stop Dana's advance.

"No more?" Dana asked. Her thighs were tensed and she looked ready to retreat.

"Just…let me get used to it for a minute."

Dana nodded and stayed still as Laurel rubbed her clit. She teased dusky pink nipples for a while, then traced her finger down the arm that worked between Laurel's thighs. She pressed a single digit inside Laurel's pussy with a low groan.

Laurel opened her mouth in a soundless cry. She felt so full, so possessed, and she found herself craving more. She brought her knees up, planted her feet on the bed, and moved farther onto Dana's dildo. Another inch, two more, and she stopped them again.

Dana kept up a steady, driving rhythm with her finger. "How does it feel, honey? Do you like it?"

Gritting her teeth, Laurel rubbed frantic circles around her clit. Now that the initial discomfort had subsided, she was feeling unbelievable things from the dildo inside in her ass. She wanted to take the rest, and then she wanted Dana to take her. "It's good. Just give me a minute—"

"Take all the time you need," Dana said. She fingered Laurel firmly, now pressing up against her g-spot. "This is all about you, baby, and making you feel good."

Laurel closed her eyes and flared her nostrils when a sudden surge of pleasure hit her low in the belly. Her thighs trembled as she tried to hold back the inevitable. She was going to come if she wasn't careful. And she didn't want to come until Dana was buried in her ass.

"More," she whispered, and opened her eyes to look into Dana's face. "Give me the rest, Dana."

So she did. Slowly, carefully, sliding in smooth and deep, in one steady motion that left Laurel gasping in pleasure. When Dana was completely inside, she stopped her hips and held still.

"Tell me when I can move," Dana murmured. Her eyes flashed with need. "And don't stop rubbing your clit."

Laurel's hand, which she'd stilled in an effort to draw out her climax, started working hard again at Dana's command. Then Dana's finger started thrusting into her pussy once more, and Laurel couldn't stand to wait any longer.

"Move," she whimpered to Dana. "Fuck me, slow at first."

Dana made careful, precise movements, easing the dildo in and out of her anus with cautious thrusts. She was slow, gentle, and her eyes never left Laurel's, ostensibly seeking out any sign of displeasure on her face.

Not that she would find anything.

Laurel's eyes threatened to roll into the back of her head. Every part of her felt like it was on fire. Her clit throbbed and swelled beneath her fingers, so hypersensitive that she could barely touch it without crying out. Dana's finger blazed a slick, hot path deep inside her pussy, searching out and rubbing at all her sensitive spots. And her ass was so full, contracting with burning pleasure around the dildo that thrust inside her body.

Faster now, and so deep. She could feel Dana's finger stroking the thin wall that separated her from the toy, and a thrill skittered down her spine.

She tried to warn Dana. "I'm going to—"

But it was too late.

The orgasm ripped through Laurel's body, stealing her words from her throat. She let out a loud cry, voice cracking, head thrown back. Her fingers made jerky, spastic movements on her clit, drawing every last bit of pleasure from herself even as she lost control entirely.

Dana stayed with her, slowing the motion of her hips but continuing to thrust with her hand. "That's it, honey. That's it. Give it to me."

Laurel's voice went hoarse as she moaned and laughed and shook and shuddered, aftershocks rumbling through her body for some time after she peaked. For a brief, dizzying moment, she almost thought she would never feel normal again. Then her body weakened and she collapsed onto the bed, nothing left to give.

"Wow," Laurel whispered. It wasn't nearly the right thing to say, but her vocabulary was severely limited at that moment. "Just wow."

"Wow," Dana echoed. She wore a look of awe, and just a little caution. "It felt like you came really hard."

Laurel shivered, contracting around Dana's finger, around the dildo. "Oh, yeah." She caressed the side of Dana's face. "You were amazing."

"You were," Dana said. "You are."

"I love you." Laurel blinked, feeling her eyes well with tears. The words weren't enough; nothing she could say would ever come close to being enough to make Dana understand. "I—"

Dana leaned down carefully, capturing Laurel's lips in a gentle kiss. "I know, baby. I love you, so much." She drew back, then reached between their bodies. "I'm going to pull out now, okay?"

"Okay," Laurel said. She closed her eyes and helped Dana expel the dildo, groaning as she felt every inch withdrawn. Then Dana's finger left, and she was empty. She grabbed at Dana's thigh as her lover pulled the bulbous end of the toy out of her with a soft groan. "I want you."

"You had me," Dana reminded with a playful smirk.

"I want you on top of me," Laurel said. "I want you to hold me."

Dana dropped the dildo off the side of the bed. "Consider it done," she said, and gathered Laurel into a strong hug. She held her and rocked her gently, murmuring nonsense words.

And Laurel fell even deeper in love.

A BAD DAY

L aurel was sitting on the couch when Dana got home from work, clutching Isis in her arms and rocking her back and forth. Her eyes were sore from the tears she hadn't been able to hold back, and she felt a wave of relief when she heard Dana unlock the door with her spare key. Looking at the clock, Laurel was surprised that it was already six in the evening. That meant she'd been crying for nearly half an hour now.

Dana's sunny smile faded as she walked into the apartment and met Laurel's eyes. "Laurel?" She walked over to the couch, clearly concerned. "Honey?"

Almost against her will, Laurel felt her lower lip poke out and fresh tears gather in her stinging eyes. "I had a bad day," she whispered.

Immediately Dana dropped her briefcase and sat down on the couch close to Laurel. "What happened, honey?" She drew her eyebrows together, studying Laurel's face. "And why didn't you call me?"

"I...lost my first patient today," Laurel whispered. Her face screwed up in pain at the memory, and she looked away from her lover's stare. "I didn't call you because you were working. I knew you were coming over tonight, so—"

"Oh, no," Dana said. She wore her sympathy plainly, and Laurel felt a slight easing of her grief at the sight. Wrapping her arm around Laurel's shoulder, Dana tugged her closer. "Do you want to talk about it?"

Laurel shook her head, but started talking anyway. "I can deal with euthanizing an animal, you know? When an animal is old or diseased, and it's suffering, there's a reason for it, and I can deal with it. But today—" She pulled Isis closer, burying her face in her silky fur. "They brought in this all-black cat. Three years old."

"What was wrong with her?"

Laurel felt a sob threaten to tear from her throat. "I'm not sure. She was poisoned somehow. We…don't know, exactly."

"Poisoned?" Dana dropped her eyes to Isis, then looked up at Laurel. "How?"

"Her owners said she was an outdoor cat. She was out overnight and when she came back, she was having trouble breathing. They brought her in to us and we basically fed her drugs while we watched the poison work its way through her system." Laurel let out a sob, scaring Isis into leaping from her lap onto the floor. With a glance backward, the cat loped away from the couch, down the hallway.

Dana scooted closer and pulled Laurel into her arms. She went willingly, collapsing into a desperate hug.

"There was nothing you could do?"

Laurel shook her head, burying her face in Dana's shoulder. "I just watched her die. Nothing we gave her seemed to have any effect. She went into respiratory failure and she was having these horrible seizures." She shuddered at the memory. "It was the most awful thing I've ever seen."

Dana shushed her and began a gentle rocking motion, soothing Laurel with soft caresses up and down her back. "I'm so sorry, honey."

Sniffling, Laurel mumbled, "I know I'm a professional and I should be able to handle this, but—"

"Handle this?" Dana frowned at Laurel. "You had to watch an animal die an ugly death today. Why should you be able to handle that?"

"She looked a lot like Isis," Laurel whispered. Fresh tears spilled from her stinging eyes. "That's all I kept thinking, the whole time. How much she looked like Isis."

Dana laid back on the couch and settled Laurel on top of her body. "Isis is just fine, honey. She's inside and she's safe."

Laurel sniffled and rested her ear on Dana's chest. She closed her eyes, lulled by her lover's heartbeat. "I get so mad when I see bad things happen to cats because they live outside. I know some people believe cats belong outdoors, but I can't even imagine." She looked down the hallway where Isis had disappeared, wishing she had her within view. "She's my little baby and I can't even imagine letting her out and putting her at the mercy of nature, human or otherwise."

"I understand," Dana murmured. She stroked Laurel's back. "You should have called me, honey. Even if you didn't want to do it at work, you didn't need to suffer alone. I could've tried to leave earlier—"

"I didn't want to bother you."

Dana sat up, dislodging Laurel from her place in her arms. "Bother me?"

Laurel turned at the sound of distress in Dana's voice, and her stomach dropped at the crestfallen expression that greeted her. "I didn't mean—"

"You thought it would bother me if you called and told me you were having a bad day?" Dana kept her hands on Laurel's hips, but it felt like some distance had grown between them. "I want to be the one to make you feel better when you're sad. I want the first thing you do when you're upset to be to pick up the phone and call me. I thought—"

"Dana," she interrupted. "Please, honey." She gave Dana a helpless shrug. "I'm sorry. It's not that I didn't think you would want to be there for me. It's just that I felt silly."

"Nothing that makes you upset is silly," Dana said. "No matter what it is."

"But—"

"And you never need to feel silly with me. I love you, Laurel. When you're hurting, I hurt. And knowing that you're choosing to hurt alone makes me want to cry."

"You're absolutely right," Laurel said after a few seconds. "I would want you to call me if you were upset about something. Of course you would want the same thing."

"Of course I would." Dana pressed her lips against Laurel's, holding the sweet contact for a number of breaths. Drawing back, she asked, "Do I not tell you well enough? How I feel?"

"You tell me just fine. Maybe sometimes I just don't listen well enough."

"Maybe I need to tell you more." Dana hugged her tight, stroking up and down her sides. "Laurel, you're the most important thing to me. I want to know everything about you. I want to be with you when you're happy, and I especially want to be with you when you're sad. I want the chance to make you feel better."

"You do make me feel better," Laurel whispered. From the moment Dana had walked in the door, her heart had been healing from her long, stressful day. "Believe me, you do."

"How can I make you feel better tonight?"

Laurel's mood shifted almost immediately and she started to smirk, then thought better of it. For once, she truly didn't feel like having sex. "We could order pizza and watch a movie on the couch." Wiping damp strands of hair away from her eyes, she said, "You could let me choose the movie. Something nice and happy and romantic."

"Done." Dana reached into her pocket and drew out a slim cell phone. "Usual place?"

"Yeah." Laurel leaned back on the arm of the couch and gazed at her. "I'm glad you came over tonight."

"Me, too," Dana said as she dialed. "Same thing? Small pizza with green peppers, onions, tomatoes, and no cheese?"

Laurel gave her an enthusiastic nod. There was such comfort in having someone who knew her pizza order by heart. Realistically, it was close to the bottom of the long list of reasons she adored Dana, but it warmed her heart nonetheless.

"Yes, I'll hold." Dana smiled at her. "You're weird, you know. Pizza without cheese? Blasphemy."

Laurel wrinkled her nose. "I started eating it like that when I was stripping. It was my way of justifying having something like pizza as long as the shape of my body determined the size of my paycheck. Turns out it's actually very good that way."

As Dana recited their standard order into the phone, Laurel retreated into her bedroom to change. Now that she knew they were staying in, she was determined to be comfortable. When she returned to the front room in her pajama bottoms and a tank top, she found Dana on the couch with Isis curled in her lap. Even from her spot across the room, Laurel could see Isis kneading her oversized paws in contentment as Dana stroked her fur. Surprised, she stopped in the doorway and watched in amused silence. It was the first time she'd seen Dana choosing to cuddle with her cat.

"Thanks for taking care of her until I got here," Dana murmured to the lounging Isis. "And I'm telling you right now: you are never, *ever* allowed to go outside. I don't care how much you beg me once I'm living with you, I'm going to be firm on that one."

Laurel raised her hand to her mouth and tried to hold back her smile. That Dana was holding a serious conversation with her cat made her entire body feel warm; that her lover had so casually mentioned living together—to Isis, of all audiences—brought joyful tears to her eyes.

She was determined to go at Dana's pace, but in this instance, she couldn't resist giving her a little nudge. Stepping into the room, she cleared her throat. "You know, Isis was asking me about that."

Dana jumped, apparently startled at Laurel's entrance. "Asking you about what?"

"When you're going to stop leaving for extended periods of time." Laurel crossed the room and handed Dana the pajama pants and T-shirt she kept at Laurel's place for overnights. Sitting down next to her, she said, "I tried to explain to her that you have your own place, but she thought it was kind of silly. We spend almost every night together, and having two places means that she just gets left alone on occasion."

"And she doesn't like being alone," Dana said. "I guess it is pretty silly. When you put it like that."

"Well, Isis thinks so, anyway."

Dana looked down at the black cat, scratching behind her ear. "You'd really share your mom with me?"

Isis didn't respond.

"Isis," Laurel cooed, in the voice she knew would get a response from her chatty cat. "What do you say?"

Blinking sleepy golden eyes, Isis raised her head and meowed.

Dana looked from cat to human, raising an eyebrow. "What did she say?"

"I think it was 'if you're having pizza, I want tuna fish.'" Laurel moved closer to Dana, slipping an arm around her shoulders. "Either that or 'stop anthropomorphizing me.'"

Dana tipped her head back and laughed out loud, which once again sent Isis scurrying out of the room. Laurel took advantage of the vacant real estate on Dana's lap and scooted closer.

"I love your sense of humor," Dana said, still chuckling. "I mean, I just love you."

"Would you love to live with me?"

Dana's eyes lit up, and she didn't even hesitate. "In a heartbeat. I don't know why we've left it this long. What's it been? Eight months?"

"The best eight months of my life," Laurel said.

Dana paused on a smile, as if delighted by a secret thought. "I think the best is still to come," she said.

"Count on it," Laurel said. "Your place or mine?"

"How about ours?" Dana said. "I wouldn't mind finding a bigger place than either of us has. And...I guess I'd really like someplace where we can start fresh together."

Before she could get too excited, Laurel felt obligated to give her proper warning. "You've never lived with someone before. I've probably got some bad habits." *I have a feeling we could be the lesbian Felix and Oscar here.*

"You've got a lot of great ones, too," Dana said. "Like loving me." Squeezing Laurel in a tight hug, she whispered into her ear. "Oh, and licking me."

"Is that it?" Laurel teased. "The extent of my great habits?"

"I doubt it. But those are two of my very favorites."

"Do you feel ready for this, sweetheart? I mean, I know I just came out of nowhere with this, and I don't want to feel like I'm pressuring you—"

"Are you kidding?" Dana asked. "I hate it every time you leave. Or I leave. I hate being away from you." She gave Laurel a serious look. "If I hadn't already been planning to come over tonight, would you have called and told me that you were upset and needed me here?"

Laurel couldn't lie. "I don't know. Probably."

"If we live together, you promise you'll always call me if something bad happens to you? Or if you're unhappy?"

"Whether or not I live with you, yes," Laurel said. "I promise." She tucked her head under Dana's neck and breathed in her scent. "I've learned my lesson. I'm feeling one hundred percent better now that you're here."

Dana pulled her close, running a gentle hand over the side of her breast. "Want to start looking for apartments this weekend?"

Laurel blinked in happy surprise. The day had just turned around, and in grand fashion. "Definitely. And I want to do something else very soon, too. Maybe after we've moved. I don't want to be distracted."

"Sounds interesting." Dana nibbled on Laurel's earlobe, and nuzzled into her neck. "What do you want, sweet girl?"

"My third fantasy."

Dana released a low, rumbling noise from deep in her throat. "I was hoping you'd say that."

A Glitch

Dana stalked out of the bedroom with a grumpy scowl on her face, looking beautiful but surly in a dark gray suit. Laurel stood in the kitchen, silently packing each of them a bag lunch to take to work. Spreading mustard on a turkey sandwich for Dana, she watched her cautiously.

Would Dana break the ice, or would she have to do it?

They'd traded sharp words just minutes ago, Dana storming around after finding a wet towel hanging over the shower door dripping onto the floor. She hated untidiness, and apparently water on the bathroom floor was a high crime. Her first words to Laurel that morning were sharp. *What the hell? Are you trying to make a mess?*

Laurel had sniped back, irritated at the reproof in the place of the hug and kiss she'd grown accustomed to. *Well, you're charming this morning, my little ray of sunshine.*

And that was the last time they'd spoken before Dana shoved the bathroom door closed and Laurel stomped away to the kitchen. Exactly seventeen minutes had elapsed. Laurel knew because she had been keeping count, her stomach uneasy because of the mood between them. She listened but kept her head down as Dana swept into the kitchen and shuffled around preparing a fresh pot of rich-smelling coffee. Dana didn't say anything as she worked. Neither did Laurel, leaving their morning routine to be carried out in silent efficiency.

It was the end of their second week in the new apartment together, and as they neared the end of unpacking all the boxes, they were going through a crash course in each other's habits. Dana was the consummate neatnik, just as Laurel had expected. Laurel was more mellow than Dana, though she guessed her lover would label her ways "messy." Laurel really had been trying to be more conscientious about her environment, and until this morning, Dana seemed to be exercising a remarkable amount of good-natured patience whenever she slipped up.

Learning all of Dana's pet peeves wasn't an easy task, and Laurel thought she deserved more credit than she'd been granted in the bathroom.

"Where's my briefcase?" Dana's voice was strained. She stood on the other side of the kitchen counter, in the dining room. "I left it by the door, but I'm not seeing it there."

Laurel lifted her eyes. "I put it in the front closet."

"The front closet. Of course." Mumbling something inaudible, Dana strode away.

Fighting off tears, Laurel stuffed a banana into one of the brown paper bags and rolled the top closed just as Dana returned. Managing a pained half-smile, she offered it to her. "Here's your lunch."

Dana's face softened a little, and she set her briefcase on the floor and took the bag, carefully avoiding Laurel's fingers. "Oh. Thanks."

"No problem." Laurel met her gaze warily. She itched to touch Dana's hand but held back, not sure the contact would be appreciated. "It's just a turkey sandwich."

Dana expelled a deep sigh and put the bag down on the counter. "I'm sorry, honey."

Despite the way her stomach ached with tension over their argument, Laurel wasn't quite ready to let it go. "Why?"

"For causing our first fight."

At the hangdog look on Dana's face, Laurel managed a faint smile. "Too late. You already apologized to me for that."

Dana tilted her head, obviously confused. "I did?"

"This isn't our first fight. I'm not even sure it's our second. The first—if you recall—was in your office, and the hallway, and the elevator. And it lasted a lot longer than this."

Shaking her head, Dana said, "Oh, yeah. So I guess I'm sorry for causing all our fights." Her expression turned glum, and she couldn't meet Laurel's gaze.

Laurel walked around the kitchen counter and wrapped her arms around Dana's shoulders. "We're not fighting."

"We're not? It felt like it, a little bit."

"We're bickering," Laurel corrected. "That's what couples do sometimes."

"Doesn't excuse my shitty mood," Dana mumbled.

"It's not a big deal. It's forgotten, okay? I forgive you." She kissed Dana on the lips, licking at the indentation below her nose with the tip of her tongue. "It happens. And I'm sorry, too."

"So it's over?"

Laurel rested her face on Dana's chest. "Yeah, it's over. Now we're going to do the whole young couple who are madly in love thing again."

A sigh of relief. "Thank God."

"I'm not sure we ever really stopped doing that, honestly." She could hear Dana's heartbeat against her ear, steady and reassuring. "At least I didn't. I love you even when we're picking at each other. I hope you know that."

"I do. And me, too." Dana placed a hand on the back of Laurel's head and cradled her close. "I can be so terrible in the morning sometimes. I guess now you know."

"I can handle you."

"All you have to do is look at me with those sad eyes and you've got me. I'd say you can handle me, all right." Dana kissed the crown of her head. "How did I get lucky enough to find a girl who will put up with me?"

Snorting, Laurel murmured, "You have a very thoughtful friend who paid to have a naked woman dance for you, that's how."

"That reminds me," Dana said, lips curling into a grin, "I need to take Scott out to dinner sometime. Again. I owe him."

Laurel giggled. So far, Scott had netted a very expensive Christmas gift, a weekend trip to Toronto for his birthday, and multiple lunches out at his favorite restaurants, courtesy of Dana. It was almost a little embarrassing how grateful her lover was for that serendipitous lap dance.

How grateful they both were.

"So do you want to tell me what's wrong?" Laurel asked. "What's got you so edgy this morning?"

"It's nothing, really." Dana shrugged, kissed her neck. "I'm just grumpy. I don't want to go to work."

Laurel pulled back, blinking in surprise. "Excuse me?" That didn't sound like Dana at all.

A petulant frown took hold of her lover's mouth. "It's been a long week. We just launched our big project and there won't be much going on today. And honestly—" She stopped and glanced away. "I want to spend time with you right now. I don't want to leave."

Laurel fought the urge to swoon. "I love you, honey. I'm sorry."

"Yeah, well, I'm an idiot." Dana shook her head in disgust. "I'm upset because I'm going to miss you today, so I act like a bitch while I've still got you here. Brilliant."

"Eh, we'll just chalk it up to one of your minor faults," Laurel said. "And letting wet towels drip onto the floor is one of mine."

"I don't care about the towel." Dana eased gently out of their embrace. She seemed fidgety. "I'm sorry I'm a jerk."

"Stop it already." Detecting something unspoken, Laurel said, "Something else is bothering you. Is it about your parents?"

The Watts were coming to dinner on the weekend. Dana had said very little when Laurel first suggested the get-together in their new apartment, but she'd been moody ever since.

"Well, you know I'm not thrilled," Dana said.

Laurel thought carefully before she spoke. She always felt she had to tiptoe in discussions about Dana's family. "What's your main concern?"

Dana's gaze faltered as though she were looking inward and didn't understand what she saw. "Things have changed," she said. "It's like I don't know how to act around them anymore. They just *love* you, and I can certainly understand that. But sometimes I feel like they're all over us. Dad's always asking me about the job and getting into conversation about stuff like home buying and 401k investments. And my mom dropping all the hints about babies? That comment the other night about your femininity was bizarre."

Laurel feigned an aggrieved stare. "Are you suggesting I *don't* have child-bearing hips?"

Dana choked on her laughter.

Before she could reply, Laurel said, "Darling, listen to me. Your parents have been closed out of your life for years and now you've let them in a little. They're excited, that's all. They're both reaching out."

She hesitated, hoping her next words wouldn't drive Dana out the door. "All I'm doing is reaching back. For both of us."

Dana was silent for so long Laurel prepared herself for the clomp of departing footsteps. But her lover stayed where she was. Something passed across her face. She looked like a woman lost in a crowd who'd suddenly spotted a friend.

In a voice as serious as Laurel had ever heard, she said, "Until you came along I didn't know how to do that. I thought I could never be close to them again. Breaking out of that habit feels strange, but the truth is, I kind of like it." She flushed.

Laurel stepped in close and hugged her again. "You'll get used to it, I promise."

Dana squeezed her tight around the middle, lifting her slightly off the floor. Laurel laughed and grabbed her shoulder until she was deposited back onto her feet. "Laurel, you make me so happy I sometimes can't believe this is happening. And I guess I've been afraid to show Mom and Dad in case it all just evaporates."

Knowing what it took to admit this insecurity, Laurel placed her hand over Dana's heart and looked deeply into her eyes. "I love you and you love me."

Chuckling, Dana pressed her nose to Laurel's hair and breathed in. "I really will miss you today."

"I'm only working until noon," Laurel reminded her. "Half shift, remember?" It was recompense for the double she'd worked the day before.

Dana sighed. "Maybe I can cut out of the office a little early."

"Or I could come and have lunch with you."

That made Dana smile. "Really? You want to go out somewhere?"

"Yeah, really. I'd love to meet you at your office." Laurel broke into a sudden grin as pure, wicked inspiration struck. "Ooh—"

"Uh-oh," Dana said, cutting her off before she could share her fantastic idea. "You're up to no good. I know that look. What are you thinking about, naughty girl?"

Laurel was caught somewhere between a laugh and a moan, hearing Dana call her naughty. She couldn't help but be amused that certain phrases they'd made their own turned her on so much. Already she could feel that her panties were damp, and she knew it was going to be a long morning.

"My third fantasy," she said. "Maybe I should redeem it today."

"Oh, really?" Dana slipped a hand under the hem of Laurel's T-shirt, and smoothed her palm up her back. "And there I was, thinking you'd forgotten all about it."

"Trust me, your bedroom repertoire has kept me rather preoccupied. But why settle for fantastic sex when I could have the perfect fulfillment of a long-held fantasy?"

"Are you trying to boost my ego or give me performance anxiety?" If Dana was attempting to hide her delight, she was failing miserably.

"I'm just trying to remind you how impeccably you granted my last fantasy. Sometimes when I have a moment to breathe at work, I close my eyes and think about how fucking good you felt in my ass."

Dana was positively beaming. "What a great way to end a long damn week."

"Is that all it takes to improve your mood?" Laurel threaded her fingers through Dana's hair, scraping her fingernails over her scalp. She grinned when Dana shivered. "You're so easy to please."

"Nah," Dana rumbled. "You're just so good at pleasing me."

"That, too."

"So what are you thinking?" Dana asked. Her hands found Laurel's bottom, cupping her gently through her uniform pants. She wore an excited smile. "I've been wondering what you'll come up with. I'm not sure how you're going to top the first two, quite frankly."

"Oh, I've got an idea." Laurel moved her hands down to tickle the nape of Dana's neck and pushed her hips into Dana's.

"I'm dying of curiosity."

"It was cruel of me to make you wait till after we moved," Laurel said without a trace of remorse. "Sorry."

"No, you're not."

Laurel glanced at the digital clock on the microwave. "Isn't it time for you to go to work?" She couldn't decide how much to tell Dana and how much to surprise her. She knew what she wanted to do, but she wasn't entirely certain how Dana would feel about it. "Do you trust me?" she asked.

"Implicitly." The response was quick, immediate. Unthinking.

Laurel smiled at the excitement in Dana's eyes. "Are you up for a quick wardrobe addition before you leave for work?"

"Oh, my. This *is* going to be naughty, isn't it?"

Laurel slowly traced a finger down Dana's chest, until she reached the waistband of her pants. "Very."

BACK WHERE IT ALL BEGAN

B y the time Laurel reached the twenty-ninth floor, she could feel slick wetness painting her upper thighs. Her nipples pressed hard against the fabric of her bra, and her breasts felt heavy and swollen. She was sure her face was flushed and her pupils dilated, and it excited her to think that anyone who saw her now would surely notice the state she was in.

She cast a fond parting glance around the elevator as she stepped out. This just happened to be the car where she and Dana had shared their first kiss. Where they'd first made love. It held a lot of very special memories for her, and she let her dreamy musings stoke the arousal she was already feeling.

With a bright smile on her face, she walked down the hallway to Dana's office. A goateed young man ambled toward her, stopping at the last minute when he realized he was about to walk into her. He gave her a slack-jawed nod and they did one of those side-to-side dances trying to get past one another. Laurel suppressed her giggle at his expression. Dana's programmers were never very subtle about their excitement at seeing a woman enter their domain. Laurel's rare visits to the office usually created quite a stir. Her biggest challenge today would be making it through the gauntlet, the name she had given to the two long rows of desks she had to walk between to get to Dana's corner office. The gauntlet, populated by staring computer geeks whose eyes would be pinned to her ass, her breasts, her face. *Don't pretend that doesn't make you just a little hot, Laurel. Trying to act natural, knowing what you're about to do.*

Hot, wet, and bare beneath her knee-length skirt, legs weak with sexual need, she worked up her courage and strode down the gauntlet. The heads swung around almost in unison.

"Having lunch with Ms. Watts today?" A dateless code monkey asked the obvious.

Laurel gave a friendly nod. *No, I'm just having Ms. Watts.*

His eyes never moved from her shirt front, which was unbuttoned far enough to show a hint of cleavage. She'd stopped at home to change out of her scrubs into something a little more alluring before leaving for her lunch date. Her panties were back at the apartment.

After all, she wouldn't be needing them.

"Is Dana in her office?" she asked.

This complex question was met with several seconds of stupefied silence before Dana's only female programmer answered, "She sure is. Have a good lunch."

Oh, I will. Laurel's pussy clenched in anticipation. She felt all eyes on her ass as she strolled through the rows of cubicles toward Dana's closed door.

Laurel knocked and stepped inside, breaking into a sunny grin when she saw Dana sitting behind her large oak desk.

"Hey, baby," Dana said in a low voice. Her gaze traveled slowly over Laurel's body. "Why don't you close that door behind you for a minute?"

Laurel stepped inside and leaned back on the door, shutting it with a gentle click. "I've missed you," she murmured. The absolute truth, never mind that it had only been a little over six hours.

Her body burned from the way Dana looked at her. She could see Dana's hands curled into fists on the surface of her desk.

"I missed you, too," Dana said.

"Have you been thinking about me?"

"You know I can't do anything but."

Laurel stepped farther into the office. "Oh, really?"

Dana's voice grew husky. "When I'm hard for you all day, it's pretty difficult to get you out of my head."

Laurel swallowed and stepped around the side of Dana's desk so she could see her lap. Sitting had the effect of stretching her dark pants tight over her hips, revealing the bulge between her legs. "How is that hard pack working out for you?"

"Good." Dana licked her lips. "Excellent."

Leaning her bottom against the edge of the desk, Laurel bent and spoke into Dana's ear. "Are you wet under that stiff cock?"

A hot, shaky exhalation blew over her neck, raising gooseflesh. Laurel closed her eyes for a beat, struggling with her desire. She wasn't done playing out this seduction scene, which was just as important to her fantasy as actually getting fucked.

"Are you?" she asked again when Dana didn't answer.

"Yes." Her lover's voice was quiet, and rough with hunger.

Laurel straightened and scooted up to sit on Dana's desk, to her left. She lifted the hem of her skirt slightly as she spread her legs. "So am I. Look."

Dana released a soft groan as she leaned back in her leather chair and craned her neck to peer up Laurel's skirt. Laurel felt a renewed flood of wetness when Dana's gaze found her swollen sex and lingered there. Reaching out, Dana stroked her fingertip along the soft skin on the inside of Laurel's knee.

As she moved up, dangerously close to the juncture of Laurel's thighs, a loud thump sounded outside the office door and Laurel brought her knees together automatically.

"Printer paper delivery," Dana explained. "There's a supplies closet next door."

Laughing softly at her own stretched nerves, Laurel slid off the desk and walked to the office door. "That's why that guy who invented locks, uh, invented locks."

"How brilliant of him," Dana replied with a lazy smile. She paused as something seemed to register. "Wait. Here?"

Laurel grinned as she secured the lock and returned to Dana. *I guess I never really made it clear that I intended to fuck her right at her desk.* She dropped to her knees on the carpet, pulling Dana's chair around. Unbuttoning Dana's pants, lowering the zipper, Laurel gave her a mischievous smile. "Tell me you've never imagined doing this."

"In my office?"

"Tell me you haven't." Laurel reached into Dana's pants and pulled out the strap-on dildo, easing it into an erect position while licking her lips. "But I'm not going to believe you."

"I have." Dana groaned deep in her throat as Laurel leaned forward and wrapped her lips around the head of the dildo, then pulled back to swirl her tongue around the tip. "Many times."

Laurel engulfed the dildo with her mouth. Just as she'd hoped, this time around, she was very much fulfilling a mutual fantasy. Bobbing her head up and down, she milked the length of the dildo with her lips, thoroughly enjoying the tease she was giving Dana. Such a mental thing, but by the way Dana's hips pumped gently beneath her and her fingers threaded through Laurel's hair, she was definitely getting off on it.

"Oh yeah, baby," Dana growled in a bare whisper. "Suck me."

Laurel continued her dutiful ministrations, curling her arms around Dana's thighs. The firm hand remained locked in her hair, not forcing her movement but keeping her close and focused on her task.

Above her, the phone rang.

"Fuck." Dana sagged back in her leather chair with a deflated sigh. "Goddamn it."

Laurel released the dildo from her mouth with a quiet pop. "Answer it," she murmured, then licked a lazy circle around the head of the toy. "Don't mind me."

The phone continued to ring.

"I can't answer it like this," Dana hissed, then gasped as Laurel reached up to grip the base of the dildo in her fist and ran her tongue down its length. "There's no way I'm going to sound normal while you're—"

"You'll be just fine." Laurel pumped the toy with her hand and lifted her eyes to give Dana a playful smile. "You're a professional." She took the dildo into her mouth again, never breaking eye contact with her panting lover.

Dana whipped the phone to her ear and greeted the caller with cool authority. Nothing about her demeanor suggested that she was receiving a spirited blow job from a woman on her knees. Laurel enjoyed watching her as she talked shop with someone who was obviously a client. Her face said it all. The challenge of keeping her composure made her eyes flash with pure heat, and she gave Laurel a stern, steamy look. It took all of Laurel's concentration not to moan out loud when the musky smell of Dana's sex registered so close to her nostrils. She inhaled deeply, sucking and licking as if Dana could feel every stroke of her tongue and the suction of her lips. Her fingers flexed on the backs of Dana's thighs, telegraphing her need. She knew Dana understood when her hand began moving over Laurel's hair, encouraging her as she worked her mouth up and down. They locked eyes as Laurel took as much in her mouth as she could manage.

Dana's thighs tensed beneath her upper arms. "Thanks, Wayne. I'll see you on Monday, ten o'clock." She waited a moment, then released a light chuckle. "You bet. Bye."

The phone clattered back into its cradle and Dana tightened her grip on Laurel's hair until she lifted her head and released the dildo from her mouth.

"Everything okay?" she asked with a wicked grin. "Did the call go well?"

"You little minx. Get up here and sit on my lap."

Laurel crawled up and straddled Dana's thighs, pulling her skirt higher so the dildo pressed firmly against her slippery labia, and leaned close to Dana's ear. "Are you going to fuck me in your office, Ms. Watts?"

Dana's hands found their way under her skirt and gripped her bare bottom. She drew Laurel against the hardness between her legs, moving her hips back and forth in slow counter-rhythm. "I think I might," she murmured.

"Are you sure?" Laurel pressed Dana's face into her cleavage so that she wouldn't see her smile. "You seemed a little uncertain earlier."

A desperate hand reached between their bodies, and Laurel felt the head of the dildo guided to her wet entrance.

"We'll make this quick," Dana whispered. "And then we'll go out."

Laurel grinned. It had been all too easy to break down Dana's inhibitions. Oh yeah, she'd definitely fantasized about this before. Tracing her tongue along Dana's earlobe, she breathed, "Fuck me, Ms. Watts. Please."

The head of the dildo slipped inside. Laurel took it in slowly, holding Dana's gaze as she was filled:

"Like that?"

Laurel nodded and gasped, "Yes." She gripped the back of the chair over Dana's shoulders, rolling her hips around. "That's perfect."

Dana rubbed lazy circles over Laurel's swollen clit. "Move for me, honey." Her eyes flicked over Laurel's shoulder toward the door. "And be *quiet*."

Laurel gave a solemn nod, and began riding the dildo that rested so deep inside her pussy. The wonderful fullness, the way she was stretched open, set her hips bucking in pleasure. The touch of Dana's hand, the careful attention of her fingers on Laurel's slick flesh, made her want to scream. She leaned forward and thrust her tongue into Dana's mouth to stifle the impulse.

Dana's fingers picked up speed, gliding swiftly over the hood of her clit. Their mouths stayed crushed together, and Laurel rocked her hips hard against Dana's body as she sought release. She was so close already, and everything was working to push her closer: the need for silence, the feeling of the edge of the desk pressing into her back as she moved, the knowledge that the only thing separating them from a room full of people hard at work was the locked office door.

Dana tore her mouth away from their kiss with a low groan. "Come for me, sweetheart."

Laurel nodded, afraid that if she opened her mouth, she would let loose and cry out her joy. She ground down on the dildo, quiet gasps escaping from between her tightly clenched teeth. Her hips jerked as the pleasure built. She felt a hand grasp at one buttock convulsively, pulling her onto the dildo again and again, forcing her to take all Dana could give her.

Laurel tipped back her head, opened her mouth, and came with a silent scream at the ceiling. Her orgasm surged through her, bone-deep and intense.

"That was fast," Dana murmured. Pride rang in her muted voice.

Laurel reached over Dana's shoulder and gave her three firm taps with her hand. "Why don't you let me pat you on the back, so you don't have to do it yourself?"

Chuckling, Dana whispered, "I was sort of hoping that you'd offer to toot my horn instead. You know, so I don't have to do it myself."

Laurel grinned. "That could be arranged."

"Want to get out of here?"

"Desperately."

With her hands on Dana's shoulders, Laurel stood slowly on unsteady legs, easing off the dildo. Glancing down, she gasped, "Baby, I'm so sorry."

Dana's eyes fell to her lap and she smiled even as her face flushed red. "Oh my God." A dark spot of wetness stained the front of her pants. "I didn't take *this* into account."

Laurel's upper lip twitched, and a snuffle of laughter escaped. "Me, neither. Oh, honey, I really am so sorry."

Dana shook her head, face growing impossibly redder. "I think, technically, that it's my fault." She stood up and tucked the dildo back into her pants, adjusting for a few moments before she zipped up. Then she pulled her jacket on and tugged it closed. Casting a hopeful look at her upper thighs, she scowled at the wet stain that was still slightly visible. "Great."

"You can barely see it," Laurel said. Flattening the material of her skirt over her thighs with both hands, she tried to fix her own appearance. "Nobody will notice."

"Damn right, nobody will notice." Dana stepped away from her desk, picking up her car keys from the corner. "You're walking in front of me."

"It's the least I can do," Laurel said. "Just act nonchalant."

"Nonchalant, right." Dana lifted her fingers to her face and inhaled. "No problem."

❖

When they finally made it to the elevator, Laurel felt like she'd just run a marathon, and Dana was grinning like an idiot.

Dana punched the Down button and leaned close to Laurel's ear. "I don't know why, but that made me so fucking hot just now."

Laurel's legs went all shaky again, and she turned her head to lick Dana's earlobe. "Me, too. I want to wear that strap-on and fuck you until you come."

Ding.

Laurel stepped inside the elevator as soon as the door opened, then turned and cocked her head at Dana. "Going down?" she asked.

She watched Dana swallow, then nod. "If I'm lucky."

After Dana moved inside the car and the doors slid shut, Laurel half turned to give her a playful look. "You know, I could just press the emergency stop button—"

"Don't even think about it." Dana laced her hands in front of the dark spot on her pants. "I'm not willing to pay Rocky for another surveillance tape."

"I'm just nostalgic," Laurel said, kicking at the floor with the toe of her shoe. "You know, you actually fulfilled one of my fantasies the first night we met. Getting fucked in an elevator."

"And you fulfilled one of mine," Dana said. She took Laurel's hand in her own. "Meeting a beautiful woman and falling in love."

Laurel blinked, for a moment unable to form a coherent response. At some point when she hadn't been looking, Dana had become a very expressive lover. Eyes filling with happy tears, she whispered, "Mine, too."

Rocky's head popped up as they left the elevator and crossed the lobby. He gave them a wink, as if they shared a secret.

Dana nodded at him as they walked past the front desk. "Until next time, man."

Every time Laurel saw him she wondered if he'd watched their tape before he handed it over. She didn't want to think about that too hard. She waited until they were outside on the sidewalk to speak again. "Brilliant performance, baby. That whole thing was absolutely perfect."

Swinging their hands, Dana wore a beaming smile. "I thought so, too." She stepped closer and bumped against Laurel's hip. "So what next, my darling?"

"The Hilton. Six minutes if you drive. Four if I do."

Dana handed her car keys over. "Let's hit it."

It took them exactly three minutes and fifty-six seconds to reach the Hilton where Laurel had booked a room that morning. She'd already checked in, so she escorted Dana past the lobby elevator to a stairwell.

"I have a friend who used to work here," she explained in response to a puzzled glance from Dana. "I know another way up."

They climbed a half flight of stairs and emerged into a short, deserted hallway. Laurel led the way to a wide, industrial gray elevator door situated at the far end, and pushed the square button on the wall. The doors slid open, revealing a large, empty car with a metal rail attached to the back wall.

"Freight elevator," she explained.

Dana's nostrils flared. "And why do you want to take the freight elevator?"

Laurel grabbed Dana by the front of her shirt and pulled her inside. "No cameras."

"You're sure?" Dana asked, glancing suspiciously around at the interior.

"I've got it on good authority." Laurel sent another silent thank-you to Rita, who used to dance at the club and now worked in the Hilton kitchen. "I made a phone call this morning. Trust me."

"Always."

Laurel hit the emergency stop button as soon as they began their ascent. Backing Dana to the wall, she pressed her against the cool metal and kissed her for all she was worth. Dana's hand found its way to her head, fingers entangling in her hair, and she held Laurel close as she kissed her back.

"I want that strap-on," Laurel murmured against Dana's lips.

"Again, honey?" Dana kissed a path from Laurel's mouth down her throat. "You're insatiable."

Laurel dropped her hands to the front of Dana's pants. Unbuttoning and unzipping with shaking fingers, she said, "No. I *want* it. I want to wear it, and I want to fuck you with it."

Dana immediately began to help, pushing her pants down around her ankles. "And you should definitely get what you want."

"Remember that, sweetheart, for future reference."

Dana wore a lazy grin as Laurel unbuckled the harness. "Why, Dr. Stanley, I think you're taking advantage of me during a moment of weakness."

"I think you're loving it," Laurel countered, hiking up her skirt to fasten the strap-on around her hips. "We've got the room for the night, you know." She gave a grateful smile when Dana took over buckling one side. "What do you say you meet me here right after you're done with work for the day?"

The dildo now jutted out from between her thighs, tenting the front of her skirt slightly. Laurel pulled the straps tight.

"I can't think of a better way to start the weekend."

Laurel eased into a slow smile as she finished tightening the other side of the harness. "Technically," she said, and gripped Dana's upper arm, "my weekend has already started. And I can think of a great way to kick it off."

Dana shivered. "How do you want me?"

Any way you'll let me have you. Laurel leered, drawing an uncharacteristic giggle from her lover. "So many choices—"

"I'm sure you have an idea about what you *really* want."

Something about Dana's inflection twisted Laurel's stomach and sent hot desire to pool between her thighs. She positioned Dana so she faced the back of the elevator car and the long metal railing. "Hold on with one hand, touch yourself with the other, and bend over so I can see your pussy."

Dana groaned at the crude request. Pants pooled around one ankle, she planted her feet wide apart and bent low at the waist. Gripping the railing with her left hand, she only hesitated a moment before reaching between her thighs. "Like this?"

Laurel groaned and squeezed the fleshy globes of Dana's bottom, pulling her open with both hands. She exposed glistening pink folds, the swollen, heavy inner lips open and inviting. "You want to be fucked, don't you?"

"Yes." Dana's hand worked between her legs, and Laurel watched fresh wetness seeping out of her opening. "Please, Laurel—"

Whimpering at the sight of her lover offering herself up, Laurel moved one hand down to grasp the base of the dildo she wore. She stood on her tiptoes and rubbed the head over Dana's pussy, then lowered herself slightly, trying to find exactly the right angle for penetration. Their positioning was a little awkward, but Laurel wouldn't be dissuaded. This was a fantasy, damn it, and she was determined to make it work.

As if sensing what she needed, Dana set her feet farther apart and arched her back. The head of the dildo slipped down over her labia and pressed firmly against her entrance. Laurel grinned in triumph and moved her free hand up to give Dana's shoulder a subtle squeeze.

"Are you ready, honey?"

Dana pushed back against her. "Stop teasing me."

Laurel rubbed the dildo up and down the length of Dana's aroused sex. "I'm not sure that you're in a position to give orders right now, Ms. Watts." She moved her hips forward and pushed just the head of the dildo into Dana's body. "What do you think?"

Dana pushed back again, but Laurel moved with her, not allowing her to draw the dildo deeper inside. A moment of hesitation, then a frustrated sigh. "No," Dana muttered.

"No, what?"

"No, I'm not in a position to give orders right now," Dana mumbled.

Laurel silently cheered. To see her composed, confident lover—always so controlled, except in these rare moments with her—to see her so wanton and needy, so willing to surrender, was breathtaking. Sliding her hand from Dana's shoulder to curl around the back of her neck, she whispered, "That doesn't happen very often, does it?"

Dana shuddered. "No."

"And you like it." Laurel grasped the dildo in her fist and swirled it around, stretching Dana's entrance in slow circles. "Don't you?"

"Yes," Dana hissed.

"Ask for it," Laurel commanded, unable to resist the opportunity to indulge in another fantasy. The need to make Dana submit overpowered her. "And don't come until I'm inside you."

"Fuck me," Dana said without hesitation. Her hand slowed, almost to a stop. "Please. Quick." She laughed lightly, then added, "Before someone realizes the freight elevator is stopped."

Laurel thrust her hips forward slowly, eyes fixed to the silicone shaft disappearing into Dana's pussy. She listened to Dana exhale, watched her pale back arch further.

"You don't want anyone to find us in here?" she asked. "You want me to fuck you fast so nobody will know how my professional woman likes to be bent over and taken?"

Dana released an explosive whimper. "Fuck, please, Laurel. I'm going to come soon." Her hand was working fiercely. "I want to feel you moving inside me."

"Say please again."

"Please, Laurel. Please."

Laurel's hips took up a steady, driving rhythm. She moved both hands to Dana's buttocks, holding her in place as she plundered her with the strap-on cock. Her eyes were pinned on the point of their joining, and her thighs shook, weak with desire.

"Are you going to come for me?" she gasped, pounding into Dana harder, aware of just how close her lover was to release. "Come for me, baby. Come on."

With a keening sound, Dana tensed and fucked back against Laurel for a few hard strokes before she threw her head back and gasped in pleasure. Laurel watched Dana's arm scissoring hard between her thighs as she used her hand to draw out her climax, mindless and primal, so fucking beautiful it made Laurel's head spin.

"Stop," Dana gasped after some time. Her damp hand flew back and gripped Laurel's hip, squeezing hard. "Please, no more."

Laurel came to a stop after a slow forward thrust, buried deep inside Dana. She held one soft buttock in each hand, keeping Dana still against her. Her breath escaped in tiny, sucking gasps.

"That was awesome," Dana murmured after a moment of shared silence.

Laurel withdrew slowly, then helped Dana straighten at the waist. Wrapping her arms around Dana's middle, she reached up and cupped soft breasts in gentle hands. "Honey, you are so incredibly hot."

Dana turned in her arms and gave her a crushing hug. "Thank you. I'm only hot with you."

Laurel kissed her hard and deep. "Let's go to the room for a few minutes before you have to get back."

"Do you think we have time?" Dana glanced at her wristwatch.

"We can make time." Laurel grinned.

They dressed in silence, and Laurel gave Dana the dildo to hide for the rest of their trip to the ninth-floor room. She wasn't about to go strutting around the hotel with that thing poking out of her skirt. Dana had long sleeves on her jacket, and the left one worked quite well to conceal their toy. The harness stayed buckled around Laurel's hips.

"That brought back some nice memories." She gave Dana a sly glance as the elevator started moving. "What a nice way to end this fantasy thing."

"Who says it has to end?" Dana curled her arm around Laurel's waist and tugged her close. "I plan on satisfying your fantasies for a long time."

Raising up on her toes, Laurel planted a loving kiss on Dana's temple. "And you're going to have to tell me some of yours, too."

"Count on it."

They found their room at the end of the hall and hurried inside. Laurel shut the door behind them and slammed Dana up against it, then captured her mouth in a hard kiss.

She felt her skirt practically ripped from her body, the harness unbuckled by impatient hands, then dropped onto the floor. Dana grabbed the hem of Laurel's shirt, tore it over her head, and threw it to the floor. An instant later her bra was unsnapped and pulled off.

Dana was still fully clothed. She kissed Laurel's ear. "I've got to get back to the office soon," she murmured. "But I want to eat you first, before I go. I want to be able to taste you on my lips while I'm finishing out the rest of the day."

Laurel looped her arms around Dana's neck. "Yes."

In a move that thoroughly surprised her, Dana scooped her up and carried her over to the bed. After tossing Laurel onto the mattress, she got to her knees on the carpet.

"This is much more fun than that proposal I was working on."

"You've come a long way, baby."

"I've had great incentive." Dana pressed her hands flat against Laurel's inner thighs and pushed her legs apart. Reaching under Laurel's bottom, she pulled her closer to the edge of the mattress. "You look delicious, baby. So wet, and you smell so good."

Laurel's stormy blue eyes sparkled. "It's time to stop talking, darling, and use that mouth for something else."

Dana pursed her lips and started to whistle a tuneless song.

"Smart-ass," Laurel said, then took a handful of Dana's hair, forcing her face between her thighs. "Licking, not whistling."

Dana pushed into the crease between Laurel's hip and thigh, dragging the flat of her tongue over her damp skin. She hummed, sending a pleasant vibration up into Laurel's abdomen. "Your skin tastes so good," she whispered.

Laurel slipped her fingers into her aroused pussy, mere inches from Dana's mouth, and rubbed her labia gently. "I taste even better here," she said.

Dana looked up. "Really."

Nodding, Laurel swirled her fingers over her clit, teasing, then lifted her hand to her face. Eyes closed, she enjoyed the taste of her own juices. "Yeah, really."

"I guess I'm going to have to try for myself," Dana said. She used her fingers to open Laurel, then lowered her face to take a long swipe across slick, engorged flesh with the tip of her tongue. "You're right," she breathed. "Yummy." Then she brought her mouth back to Laurel's wetness, and didn't pull away again.

Laurel closed her eyes and focused on the magic of Dana's tongue on her pussy. She was being licked like there was all the time in the world for this, for her pleasure, and her muscles turned to jelly at the absolute decadence of the feeling. Dana's hair was silky soft in Laurel's fist, her face warm against her center.

She groaned and curled her toes, already close to orgasm after only a couple of precious minutes. "You're too good at that."

"Too good?" Dana lifted her head and gave a playful smile. "Is that possible?"

"It is when all I want to do is prolong this feeling, but you're about to make me come again. Already."

"Do you want me to stop?" Dana sat back on her ankles.

Laurel propped herself up on her elbows, shaking her head adamantly. She could feel cool air blowing over her exposed clit, and her pussy throbbed in the absence of Dana's touch. "No. I was just… saying."

"You want me to be less good?" Dana asked. She brought her lips back to Laurel's sex, kissing her neatly trimmed mound, then slid her tongue down over her labia in a crazy, aimless pattern. "Like this?" Up and down, side to side, never staying in one spot long enough to induce orgasm, but exploring her thoroughly, every fold and crevice.

Laurel pumped her hips in a frantic effort to force Dana's tongue to the places that felt best. She felt the sharp edge of her pleasure fading, becoming duller, while a burning fire rose low in her belly. This was doing nothing to dampen her arousal, and only drove her further from release.

"Wait," Laurel gasped. "Please."

"You want me to stop altogether?" Dana drew back as if to retreat. "I'll confess, I'm surprised. But if you don't want—"

Laurel tossed her head back and forth on the pillow, dazed and vaguely frustrated. "No. No, don't stop."

"Then what do you want?" Dana's voice was quiet, commanding. "Tell me what you want and I'll do it. Anything for you."

Laurel struggled with a moment of indecision, with the conflicting desires to draw this out or to come hard, now, this instant. She was so wet, so swollen and heavy, and the faint traces of orgasm were already curling deep in her belly. *I could ask her to make me come now, then try and make it last when she gets back from work later.*

Swallowing, she said, "Make me come. Now."

With a nod, Dana pressed the palms of her hands against Laurel's inner thighs, pinning her so she was spread wide. Her pussy shone with her juices, and as Dana watched, her opening contracted, as though anticipating the orgasm Dana would induce.

Laurel had to close her eyes, moved more than she could bear by the look of intense, soul-deep desire on Dana's face before she lowered her face and began licking in earnest once more. When she came, it was with a mournful cry of pleasure. Her climax was bittersweet; intense, dizzying, but ultimately fleeting, and the moment the spasms began to subside, she wished she were poised on the brink again.

Dana moved up and took her mouth in a deep kiss, sharing Laurel's musky-sweet taste on swollen lips. She pulled Laurel into a tender hug, cradling her naked flesh against her own fully dressed form.

"I hate to say it," she whispered after Laurel's breathing had slowed a little, "but I should get going. The sooner I do, the sooner I can leave and come back to you."

Laurel managed a reluctant nod. "I know." She encircled Dana's shoulders with her arms, kissing her cheek. "I'll miss you."

"I'll miss you, too," Dana murmured past the lump in her throat. She meant the words more than she could ever make Laurel understand.

Laurel felt a gentle hand move between her legs, fingertips sliding over her labia, swirling close to her entrance.

Dana brought her hand to her face, inhaling deeply. "But now I've got something to take with me."

Laurel flushed at the erotic gesture. "Hurry back. I love you."

"I love you, too." Dana left her with a last, soulful kiss and an adoring smile. "Always."

TWELVE MONTHS TOGETHER

D ana sat back on Laurel's couch with a grin, watching as Isis came nose to nose with a black-and-white Great Dane puppy who was already five times her size. The puppy's tail wagged frantically as he sniffed Isis, and he lowered his chest to the ground in a position Laurel said was called a "play bow." Dana gazed over at Laurel, who watched the scene with a delighted expression.

"I didn't realize when I hooked up with you that I was signing up for life at a doggy orphanage," Dana said good-naturedly.

She chuckled as Isis swatted the puppy's nose with her oversized paw, making him stumble backward before seeking refuge in Laurel's lap. At fifty pounds, he was all baby, but far too large to be cowering on top of Laurel like a scared little mouse.

"Not an orphanage." Laurel laughed as the puppy showered her face with kisses. "Just a foster mom."

Dana watched Laurel's joy as she interacted with her beloved cat and the homeless puppy she had just diagnosed with elbow dysplasia. A year ago, she would never have guessed that she could so quickly and easily fall in love, and with someone like Laurel. She had the biggest heart Dana had ever known, especially with animals. Dana had found herself becoming an animal lover, just because Laurel's enthusiasm for them was so infectious.

Laurel liked kids, too. And though Dana had always felt intimidated by babies, more and more she found herself sneaking peeks at women holding the little squirming, bald creatures, wondering whether her future might hold even more surprises for her. She had to admit, when she thought about starting a family with Laurel, the idea held a lot of appeal. And her mother would be ecstatic.

"Well, you're a wonderful foster mom," Dana murmured. She met Laurel's grin with a tender smile of her own. "Hamlet seems to think so, at least."

"Isis isn't so sure. She's never thrilled about sharing me."

Dana settled back against the couch cushions with a contented sigh. She was pretty sure this was the happiest moment of her life. It wasn't as though she hadn't enjoyed countless other happy—even blissful—moments since that first night in the elevator with Laurel. And it wasn't even like this particular moment was specifically happier than any of those. It was just that ever since she met Laurel, every day was better than the last, and with each moment they were together, Dana felt her hope and excitement about the future grow. Tomorrow she would be even happier than today, and even more in love.

After everything they'd experienced together, she trusted Laurel more than anyone else in the world. And she knew Laurel felt the same way, which was the most powerful gift Dana had ever been given. Yet Dana yearned for something more.

She watched Isis make a tentative circle around Laurel's feet, flicking her tail in what looked like irritation. She meowed while Hamlet wriggled around on Laurel's lap. With a smile, Dana said, "I'm glad Isis learned how to share you with me."

"Yeah, she says you're family now."

Dana felt an unexpected rush of emotion at the sentiment. She did feel like they were a family now. It was amazing how much she had come to depend on the idea of sharing her life with someone. Knowing now how wonderful it was to trust another person, she marveled at how much she missed out on those many years she spent alone. She could find that depressing, except that it all led to her meeting Laurel. She couldn't imagine wanting to be with anyone else.

Thinking about the possibility of starting a family with Laurel some day brought up thoughts of her parents, and even her brother. She had been close to all of them once, and all the recent changes in her life made her yearn to repair some of the damage she had done to their relationship by closing herself off from them after college. Part of her new desire to build bridges was knowing how important family was to Laurel, and seeing how happy it made her when Dana reached out. Besides, if they did do something crazy like have kids some day, those babies deserved to have grandparents.

Dana's musing came crashing to a halt when Hamlet leapt onto the couch and clambered onto her lap. Large, clumsy paws gripped at her thighs, and a wet nose pressed against her cheek. She could feel the wagging of his tail vibrate throughout his entire body.

"Hamlet!" Laurel said, and rushed to the couch to take hold of his collar. "Off."

Dana couldn't imagine what her reaction to the puppy's playful enthusiasm might have been before she met Laurel. Now she laughed instinctively, even as she gasped for breath when a large paw landed on her stomach. The dog came home with Laurel a week ago, and it was already clear that he had decided to bond with Dana. She didn't know what to make of that, but to her surprise, it made her feel pretty damn good.

"I'm so sorry," Laurel said. "He definitely needs to learn some manners."

"It's okay," Dana said as Hamlet finally hopped off the couch and struck a loyal pose next to her on the floor. She reached out and fingered his floppy ears, then gave his head an affectionate stroke. "I get it. I was socially awkward before I met you, too."

"And look at you now." Laurel leaned over and kissed her, smiling against her lips.

Dana considered her life: a former workaholic desperately in love with a sexy stripper-turned-veterinarian, flanked by a giant puppy and a spoiled cat, having idle thoughts about family and babies on an uneventful Wednesday evening. With a grin, she agreed, "Look at me now."

❖

That weekend, Dana tested her resolution. They were having dinner at her parents' house, these days a regular happening. From the moment her father opened the door and invited them in, Dana forced herself to relax and reach out to her family. She greeted her father with a hug, then gave her mother a kiss on the cheek.

Trevor earned a mock punch to the arm, which he deflected with an expert block. Dana grinned at him, allowing herself to take pleasure in the familiar routine. To her surprise, he returned her warm smile.

"You guys really got a Great Dane puppy?"

Dana blushed. Obviously her mother had shared some of their phone conversation of the day before. She caught Laurel grinning at her, and said, "We're *fostering* a Great Dane puppy. Until we can find him a good home."

"That's so cool. Maybe I could meet him? I've been thinking about getting a dog."

"Think about it once you've moved out of here for good," Dana's father said as he shut the door behind them. "Until then, you can visit Dana's dog."

"Well, he's not really—" Dana protested, until she could see that nobody was listening to her.

Laurel gave her a long-suffering shake of the head, and Dana rolled her eyes. Like Laurel would be devastated if Dana decided she didn't want that big lug of a puppy to leave.

"Is there anything I can do to help with dinner, Vicki?" Laurel asked.

Dana's mom lit up at the suggestion and took Laurel by the arm. "I have some potatoes that need peeling, if you're interested."

"Sounds like fun," Laurel said, and let herself be led to the kitchen. "I used to be the official potato peeler for my mom, too."

Dana could hear her mother ask Laurel a question, but didn't catch the words. She watched her lover go with a smile, unable to believe how quickly her parents seemed to have accepted her into the fold.

As though sensing Dana's thoughts, her father stepped close and wrapped an arm around her shoulders. "You look happy."

"I am," Dana said honestly. "Things are going really well."

"And I suspect we have Laurel to thank for that?"

Trevor shot her a grin full of insinuation but kept a lid on the rude comments. Dana sensed that he was trying hard to get along with her, and that it was probably due in large part to how hard she was trying to get along with him. She gave both Trevor and her father a smile, and said, "We definitely have Laurel to thank for that."

"Tell me, does Laurel like playing Boggle?"

Dana laughed at the mention of her father's favorite word game. "I don't know that I'm aware of Laurel's feelings on Boggle."

Her father widened his eyes and led her into the den. "You two have never played?"

Dana raised her eyebrow at Trevor, warning him not to go anywhere with that comment, then told her father, "No, we haven't."

"Well, Dana," her father said in a serious voice, "she has to play Boggle if she's going to be part of this family. I'm still looking for someone to dethrone me."

Dana's heart swelled at her father's acceptance of Laurel's role in her life. She could see he was fast pushing past the initial discomfort of this new part of his daughter's life, and she was grateful for it. "Don't I get another shot at taking the title?"

"Of course you do," her father said. He looked extraordinarily pleased, and Dana wished she had thought of inviting him to play a game of Boggle sooner. They used to play all the time when Dana was a teenager, and she loved it. Why had they ever stopped?

"Am I going to be able to get in on this action?" Trevor asked.

"Only if you're ready to get your ass kicked," Dana said. She sat down at the round oak table in their den, staring Trevor down as her father got the well-worn box out of their gaming cabinet.

"We'll see," Trevor said. He cracked his knuckles, drawing a wince from Dana. He knew she hated that.

"It's cute to see you two fighting over second place," Dana's father said, and opened the game.

Dana looked up to see Laurel watching them from the kitchen, gazing out over the bar to meet Dana's eyes. She was laughing at something Dana's mother was saying, and her face shone with happiness that Dana could see from across the room.

I love you, Laurel mouthed silently.

I love you, Dana mouthed back. She caught her brother looking at her, but he just gave her a friendly smile, and she couldn't help but smile back. When she returned her gaze to Laurel, she was busy at work in the kitchen with Dana's mother.

And she was positively radiant.

Dana was filled with a joy she had never known before. She felt almost wholly content, surrounded by people she loved and who loved her in return. As her father set up the game on the table, handing out pencils and paper, Dana made an important decision.

She couldn't imagine her life without Laurel. And she was going to do whatever it took to make sure she wouldn't need to.

❖

Laurel lay on her side in bed, gazing at the alabaster skin of Dana's shoulder bathed in soft moonlight. The ethereal light made her look as though she were glowing, which seemed appropriate, given the amazing time they'd had with Dana's family that evening. Unlike their early visits with Dana's parents and brother, when Dana had been uncomfortable and everyone seemed closed off, tonight was like being part of a real family again.

Watching Dana and Trevor tease their father for winning yet another Boggle game warmed Laurel thoroughly. And helping Vicki prepare dinner was a great time. She got to hear stories about Dana that she wasn't sure her lover would have ever disclosed, and she also had an opportunity to tell Vicki more about herself. Laurel wanted so badly for Dana's family to like and accept her, because she planned on being in Dana's life for a very long time.

Dana mumbled, a small, sleepy sound, and turned slightly so that the comforter slipped off her upper body. Laurel touched her back gently, not wanting to wake her but eager to reconnect. Her skin was soft and warm, luring Laurel forward so she could plant a feather-light kiss on the nape of her neck. Funny, but when Dana slept, Laurel missed her.

So much had changed since they'd met. Dancing at the club was a distant memory, and she was finally a veterinarian working at an incredible practice, making a difference and helping animals. She was also deeply in love, and madly in lust. Nobody ever made her feel like Dana did, in bed or otherwise. At some point in the past few months, Laurel had almost stopped expecting the other shoe to drop. She found herself able to enjoy where life was taking them, and though the fear of losing someone she loved would never disappear completely, she could do nothing but hold on tight and let things happen. Dana had shown her so much courage, Laurel knew she had to do the same.

Dana. If Laurel felt different now, Dana was practically a brand-new person. Laurel had watched the past few months with breathless delight as her lover transformed before her eyes from a tightly controlled workaholic to a warm, passionate partner who made her feel safer than she ever had before. With the difference their time together had made already, Laurel was certain they both had much to look forward to.

No doubt more than either of them could imagine.

HAPPILY EVER AFTER

Dana returned to their hotel room with a colorful bouquet of roses in her hand. When she walked into the bathroom, she was wearing a wide, crooked grin. "Best Friday of my life," she said in a slow drawl.

Laurel rose from beneath a layer of foam and sat up in the large tub. The sight of the roses—red, pink, and white—made her smile, and she stretched out a hand for Dana. "They're beautiful, honey."

Dana knelt beside the tub and gave her a lingering kiss. "So are you, darling."

Locking her hand in Dana's hair, Laurel brought her back for another kiss. Their monthly lunchtime encounter had left her incredibly horny and needy for more. Now that her body had recovered and she'd spent the last four hours thinking about how crazy in love she was, she couldn't get enough of her lover.

Dana placed the roses absently on the toilet lid and caressed a slow path over Laurel's soapy skin, down into the fragrant bubbles to cup her breast. Her fingers found Laurel's nipple, which was growing stiffer despite the heat of the water. When she gave it a gentle pinch Laurel gasped and whispered, with a catch in her voice, "So you had a good day?"

"The best." Dana stroked along the curve of her other breast, into her cleavage. "I couldn't stop thinking about you all afternoon."

"I know the feeling." Laurel felt fingertips tracing the shape of her belly button.

"I stopped by the apartment and picked up an overnight bag,

then dropped Hamlet off for his overnight with Trevor. And I brought Chinese food."

Really, Dana couldn't be more perfect if she tried. "I knew I kept you for a reason," Laurel murmured with absolute love. "Cashew chicken?"

"Of course. I know what you like, baby. And I always try to give you what you want." Dana worked her way lower to cradle Laurel's soapy-wet center.

"You're getting your shirt wet," Laurel said.

Dana joined in her study of the slowly moving arm and the shirt sleeve now fully submerged in the soapy water. "Indeed I am."

Laurel blinked at the mild tone of her lover's voice. Not so long ago, Dana would have been most unhappy about something like that. "I love you," she said, in an effort to give voice to the intense feelings that consumed her at moments like these. "So much."

Something flickered across Dana's face, a happiness that lit her eyes and seemed to tug at the corners of her mouth. "I love you, too."

"Do you want to eat dinner?"

Dana nodded but planted a hand on Laurel's upper chest when she tried to lean forward and open the drain in the tub. "Wait."

"For what?"

"I was hoping you could make one of my fantasies come true."

Laurel chuckled. "Ooh, sounds like fun." She wondered at the sudden emotion that shone in Dana's eyes, so much more complex than simple desire. Her heart began to thump hard and fast as she sensed something important was about to happen. It was written all over Dana's face—hope and fear and nervous anticipation. "What's your fantasy?"

Dana started to dig around in her pockets. "I was going to wait until later, but…"

Laurel sat up straighter in the tub. Her breath caught when Dana produced a small black ring box from her pants pocket.

Clearing her throat, Dana said, "I want you to have this."

Laurel's eyes were glued to the deep red ruby set in a white gold band when Dana flipped open the lid. The ring was gorgeous, and perfect.

"Dana…" She could hardly speak. If Dana was about to do what she thought she might, Laurel was sure she wouldn't be able to stop herself from crying.

"My fantasy is to wake up with you every morning." Dana took the ring from its velvet home. "And go to bed with you every night, and be with you for the rest of our lives. It's what I want more than anything." She slid the ring onto Laurel's wedding finger. "Will you give me that?"

Laurel met her eyes. "Yes," she said without hesitation. There was nothing to think about. She'd wanted this for months. Tears of happiness spilled from her eyes. "Yes, Dana."

Dana was trembling as she swept Laurel into a tight hug. "You like the ring?"

"Almost as much as I like you," Laurel breathed into Dana's ear. "Which is a whole lot."

She knew she was getting Dana's shirt even wetter with soapy bathwater and tears, but she didn't care.

Dana tightened her embrace. "Good. Fantasy complete."

Laurel placed her hand on the small of Dana's back, holding her close. She wanted never to let go. "That was an easy fantasy to fulfill."

"I'm not very difficult to please," Dana said with deep tenderness.

Laurel stared down at the first gold band she'd ever worn entirely for love. All at once, every random piece of her life seemed to fall into place, and she felt whole and complete in a way she could never remember feeling before.

She looked up at Dana. "Are there any other fantasies I can help you out with tonight?" With a mischievous smile, she added, "I hardly think it's fair for this one to count as your turn, since it was mine, too."

Dana's face took on a now-familiar expression of lust, made that much more intense by the moment they had just shared. "Well…there *is* the little matter of the warrior queen and her body slave."

Laurel felt a sudden surge of wetness between her legs, and it had nothing to do with her bath. "That, my queen, can most definitely be arranged."

About the Author

Meghan O'Brien is a twenty-year-old software developer who lives in Northern California with her partner Angie, their son, three cats, and one dog. A native of Royal Oak, Michigan, she is thoroughly enjoying the weather in her new locale.

Meghan is the author of two previous novels, *Infinite Loop* and *The Three*. She has had selections included in the BSB anthologies *Erotic Interludes 2: Stolen Moments*, *Erotic Interludes 3: Lessons in Love*, *Erotic Interludes 4: Extreme Passions*, and *Erotic Interludes 5: Road Games*. Meghan is extremely excited to have joined the Bold Strokes family and plans to continue writing for as long as humanly possible.

Look for her new Ebook version of *The Three* from Bold Strokes in 2008.

Books Available From Bold Strokes Books

Love on Location by Lisa Girolami. Hollywood film producer Kate Nyland and artist Dawn Brock discover that love doesn't always follow the script. (978-1-60282-016-6)

Edge of Darkness by Jove Belle. Investigator Diana Collins charges at life with an irreverent comment and a right hook, but even those may not protect her heart from a charming villain. (978-1-60282-015-9)

Thirteen Hours by Meghan O'Brien. Workaholic Dana Watts's life takes a sudden turn when an unexpected interruption arrives in the form of the most beautiful breasts she has ever seen—stripper Laurel Stanley's. (978-1-60282-014-2)

In Deep Waters 2 by Radclyffe and Karin Kallmaker. All bets are off when two award winning-authors deal the cards of love and passion… and every hand is a winner. (978-1-60282-013-5)

Pink by Jennifer Harris. An irrepressible heroine frolics, frets, and navigates through the "what ifs" of her life: all the unexpected turns of fortune, fame, and karma. (978-1-60282-043-2)

Deal with the Devil by Ali Vali. New Orleans crime boss Cain Casey brings her fury down on the men who threatened her family, and blood and bullets fly. (978-1-60282-012-8)

Naked Heart by Jennifer Fulton. When a sexy ex-CIA agent sets out to seduce and entrap a powerful CEO, there's more to this plan than meets the eye…or the flogger. (978-1-60282-011-1)

Heart of the Matter by KI Thompson. TV newscaster Kate Foster is Professor Ellen Webster's dream girl, but Kate doesn't know Ellen exists…until an accident changes everything. (978-1-60282-010-4)

Heartland by Julie Cannon. When political strategist Rachel Stanton and dude ranch owner Shivley McCoy collide on an empty country road, fate intervenes. (978-1-60282-009-8)

Shadow of the Knife by Jane Fletcher. Militia Rookie Ellen Mittal has no idea just how complex and dangerous her life is about to become. A Celaeno series adventure romance. (978-1-60282-008-1)

To Protect and Serve by VK Powell. Lieutenant Alex Troy is caught in the paradox of her life—to hold steadfast to her professional oath or to protect the woman she loves. (978-1-60282-007-4)

Deeper by Ronica Black. Former homicide detective Erin McKenzie and her fiancée Elizabeth Adams couldn't be happier—until the not-so-distant past comes knocking at the door. (978-1-60282-006-7)

The Lonely Hearts Club by Radclyffe. Take three friends, add two ex-lovers and several new ones, and the result is a recipe for explosive rivalries and incendiary romance. (978-1-60282-005-0)

Venus Besieged by Andrews & Austin. Teague Richfield heads for Sedona and the sensual arms of psychic astrologer Callie Rivers for a much-needed romantic reunion. (978-1-60282-004-3)

Branded Ann by Merry Shannon. Pirate Branded Ann raids a merchant vessel to obtain a treasure map and gets more than she bargained for with the widow Violet. (978-1-60282-003-6)

American Goth by JD Glass. Trapped by an unsuspected inheritance and guided only by the guardian who holds the secret to her future, Samantha Cray fights to fulfill her destiny. (978-1-60282-002-9)

Learning Curve by Rachel Spangler. Ashton Clarke is perfectly content with her life until she meets the intriguing Professor Carrie Fletcher, who isn't looking for a relationship with anyone. (978-1-60282-001-2)

Place of Exile by Rose Beecham. Sheriff's detective Jude Devine struggles with ghosts of her past and an ex-lover who still haunts her dreams. (978-1-933110-98-1)

Fully Involved by Erin Dutton. A love that has smoldered for years ignites when two women and one little boy come together in the aftermath of tragedy. (978-1-933110-99-8)

Heart 2 Heart by Julie Cannon. Suffering from a devastating personal loss, Kyle Bain meets Lane Connor, and the chance for happiness suddenly seems possible. (978-1-60282-000-5)

Queens of Tristaine by Cate Culpepper. When a deadly plague stalks the Amazons of Tristaine, two warrior lovers must return to the place of their nightmares to find a cure. (978-1-933110-97-4)

The Crown of Valencia by Catherine Friend. Ex-lovers can really mess up your life…even, as Kate discovers, if they've traveled back to the eleventh century! (978-1-933110-96-7)

Mine by Georgia Beers. What happens when you've already given your heart and love finds you again? Courtney McAllister is about to find out. (978-1-933110-95-0)

House of Clouds by KI Thompson. A sweeping saga of an impassioned romance between a Northern spy and a Southern sympathizer, set amidst the upheaval of a nation under siege. (978-1-933110-94-3)

Winds of Fortune by Radclyffe. Provincetown local Deo Camara agrees to rehab Dr. Bonita Burgoyne's historic home, but she never said anything about mending her heart. (978-1-933110-93-6)

Focus of Desire by Kim Baldwin. Isabel Sterling is surprised when she wins a photography contest, but no more than photographer Natasha Kashnikova. Their promo tour becomes a ticket to romance. (978-1-933110-92-9)

Blind Leap by Diane and Jacob Anderson-Minshall. A Golden Gate Bridge suicide becomes suspect when a filmmaker's camera shows a different story. Yoshi Yakamota and the Blind Eye Detective Agency uncover evidence that could be worth killing for. (978-1-933110-91-2)

Wall of Silence, 2nd ed. by Gabrielle Goldsby. Life takes a dangerous turn when jaded police detective Foster Everett meets Riley Medeiros, a woman who isn't afraid to discover the truth no matter what the cost. (978-1-933110-90-5)

Mistress of the Runes by Andrews & Austin. Passion ignites between two women with ties to ancient secrets, contemporary mysteries, and a shared quest for the meaning of life. (978-1-933110-89-9)

Vulture's Kiss by Justine Saracen. Archeologist Valerie Foret, heir to a terrifying task, returns in a powerful desert adventure set in Egypt and Jerusalem. (978-1-933110-87-5)

Sheridan's Fate by Gun Brooke. A dynamic, erotic romance between physiotherapist Lark Mitchell and businesswoman Sheridan Ward set in the scorching hot days and humid, steamy nights of San Antonio. (978-1-933110-88-2)

Rising Storm by JLee Meyer. The sequel to *First Instinct* takes our heroines on a dangerous journey instead of the honeymoon they'd planned. (978-1-933110-86-8)

Not Single Enough by Grace Lennox. A funny, sexy modern romance about two lonely women who bond over the unexpected and fall in love along the way. (978-1-933110-85-1)

Such a Pretty Face by Gabrielle Goldsby. A sexy, sometimes humorous, sometimes biting contemporary romance that gently exposes the damage to heart and soul when we fail to look beneath the surface for what truly matters. (978-1-933110-84-4)

Second Season by Ali Vali. A romance set in New Orleans amidst betrayal, Hurricane Katrina, and the new beginnings hardship and heartbreak sometimes make possible. (978-1-933110-83-7)

Hearts Aflame by Ronica Black. A poignant, erotic romance between a hard-driving businesswoman and a solitary vet. Packed with adventure and set in the harsh beauty of the Arizona countryside. (978-1-933110-82-0)

Red Light by JD Glass. Tori forges her path as an EMT in the New York City 911 system while discovering what matters most to herself and the woman she loves. (978-1-933110-81-3)

Honor Under Siege by Radclyffe. Secret Service agent Cameron Roberts struggles to protect her lover while searching for a traitor who just may be another woman with a claim on her heart. (978-1-933110-80-6)

Dark Valentine by Jennifer Fulton. Danger and desire fuel a high-stakes cat-and-mouse game when an attorney and an endangered witness team up to thwart a killer. (978-1-933110-79-0)

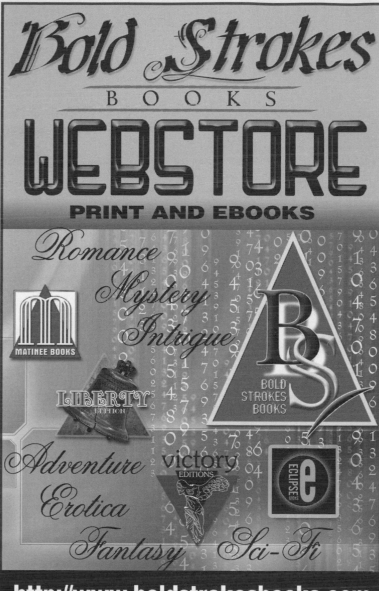